Angela
MARSONS

A D.I. Kim Stone NOVEL

FATAL
PROMISE

SPHERE

SPHERE

First published in 2018 by Bookouture, an imprint of Storyfire Ltd.
This paperback edition published in 2022 by Sphere

1 3 5 7 9 10 8 6 4 2

A CIP catalogue record for this book
is available from the British Library.

ISBN 978-0-7515-7754-9

Printed and bound in Great Britain by
Clays Ltd, Elcograf S.p.A.

Papers used by Sphere are from well-managed forests
and other responsible sources.

MIX
Paper from
responsible sources
FSC® C104740

Sphere
An imprint of
Little, Brown Book Group
Carmelite House
50 Victoria Embankment
London EC4Y 0DZ

An Hachette UK Company

www.hachette.co.uk
www.littlebrown.co.uk

has taken many novels to find that one character who just refused to go away. And so D.I. Kim Stone was born. The D.I. Kim Stone series has now sold over five million copies worldwide and been translated into twenty-eight different languages.

ALSO BY ANGELA MARSONS

DETECTIVE KIM STONE SERIES PREQUEL
First Blood

DETECTIVE KIM STONE SERIES
Silent Scream
Evil Games
Lost Girls
Play Dead
Blood Lines
Dead Souls
Broken Bones
Dying Truth
Fatal Promise
Dead Memories
Child's Play
Killing Mind
Deadly Cry
Twisted Lies
Stolen Ones
Six Graves

Other Books
Dear Mother (previously published as *The Middle Child*)
The Forgotten Woman (previously published as *My Name Is*)

This book is dedicated to Keshini Naidoo without whom Kim Stone and her adventures would live only in my head. My fairy godmother, always.

PROLOGUE

The late April sunshine bounces off the bluey black denseness of the hearse that is too vast to hold the coffin despite the array of mockingly bright blooms swamping it.

A coffin that is sickeningly small. Pure white with brass hinges, carried on the shoulders of four family friends, when in truth it could be carried by fewer. One strong pair of arms would do.

Tears stream down their faces; four burly men who try to outdrink each other every Friday night. Four men's men that burp and fart and congratulate each other.

But now they weep and make no effort to hide it. It's acceptable. They will not be judged.

The church is deathly silent as they reverently traverse the aisle to the top of the space. Despite their tears, grief, and sadness there is great concentration. The coffin is small and light, no match for the combined strength of mates who met on the rugby pitch. But who would want to trip, stumble over the raised edge of a carpet, or entangle their foot in the strap of a handbag spilling carelessly out of the aisle?

Who would want to drop the coffin? Who would want that as their claim to fame? Who would want to be the subject of that drunken Friday night anecdote?

And as I well know, the tighter you try to hang on to something, the more you focus on it, the easier it can slip from your grasp.

Every gaze follows the small white box as it passes by. There is something repulsive about such a tiny burial coffin. But what repulses *also fascinates, I realise as I watch people crane their necks from the far sides of the church. People want to see the incongruous oddity. The macabre short journey of life and death.*

A strangled sob sounds somewhere behind me, but most people's horror has rendered them mute.

The sorrowful glances slide from the coffin to me.

I don't react to their stares or the sympathetic expressions, held too long in case I glance their way and they can show me how deeply they mourn. I don't wish to share their grief and I'm not willing to share mine.

Mine has become useful. It is a living breathing entity that has changed in shape, size, and colour. It no longer weighs me down like a burden, it feeds me. It is like the air that I breathe. It enters my body as oxygen, something pure, something good. But then it transforms and expels as something different, poisonous.

Eventually, the crowd follows morosely on the short walk to the corner of the cemetery that is filled with colour, flags, cuddly toys, angels and cherubs.

Mourners are speaking in hushed tones behind me. I know that they cling to each other for support. Arms entwined as they make slow respectful steps.

The minister appears at the grave, a hole more suited for a decent-sized tree. Not a life. A plant, a bush, but not a life.

He reads from the bible as the coffin is lowered.

The sobs behind me turn to grief-stricken howls, shrieks that could not be contained inside now set free to disperse amongst the trees.

And it is done.

The coffin is in the ground.

Hands land all over my back, reassuring, comforting. Some brief, some linger.

Everyone wants to offer something, some indication, a token of their grief. They want me to know. They want me to share. They offer it as a gift of their own humanity.

And I don't give a fuck.

My comfort doesn't come from them.

Neither does it come from the knowledge of eternal peace.

It doesn't come from the platitudes and clichés, the well-wishers, cards, flowers or the phone calls. It doesn't come from the short time we had together.

It comes from the rage. It comes from the white, hot anger that burns in every pore of my body, every atom of my being.

My comfort comes from the plan.

My comfort comes from the knowledge.

The knowledge that everyone responsible will die.

CHAPTER 1

Kim breathed a sigh of relief as the nurse completed the cut of the fibreglass cast with a cast saw. All five toes appeared to be intact.

Finally, she could feel fresh, clean air circulating around the mummified skin.

She groaned out loud with pleasure as she reached down and scratched a spot halfway down her shin. A taunting itch that had been driving her mad for six long weeks.

'Feel good?' asked the nurse, smiling.

'Hell, yeah,' Kim said, raking the area so hard it was reddening beneath her nails.

And yet, after six weeks of torture the scratching of her flesh was not producing the level of satisfaction of which she'd dreamed. There had been nights she'd been tempted to use her own circular saw to release her limb for a scratch but she'd resisted, anticipating the pleasure of this moment. It was over all too soon.

The nurse passed her a wet wipe which she gratefully wiped all over the flesh indented from the cast.

The nurse threw the cast to the side as Kim moved her right leg to the edge of the bed. After six weeks of additional weight attached to it she had the sensation that her left leg was going to rise up and float away.

A steadying hand rested on her thigh. 'Not so fast, Inspector,' said the nurse with a knowing look. 'Doctor Shah will be with you in a minute. The cast is off but you're not out of the woods yet.'

She finished with a soft tap as though speaking to a child.

'Yeah, and I've got places to—'

'Aah, Miz Stone,' said Doctor Shah. 'I see you are your usual patient self this afternoon.'

'Doc, I just want to get back—'

'It is frustrating when the body is not so easily commanded by the will of the mind, no?'

Kim narrowed her eyes at his light breezy tone.

Doctor Shah peered at her over his glasses, as he had done the day she'd been wheeled in following the death of her colleague.

His calm, soft voice had punctured her rage as she'd fought to get off the hospital bed and flee. She'd had no idea where she wanted to go. All she'd known was that her colleague lay broken at the bottom of a bell tower and she'd been forcibly removed from the scene.

She shook herself back to the present, as Doctor Shah placed a hand on each ankle, as though gently holding her in place while he spoke.

'Lift,' he said, tapping her left ankle and then hovering his hand in mid-air.

There was a delay of a few seconds as her brain sent the instruction to muscles that had lain dormant for weeks.

The leg lifted and touched the outstretched hand. It faltered in mid-air before her upper thigh muscle controlled the descent back to the bed.

'To the left,' he instructed.

'And to the right,' he said.

'There will be muscle weakness and this should be built up slowly. The leg is not normal yet,' he said, again peering over his glasses.

And didn't she know it? Her milky white flesh bore the marks of the plaster imprinted into her skin. A two-inch scar ran down her shin where the fractured bone had forced itself through.

'The X-rays show that the bones have healed well, however...' he said, pausing.

Nothing good ever came from however, Kim thought.

'You still need to be careful. There will be pain and the leg muscles will be weak from inactivity. I'd like you to come to physiotherapy three mornings—'

'Doc, you know what I'm going to ask?' she said, cutting him off.

'You need to understand that your leg needs time and gentle exercise to repair properly. The mending of the bones is only the first step—'

'Doctor Shah,' she pushed.

He sighed dramatically in the face of her impatience.

He nodded towards the crutches she'd leaned against the paper towel dispenser to the right of the door.

'I'd like you to continue using them until you've completed a couple of physio sessions.'

'Doc,' she pushed again.

'Providing you stick to light duties, preferably behind a desk, then I see no reason for you not to return to work.'

Kim swung her right leg to the edge of the bed and shimmied her left one along using her hip and buttock muscles.

'So, I'm officially signed off, right?'

He nodded gingerly as though he felt it was a decision one of them might live to regret.

Kim lowered herself and held up a hand when both Doctor Shah and the nurse moved forward to assist.

She placed her right leg down then followed with her left.

A jolt of pain shot from her shin bone right into her hip.

She stumbled.

The doctor reached to stabilise her but she shook her head and hung onto the bed.

She did it again trying to ignore the sensation of weightlessness that made her think her leg was going to levitate of its own accord like a stage show magic trick.

She understood that her leg had spent six weeks encased in safety and the feeling of instability now unnerved her.

She focussed hard and took another step forward.

Still pain but not as blinding and this time she was expecting it. She ignored the sweat beads forming on her forehead as she took another step.

Doctor Shah had stepped back and was watching her movement.

She took another step. Towards the door.

'Don't rush your recovery,' he said, as she took another step.

Her hand was on the door handle as she thanked him.

His kind eyes acknowledged her words as she stepped out into the corridor. She closed the door, leaving the crutches firmly behind her.

She moved slowly along the hospital corridor. She had forgotten how far she was from the main entrance. She had entered the hospital with two additional legs and six weeks' experience in using them.

Ten steps she counted as she reached a set of lifts. Each time she placed her foot down it felt a little more natural, like a distant memory returning, but the effort had brought on a wave of nausea.

She took a second to rest against the wall, frustrated that her muscles were still waking up.

'May I help you, miss?' asked a red tee-shirted volunteer. His name plate announced him as Terry.

She shook her head as he opened a door to the right of where she stood.

'There's a chair,' he said, pointing inside to the small space. 'Just take a minute,' he said. 'You look like you're about to pass out.'

'Thank you but I'm fine,' Kim said, moving away from his kindness and towards the hospital main entrance.

As she neared the automatic doors she spotted the taxi she'd instructed to wait.

She couldn't reach it fast enough.

It was time to return to work and her team. And although her team would never be the same again, she'd been away from them for long enough.

CHAPTER 2

Doctor Gordon Cordell pulled up in front of the apartment block and marvelled at the speed of his change in fortunes.

There was nothing about his life that hadn't altered in the six weeks since the investigation into the death of Sadie Winters at his old school, Heathcrest Academy. Every aspect of the elite facility for the privileged and wealthy children of the Black Country had been investigated. That same investigation had uncovered the fact he'd performed an illegal abortion on Sadie's sixteen-year-old sister.

Not that he'd had a choice. When presented to him by her father, at least three weeks over the twenty-four-week legal limit, he had foregone the mandatory agreement of another doctor to satisfy the Abortion Act requirements and performed the termination anyway.

Thank God he had kept no records of the procedure and what was left of the Winters family weren't shouting about it from the rooftops.

But that bitch detective and her team from West Midlands Police had tried their hardest to bring charges against him. And had failed.

The secret society of the Spades had come together and protected him. He had been grateful for the day when he was eleven years old and had been invited to join one of the four secret societies that existed at Heathcrest. He had relished the prestige of being a chosen one and had enjoyed all the benefits and connections of the brotherhood that continued beyond school. Once a Spade, always a Spade. And as expected his fellow Spades in high places had come forward and shielded him. Until the danger had passed.

And then they'd sent him the card.

The satisfied sigh of relief that he was untouchable had been silenced when he'd opened the envelope to find a ripped playing card. The nine of spades had been torn into bits and sent to him. No note. No explanation. Not that he'd needed one. He'd understood the message loud and clear.

The Spades had protected him for one reason only: they hadn't wanted the police to destroy him because they had wanted to do it themselves.

Within forty-eight hours of opening the envelope he had been fired from his job as head surgeon at the private Oakland Hospital in Stourport-on-Severn. His brand new Lexus had been collected the same day, and his wife had thrown him out two days later when she'd learned why he had lost his job. The Spades were not upset because he'd performed the illegal abortion. They were upset because he'd been caught.

Within a week of expulsion he had been employed by Dudley Health Authority who were pleased to have him on board.

As well they should be, he reasoned. He had been educated at the best schools in the country and his record was impeccable. His official record, of course.

While not even close to the high six-figure sum he'd commanded at Oakland, the salary afforded him the opportunity of paying the mortgage on the home occupied by his wife with enough left over for rent on the one-bedroom apartment in Dudley and the nine-year-old Vauxhall he now drove.

It was all temporary. He knew that. This was his penance for being found out. This was his punishment for the police having got too close and bringing the whiff of scandal to a secret society that was steeped in tradition. But his fortunes would change in good time. Soon there would be a Spade that wanted his help. There would be some Lord or member of the cabinet with a careless teenage daughter who had a problem that needed taking care of by someone who could keep their mouth shut.

And that was when they'd bring him back. His old job would suddenly be available again. His Lexus would appear on the drive of his five bed, four bath barn conversion in Hartlebury, and his wife would welcome him home. His home once more.

But for now he would perform routine surgeries on the dregs of humanity for the NHS for a pittance of what he was worth.

'Oh Doctor…'

'Not now, Mrs Wilkins,' he snapped, passing by the front door of flat 1A as the elderly woman peered out.

Ever since he'd foolishly mentioned that he was a doctor she had assaulted him with an ever-changing list of symptoms almost on a daily basis.

'But, I just—'

'Sorry, can't stop,' he said, reaching the first flight of stairs. He could still hear her protests but he wasn't going back. He was just glad she didn't have access to the internet. She'd have found one life-threatening disease after another.

He mounted the two flights of stairs while adjusting his breathing. His bulk didn't take well to the absence of a lift, but in a month, he had shaved over sixteen pounds from his twenty-two stone weight. And although he didn't wish to prolong his excommunication from his real life for longer than necessary, he secretly hoped he could shift another stone before returning home. His wife, Lilith, had tried dozens of diets, without success, and he had constantly told her less food and more exercise was the only way. He enjoyed a certain smugness and anticipated the 'I told you so speech' with relish.

These stairs, and not having his meals readily cooked for him, were working a treat.

He ignored the laboured breathing, white stars behind his eyes and the sweat on his forehead as he opened the door to his temporary home. It was a flat he'd kept for some years but only for a night here and there.

He stepped straight into the lounge which he swore got smaller each day.

An archway led to a boxy kitchen with no window and too many wall cupboards.

A door led to the bedroom which then led to the shower room behind.

It was still the stark empty box it had been the day he'd taken the keys.

He walked straight through to the bedroom loosening his tie as he went. After the first few days, Lilith had allowed him to return for a suitcase of clothes. She'd told him to take them all but to touch nothing else.

He smirked. She hadn't noticed him swipe the bedside photograph of his two boys, Saul, already a surgeon and Luke in medical school. Small triumph, but a triumph all the same.

He reached into the bottom of his case to take out the photo, as he always did.

Placing it beside his bed admitted a permanence about his current situation that he was not prepared to acknowledge.

His pudgy fingers met with the silk lining of the case.

He frowned as he moved aside his spare pair of shoes and two pairs of socks.

He felt nothing but more silk and the securing strap.

He looked around the room even though he knew he had not removed it from its safe place in the suitcase.

'Where the hell?…'

His words were cut off as a blinding pain shot through his head.

He fell forward as the sound of shattering glass reverberated in his ear.

Stars darted in front of his eyes as the nausea rose in his stomach. His consciousness threatened to desert him. He swallowed the saliva in his mouth to ward off the sickness.

He blinked rapidly hoping to outrun the descending darkness.

'Hello, Doctor Cordell,' said a smooth, calm voice behind him.

He fought off the nausea to turn and view his attacker.

The voice was not familiar, but as he turned, he realised that the face was. It was a face he had seen before but he couldn't recall where.

'What the—'

'Shut up, Doctor Cordell,' said his attacker cutting him off.

'Lovely boys you have,' Cordell heard, as he tried to blink his wavering vision back to normal.

Only then did he realise he'd been struck with the photo. The picture of his wonderful sons.

The photo was thrust into his face.

'The time has come for you, Doctor Cordell. It's time for you to make a choice.'

CHAPTER 3

Kim pushed aside the feeling of unease as she approached the doors to the station. She hadn't set foot in the place for over a month. At first, she had railed against sick leave, insisting that she could function close to normal, but Woody's risk assessment said otherwise.

Jack offered her a nod and a half smile as she passed the front desk. 'Welcome back, Marm,' he offered.

She nodded in return but said nothing.

She walked the familiar corridors busy at evening shift change-over, the air crackling with both cheer and misery.

Normally she took the stairs two at a time up to her boss's office on the third floor without a moment's thought. Today she took the lift. She passed two other executive offices before knocking on Woody's door.

Again, the unease returned. An activity she'd performed many times over the last few years without a moment's thought or hesitation no longer held the same familiarity.

His low steady voice told her to enter just as she shifted weight onto her right leg.

She pushed the door open and suddenly realised that this man was a constant in her life.

Never did she doubt that he would be sitting behind his desk, his smooth brown skin and shaved head accentuating the smart white shirt. The wedding band still on his finger despite the loss of his wife three years earlier.

He removed his glasses and placed them in front of a framed photograph of his granddaughter, Lissy.

'So, you're back, Stone?'

Exactly the words she would have expected but a difference in tone. There was an edge, an element of tolerance. Forced through gritted teeth as though the moment had arrived too soon.

'Fighting fit, sir,' she said, taking a step forward.

He regarded her coolly. As well he should. There was an issue between them that hadn't yet been addressed.

She took a breath. 'Sir, there's something I've been meaning—'

'Counselling, Stone,' he said, cutting her off. Clearly his urgency was focussed on a different priority to hers.

'Not necessary,' she retorted, automatically.

'In whose opinion?' he asked.

'Mine, sir. I'm fit to return to work.'

'As I wouldn't accept your judgement on your own physical fitness, why would I accept your assessment of your psychological readiness?'

'Because I know my mind better than anyone,' she said, simply.

'Stone, I enjoy a good steak but it doesn't make me a butcher. An appointment has been made with a force psychologist for—'

'No,' she said, simply.

His face hardened. 'This is not negotiable.'

She took her warrant card from her pocket and placed it on his desk.

'You're right, sir, it's not.'

Never would she allow the force psychologists near her again. Ten years earlier, during her time as a constable, she'd been involved in a child abuse case where a young boy had been found dead on the day she'd accompanied Child Services to remove him from the home.

A routine visit to the force psychologist after the investigation had turned into much more when he had tried to link her feelings of anger to the death of her twin brother when she was six years old. That he'd gleaned the information from her personnel file had been bad enough but his insistence that she had relived her own brother dying of starvation as they had lay chained to the radiator together had boiled the blood that ran through her veins. Yes, she relived Mikey's death and her inability to save him regularly but only in her dreams.

Despite her protestations that she was angry because the difference between the child's life and his death was owing to the paltry two hours it had taken to get the authorisation letter signed, the force psychologist had filed a report stating she was 'not addressing key issues that may be problematic in the future'.

Luckily her sergeant had been overworked and understaffed and had filed the report under 'unlikely to be my problem by then'. But had he taken it more seriously she would probably have been out of a job.

Woody tipped his head and waited for her explanation.

'I'm not going to open up to anyone and you know that. I'm not going to explore anything and, trust me, sir, you don't really want me to.'

His expression told her he was not backing down. 'It is a requirement of the—'

'Sir,' Kim interrupted. 'The basics are that you need to be sure I'm able to do my job.'

'There is significantly more to it than that,' he argued. 'One of your team members lost his—'

'I don't need reminding of that,' she snapped before she could stop herself. She amended her tone before continuing. 'But ultimately, that's your main concern, isn't it? Can I function?'

He nodded.

'In which case, there will be a report on your desk by the end of the week from a qualified psychologist with an answer to

your question, but in the meantime you know me well enough
to allow me back to work.'

'With Bryant?'

She just about managed to stop her eyes rolling upwards. Her
boss sure liked keeping her attached to her steady, pragmatic
partner. She wasn't sure how Bryant would feel about that. She
hadn't seen him in weeks.

'Of course,' she answered, hoping she was speaking for Bryant
as well as herself.

He thought for a moment before nodding and pushing her
warrant card back towards her.

'And dramatics don't suit you, Stone.'

She took her identification back and said nothing. It was no
drama. She would have walked.

She took a deep breath.

'Sir, I'm sorry,' she said forcing the words out of her mouth.
They did not leave her lips often.

'Leave it, Stone,' he said, through a tightening jaw.

'No, sir, I won't,' she said, stubbornly. 'My apology may be
six weeks overdue but I shouldn't have doubted you during the
Heathcrest investigation. I should have known that your first
and only priority was for those children. It's not a mistake I'll
make again.'

During their last major investigation she had urged him to
announce the death of a child as murder to protect other families
at the Heathcrest facility, but he had been forced by higher powers
to keep that word firmly out of the press conference. She had
questioned his integrity while being unaware of an arrangement
he'd made with Frost, the reporter for the *Dudley Star*, that Frost
would raise the question of murder during the press conference
which had produced the exact response that Kim had wanted
but without him having to defy a direct instruction. She felt
bad in part that she hadn't realised herself what he'd been up to

and just as bad that it had taken Tracy bloody Frost to point it out to her. And it had all served to remind her of the reasons she aspired to no higher position in the police force. Woody could keep the office politics.

His mouth twitched. 'Feel better after that, Stone?'

'Actually, sir, yes, I do,' she said honestly.

The air between them had been tense since the press conference, despite the loss of Dawson, but she was hopeful that in their working relationship they could get back to the mutual respect and trust they'd always had.

'It's been pleasantly quiet here without you, Stone,' he said, as the expression in his eyes warmed up a degree or two.

'Don't doubt it, sir,' she said, nodding. 'But I'm back now, so where the hell is my team?'

CHAPTER 4

Kim opened the door to the squad room and turned on the light. She faltered and took a step back as her gaze fell immediately on to Dawson's empty desk. For some reason, she expected to see his belongings still sitting there. She'd expected to see his photograph of Charlotte. The paperweight under which he'd filed anything he classed as not urgent. The solar-powered nodding alien Stacey had bought him after he'd admitted he detested the things. He had hated it but kept it anyway.

Someone had found the strength to remove his stuff and it was now nothing more than a desk. An empty desk. Just a workspace. As though he'd never been there.

She pulled herself away and headed for the glass bowl in the corner. The eight feet square space which housed only a desk, chair, and filing cabinet seemed to have shrunk in her absence.

She threw her leather jacket over the back of her chair as Bryant arrived. The first of her team to return. And now fifty per cent of her team. He stole a glance at the empty desk before smiling in her direction and offering his hand.

'Evening, Marm, my name is…'

She shook her head indicating that it wasn't funny or appropriate.

'How's the leg?' he asked, taking his seat.

'Not bad,' she answered, on safer ground. 'But you'll be happy to know I can't drive.'

'I already know that, guv. Oh sorry, you meant you're not allowed to drive. My mistake.'

Kim couldn't help but smile as they quickly settled back into their bantering relationship. She supposed that's what happened with friends. Even ones you hadn't seen in over a month.

And that had been her choice not his.

She was sure her withdrawal would come up at some stage but not right now and for that she was grateful.

'So where's?...'

'Hey, boss,' Stacey said, with forced brightness as she barrelled into the office. She removed the satchel that crossed her body before throwing herself into her seat.

Kim noticed that she hadn't glanced at the desk opposite.

'So, you two had a good holiday?' she asked, perching on the spare desk.

It occurred to her this was the first time they'd all been in the office together since Dawson's death. There was a sense of imbalance resting around her. There were many times it had just been the three of them but it reminded her of when she'd been on sick leave. When Barney was just in another room she never gave it a thought and just carried on with her business as though he was right behind her. But two weeks ago her dog's groomer had collected him and taken him for his bi-monthly detangling and the sense of emptiness in the house had been overwhelming. She had been able to focus on nothing and had just paced and checked her watch until the doorbell signalled his return.

It wasn't that Dawson wasn't sitting there right now that caused the imbalance in her mind. It was that he wasn't sitting anywhere.

'Well, I've been to Costa del Brierley Hill,' Bryant answered. 'Desk duties mainly. They like their bloody paperwork trails,' he said, shaking his head.

'Cote D'Sedgley for me, boss,' Stacey said. 'Mainly CCTV stuff.'

Kim had known her small team had been reassigned to new teams in her absence. And neither placement seemed to have known what to do with the additional resource and so had put them on 'mug's work' as she liked to put it.

'Anything of interest?' she asked, aware that all their desks were relatively empty as the cases would have been distributed around neighbouring teams.

They both shook their heads but Stacey's response was just a nanosecond too slow.

'And what about?...' Bryant asked, nodding towards the empty desk.

'Woody's on it,' she said, holding up her hands. He'd told her no more than that.

She glanced up at the clock. It was almost seven but she'd wanted to just touch base with them both before starting work the next day.

'Well, thanks for...'

Her words trailed away as her mobile began to ring.

She answered, listened and then ended the call.

She turned to what was left of her team.

'Well, I hope you both had a good holiday because now we're back at work.'

CHAPTER 5

'Look, I just wasn't ready, okay?' Kim said as Bryant eased the car out of the station.

The Halesowen ring road had quietened after rush hour.

'Never said a word, guv.'

'You didn't have to,' she said, adjusting her leg to a more comfortable position. 'I can feel your accusation from here.'

'Guv, you're projecting. You needed space and I gave it to you. Simple.'

She glanced to her right and found no pretence in his expression.

Twice he had called and invited himself around and twice she'd refused. He would have wanted to talk and she would not. Could not.

'Your loss at the end of the day,' he said, putting her at ease as they left the A458 and turned towards the entrance into Leasowes Park.

Yep, he was probably right about that.

'Any idea where we're…' His words trailed away as he spied three squad cars parked by the warden's base at the edge of the car park, blocking the entrance.

Leasowes was a 141-acre site east of Halesowen. Designed by the poet William Shenstone in the mid-1700s, it had surfaced footpaths, woodland, grassland, streams, waterfalls and large ponds. The Grade 1 listed public park was considered to be one of the first natural landscape gardens in England. Not a fact normally respected by the kids that congregated on the benches to smoke and drink cider or the drug pushers making sales in a couple of known locations at the boundary edge.

Other than the uniforms, Kim realised they were the first to arrive. The drive from the station to the park had taken them less than five minutes.

'Here, guv,' Bryant said, passing her a pair of blue shoe coverings from the boot of his car. It was good to see he was as prepared as always.

They approached a collection of yellow jackets at the edge of the western treeline as crime scene tape was being pulled across two trees.

The officer waited for them to pass.

'Just in there, Marm,' said a portly constable nodding towards the woods. 'Not been touched.'

'Not even to check for a pulse?' she queried.

He shook his head. 'No need, Marm.'

She followed the path through the pause in the treeline. Twenty feet in beside a single bench she saw what she was looking for.

She approached the body as a raindrop landed on her hand. It was warm and heavy.

She felt Bryant stiffen beside her and followed his gaze. Immediately she understood his train of thought. The placement of the body before them bore a resemblance to the position in which they had found Kevin Dawson at the bottom of the bell tower. She wondered if they would see their colleague in every crime scene.

'Go find out what they know,' Kim instructed Bryant, nodding towards the milling constables.

He took one last look before moving away.

She took a breath, pushed Dawson from her mind and took a step closer to the body.

The figure lay face forward with his head turned. His left cheek was resting in a pool of mud from an earlier shower. A patch of dried blood had matted together his dark hair on the back of his head.

More spots landed on her head telling her another storm was imminent.

Kim understood the constable's assessment of the scene. The grass around the body was stained a deep red and the eye she could see was staring, glazed, along the line of the ground.

Another spot of rain landed on her neck.

Damn it, the techies weren't here yet with a tent, and she suspected that as prepared as Bryant was he didn't have one of those in the boot of his car.

She already knew that rain was a forensic investigator's enemy. That and careless officers.

She had to think quick. Use your resources, she thought looking around.

In the immediate vicinity were six uniformed police officers. She had a choice to make. Preserve the area around the body or preserve the body itself. Which had the potential to offer them the best chance of evidence?

'Get in here and take your jackets off, guys,' she called out, as the raindrops fell. 'Gotta protect the body.'

She knelt beside the figure on the ground as high-vis jackets rustled all around her.

She winced as a pain shot from her shin to her groin.

Already, despite the trench coat, she could see the man was overweight. His jacket was good quality, as were his shoes. His arms lay straight at his sides, landed where they'd fallen with no attempt to stop his body pitching forward. Dead before he hit the ground.

Kim squinted and then took out her torch as the coats began appearing over her head, blocking out her light but keeping the body dry.

She heard a car somewhere behind her and hoped it was either Keats, the pathologist, or Mitch, who normally headed up the forensics team.

She probably just about had time to reach into his front pocket and gently search for a wallet before they arrived and told her she couldn't.

The fabric inside his pocket reminded her that the wet ground was seeping through her black canvas trousers and into her knees.

She briefly wondered what Doctor Shah might think if he could see her now. *No driving, light duties and desk confinement*, he'd said.

Hmm… not so much, but one out of three wasn't bad.

She flicked open the quality leather wallet and instantly ruled out the most obvious motive. This man hadn't been killed for his money. At least eighty pounds sat undisturbed in the billfold section.

The beam of light from her torch landed first on a small photograph of two young boys: dark haired, laughing and unmistakeably brothers.

She frowned at the photo on the driving licence and pulled it closer. She shone the torch on the name.

'Bryant,' she called out as she checked again.

'Yeah, guv,' he said, crawling into the makeshift tent.

Her eyes hadn't deceived her at all.

'Jesus Christ,' she breathed. 'We bloody know this guy.'

CHAPTER 6

Stacey forced herself to look at the empty desk and the feelings came flooding back as if it had happened yesterday.

Being away from the office in a place she couldn't visualise her colleague and friend had at least distracted her through the day. She was pretty sure the psychologists had called it avoidance. Although the reverberations of the nightmares had stayed with her like ripples in a pond.

The dreams were always the same. She reached him, held his hand, almost pulled him to safety before he smiled and loosed her hand.

She didn't know which was crueller, reliving his death over and over like a torturous groundhog day, or almost saving him in her dreams only to wake and face the truth. Again.

Despite the weeks that had passed Stacey couldn't prevent the tears blurring her eyes as she realised that he would never sit opposite her again. He would never give her that boyish, mischievous smile when he wanted something from her. He would never roll his eyes at Bryant's overcautious and fatherly advice or wink at her when he was deliberately winding up the boss, or completely ignore her when something had commanded his attention.

She tapped her fingers on the desk waiting for her vision to clear.

The boss and Bryant had headed off at speed following the report of a body found. Normally there were two of them sitting here awaiting further instruction. Now it was just her. She had the strangest feeling of being left behind.

She pushed the thought away and remembered her own hesitation when the boss had asked if she'd been working on anything in particular.

She had lied.

She reached into her satchel and took out the printed photograph of a fifteen-year-old girl named Jessie Ryan.

CHAPTER 7

Only when Mitch and his colleagues had erected the tent did Kim give the instruction for the coats to be removed.

'Quick thinking,' Mitch said, coming to stand beside her. 'Thanks for that.'

Kim acknowledged his words while trying to keep the agony emanating from her leg showing on her face.

She always hoped to land Mitch as the crime scene manager. His speed and accuracy in prioritising and coordinating a crime scene in consultation with herself as the investigating officer was something she'd never had to question. And in turn she ensured she followed the ISP rules as soon as she arrived. Identify, Secure and Protect.

Add in the role of the pathologist, normally Keats, it was up to the three of them to determine the six Ws: Who is the victim? What happened? Where did it happen? When did it happen? Why did it happen, and hoW did it happen?

'Your best mate's here,' Mitch said, nodding towards Keats who was passing by the squad cars.

The pathologist approached looking from her to Bryant. He began singing the song 'Reunited'.

'Good to see you too, Keats,' she offered.

He regarded her for a moment. 'Is that grimace you're trying to hide due to my arrival or your recent injury, Inspector?' he asked.

'Well, both are a bit of a pain in my—'

'Keats, good to see you,' Bryant said, stepping in and offering his hand.

'Who do we have here?' Keats asked, taking a step forward, underneath the tent. 'That was a question to you, Inspector, as I'm reasonably sure you would not have resisted the temptation to have a look in my absence.'

Yep, he knew her well.

"Doctor Gordon Cordell, gynaecologist to the stars.'

'Really?'

'Not so much the stars but definitely the affluent,' she said.

'The name seems familiar,' he observed, taking the driving licence from her outstretched hand.

He glanced at the photo and shook his head. 'Can't place him.'

'In the papers, a few weeks ago. In connection with the Heathcrest investigation,' she offered.

A wave of sadness washed over his face. 'Yes, how could any of us forget that one?' he asked of no one in particular.

Keats had been the one to attend Heathcrest and pick up the pieces, literally, of a man he had come to know as a colleague. And although she had been forced away from the scene prior to Keats's arrival, she knew that however deeply affected he'd been by the sight of Dawson lying broken on the ground, he would have swallowed it down and done his job.

'Didn't you suspect him of carrying out illegal abortions?' Keats asked, bringing her back to the present.

Indeed.

And Kim had been appalled that the team had been unable to bring any charges against him. The scandal that had stained the Winters family was deep enough and neither Saffron nor her father had been prepared to make him pay. But he'd paid for something now.

'Okay, let me at him,' Keats said, lowering himself to the ground.

At the first sight of the rectal probe, Kim stepped away.

Bryant followed.

'You don't think this is connected to the Heathcrest investigation, do you?' he asked.

Kim shrugged as she took out her phone.

Stacey answered on the second ring.

'Stace, our victim is Doctor Gordon Cordell.'

'From Heathcrest?' she asked with a brittle edge to her tone, as though even saying the name of the place was like speaking around shards of glass in her mouth.

'The very same,' Kim answered. 'Do some digging, Stace. See what he's been up to since we last saw him.'

'Will do, boss.'

Kim ended the call, her mind already working overtime. Were the Spades, a secret society at Heathcrest, involved in his demise? Had he operated on the wrong girl? Had he spoken out of turn or did he know something about someone? Jeez, the list was endless.

'We're ready to turn him, Inspector,' Keats called to her over his shoulder.

Due to the victim's size, Mitch and two of his colleagues had gathered to help.

Gently they turned him onto his side and then onto his back with a cloth laid to catch any evidence from the wound to the back of his head.

'Bloody hell,' Kim said, her eyes widening at the sight before her.

'Literally,' Bryant added.

A line had been sliced across his throat from ear to ear. The bottom skin hung down like an open mouth. The blood had escaped the wound and saturated the loose skin, travelling down his chest and colouring his clothes scarlet.

Crime scenes very rarely, in her experience, mirrored horror films but this was the exception.

As Keats had turned him the ground beneath had been revealed. A red river glistened up at them.

'From behind?' Kim asked the pathologist.

Keats nodded. 'I'd guess, at this point, that the victim was kneeling, his head was pulled back to expose the neck and then…'

Keats made the sign across his neck.

'I'm pretty sure I can deduce cause of death myself,' Kim admitted. 'But a time would be—'

'No more than two hours,' Keats answered.

Somewhere around six o clock, she noted.

She narrowed her gaze.

'What is it, guv?' Bryant asked, reading her expression.

'How did they do it?' she asked.

'With a pretty sharp knife,' he answered.

She ignored him as she looked around.

'I don't see any cars around, so how did our killer get him to this spot without a fight?' She pointed to the ground. 'No drag marks in the grass. He's a big man, I'd guess around twenty stone. He would have taken some forcing.'

'There's that wound to the back of the head,' Bryant observed. 'He could have been knocked out or even semi-conscious.'

She shook her head. 'He'd have been just as difficult to move as a dead weight.'

'More than one killer?' he asked.

'Maybe,' she answered. But he would have still taken some moving.

'Told to meet someone here. Knew his killer?'

'And just got into the position on his knees and calmly waited to be murdered?' she asked.

Bryant shrugged. 'You think this means something?'

'Dunno, Bryant,' she admitted and then turned to Keats. 'Can you look more closely for any defensive wounds when you get him back?' she asked.

He raised one eyebrow. 'Of course I needed you to ask me to do that, Inspector, as I haven't already been doing this for twenty-three years. One has to wonder how I've managed in your absence.'

Her brief smile accepted his rebuke while she quietly enjoyed his annoying consistency despite recent events.

'I think your time off has addled your brain,' he observed, turning away.

She didn't disagree.

'But I do have something interesting to show you,' he said, pointing to a spot on Cordell's jacket.

'Is that a boot mark?' she asked.

'It is, and we already have a dozen photos of it but look more closely.'

She did and saw what he was referring to.

'Stab wounds?'

Keats nodded. 'And so far, I've counted twenty-seven. All inflicted after death.'

Why so many times once the man was already dead?

'Well, Inspector, I'm guessing your killer knew his victim and really didn't like him.'

Kim agreed and knowing what she did about Gordon Cordell, she had the feeling that information was not going to help her narrow it down one little bit.

CHAPTER 8

Kim perched on the edge of the spare desk with a strong black coffee in her hand. Pain and nightmares had kept her awake until well after 2 a.m.

Her team waited expectantly as they began their first day of a new investigation without Detective Sergeant Kevin Dawson. She didn't know if they expected her to say something. To mark the occasion in some way; formally acknowledge his absence. She would not.

'Before we start, new guy will be here shortly. Apparently we need to be at full strength for this investigation.'

She chose not to inform her team that her immediate response to Woody's news had been to refuse. But her boss was right. They had a body and their personal feelings were not the priority.

She waited for a moment for her team to digest that there would be a fourth that wasn't Dawson.

Kim glanced at the empty desk.

'Stacey, move,' she said.

'Boss?'

She nodded towards the offending desk.

Stacey followed her gaze and understood.

'Yes, boss,' she said, gathering her stuff together.

None of them could tolerate the thought of a stranger sitting in that spot.

'Bryant, get the board,' she said, as Stacey focussed on moving desks.

Bryant took four photos from the printer.

He wrote Cordell's name on the top and taped up the pictures. The first was a close-up of the neck injury, no less horrific in the cold light of day.

'Ugh,' Stacey said as she wheeled her ergonomically designed chair into position.

The second was a long shot of the body before he'd been turned, and the third was a close-up of the shoe print. As yet their only clue. And the fourth was the gash to the back of the head.

With her belongings moved, Stacey logged on to the computer and rejoined the conversation.

'Okay?' Kim asked.

Stacey smiled. 'Yeah, boss.'

The change of scenery would also alter the landscape for the constable. She would no longer have to stare at the empty space, picturing him right there.

'Okay, so we know that Cordell had his throat slit from ear to ear, but what these photos don't show is the numerous stab wounds inflicted to the body after death. Approximately twenty-seven.

'Cordell's car was not found at the scene, so our attacker either took the man's vehicle or Cordell made his way to the park by other means. No evidence of a struggle to the kill spot, so there may have been more than one person involved. Cordell appears to have lost a little weight since we last saw him but still a substantial man to push around.'

'So many stab wounds?' Stacey asked.

As a team, one of the first things they considered were the motivational categories. Anger, criminal enterprise, ideology, power and thrill, psychosis, sex and financial gain. The first category was a certainty given the abuse of the body after death but it didn't automatically rule out the rest.

'Frenzy,' Kim said, following her gaze. 'Killing him once wasn't enough. Our killer wanted to do it all over again.'

'Jeez, what did he do?' Stacey asked.

'We do know of his involvement with Heathcrest, the Spades, and illegal abortions, which is where we begin our search. Bryant and I will attend the post-mortem at nine and then speak to his family; if you can get me his—'

'Got it,' Stacey said, passing a piece of paper to Bryant.

'Two addresses?' he asked.

'Yep, very nice house in Hartlebury and a one-bed flat in Dudley.'

'Strange,' Kim said.

'And I'm pretty sure he dow work at Oakwood no more,' Stacey said, tapping a few keys.

Kim moved to stand behind her.

'Because he ain't on the who's who family tree on the clinic's website.'

Hmm… Even stranger, Kim thought as a sudden notion occurred to her.

'Ahem,' she heard from the doorway.

Three heads turned to look in the same direction.

It took Kim just three seconds to connect the dots.

They were all now looking at Kevin Dawson's replacement.

CHAPTER 9

'But why him?' Kim raged, pacing in front of Woody's desk. 'Why fucking Penn?'

'Would you like to try that again, Stone?' Woody asked, regarding her coolly. 'I'll make one allowance for your shock at Dawson's replacement and that was it. Now, I suggest you guard your tone.'

Kim swallowed down the bitter taste in her mouth.

'If you've calmed down enough to recall where you are, I'll explain.'

Kim nodded although she couldn't imagine anything that would persuade her to agree.

The bandana-wearing detective sergeant from West Mercia had audaciously appeared in the doorway to her squad room with his man-bag crossing his chest and a Tupperware container in his hand.

'Hi, I'm the new guy and I brought home-made cakes,' he'd said.

As ever Bryant's manners had won the race as he'd offered his hand and welcomed Penn to the team. Stacey had stared at him in stunned silence, and Kim had nodded cordially at him, saving her rage for her boss.

'He put in a request to transfer back to West Midlands after working with the team in January. He's moved in with his parents, so he's back in the—'

'What is he, a bloody yo-yo?' she asked. He'd already transferred from West Mids to West Mercia and now he was back again.

'Where next – South Staffs, Derbyshire? And why's he back with his parents?' she scoffed. He was a grown man.

'His reasons are not my concern and nor should they be yours. There was no space for him with any other—'

'Well, I'm so pleased we could bloody accommodate him by losing one—'

'Stone,' Woody thundered, cutting her off. 'That's not what I meant and you know it.'

She stopped pacing and sat. He was right and that had been unfair. A cheap shot born of frustration.

'It won't work, sir,' she said honestly.

'I don't see why not. He's known to you all. Twice now he's assisted the team, and he is a damn good officer.'

She couldn't disagree with the facts as he stated them. She had first worked with Penn when seconded to West Mercia to work alongside DI Travis on a Hate Crimes case. The sergeant had been instrumental in uncovering the group behind the attacks, which in turn had helped her to save Stacey's life. More recently he had been seconded from West Mercia to assist on a string of murdered prostitutes, his data mining skills imperative to the case while Stacey and Dawson had been following a lead on forced migrant labour.

But temporary assistance wasn't permanent placement.

'The dynamics are all wrong,' she said, trying to imagine Penn fitting in with her team and failing miserably. 'Too many sharp points,' she said, frowning.

'Explain.'

'Well, it's a new team member who immediately comes in above Stacey. He's a sergeant and she's a constable. It's not fair.'

'You know how I feel about that, Stone. You've got to start pushing her along. She needs to be considering promotion. She's ready.'

'Kick me while I'm down, why don't you?' she asked.

'You know it.'

'They're too similar,' she explained, changing the subject. 'Stacey's more experienced out in the field now but brilliant at data mining. Penn is the same.'

'Well, forgive me for trying to equip you with the best team possible,' he said. 'And that's about team management not team fit, which is your problem, not theirs. Just because they don't fit into your tidy little mould doesn't mean Penn isn't the right person for the job.'

'He's not,' she insisted, stubbornly.

He considered her for a moment before a sad smile lifted his mouth.

'Who would be, Kim?' he asked, using her first name for only the second time since she'd known him.

The name Dawson instantly sprang into her mind but she shrugged in response. Failing that, she honestly didn't know.

A moment of understanding passed between them.

Woody laced his fingers beneath his chin. 'Okay, use him on this one case. You've got a body and you need all the help you can get. If it doesn't work out, I'll move him to another unit and we'll find someone else. Agreed?'

Kim felt the tension begin to ease out of her. She'd felt backed into a corner by her boss, who had now taken a step to the side and given her a way out.

That was enough. For now.

She nodded her agreement. 'Now about that body, sir,' she said, returning to the thought she'd had in the squad room.

CHAPTER 10

'Bloody chilly in there, guv,' Bryant commented as he pulled off the station car park.

'Spoke to him, didn't I?' she asked.

'Barked *at* him is probably more accurate.'

'I asked him to start looking at the footprint,' Kim said.

'Wasn't exactly posed as a question, guv, but you're technically right, I suppose.'

Well, technically right would do for now. At least until she could tolerate the thought of his arrival. She wasn't proud of the way she'd spoken to him but somehow a stranger would have been better. Perhaps, thinking of him as a temporary solution to their current manpower problem would help her mind process his presence.

'Just don't get too attached. That's all I'm gonna say,' she stated, as a few drops of rain landed on the screen.

Bryant opened his mouth and closed it again.

She watched as the raindrops fell heavier and pedestrians started fishing out cardigans to cover prematurely bare arms.

She knew many people favoured spring as their season of choice. Warmer days, more light, rebirth, new beginnings. Personally, she hated it. To her it signalled the end of winter, her favourite time. Everything was clear in the winter. Cold, crisp days that left no doubt where you were. Spring was limbo. Neither one thing nor another.

'So, what else did you say to Woody?'

'I asked him to try and find out if the Spades were involved in Cordell's murder.'

Bryant laughed out loud.

During their last investigation into the deaths at Heathcrest it had become increasingly clear that someone high up in the police force was connected to the secretive group.

'And what, Woody's gonna ring up Lloyd House, ask who is a Spade and then accuse them of murder?'

'Not exactly,' she replied, rubbing her shin bone.

'Well, how the hell is he going to find out?' Bryant asked.

'He's not,' she explained, patiently. 'All he's going to do is call Chief Super Briggs and drop out that it's a line of enquiry we're following.'

'And?'

'See if the Spades react.'

His head snapped around. 'You're trying to bait them?'

'A little bit,' she admitted. 'Look, we both know that if they're involved they'll react to the fact we're trying to link them; if not they'll just leave us alone.'

'And when you say, react, what do you mean exactly?'

She shrugged. She really had no idea.

'Guv, did you just put a whopping great target on our backs?'

'Probably,' she admitted.

'Jeez,' he said, shaking his head.

She smiled and stretched her left leg into the footwell.

'See, now wasn't it just boring without me?'

CHAPTER 11

Stacey had lost count of the times Penn had irritated her already and the boss had only been gone ten minutes.

Sitting down had been his first mistake, followed by throwing his bag haphazardly under the desk; offering her one of the weirdest-shaped cookies she'd ever seen from his Tupperware box and making a fresh pot of coffee had been the final straw.

And now she had to look across the desk at him wearing those stupid oversize headphones. And they weren't even playing anything, she marvelled, remembering the time she'd told him the boss wouldn't be pleased.

He'd been given the task of researching the footprint, and she was on CCTV duty.

He'd donned the headphones, started tapping and hadn't glanced her way since. He appeared impervious to the fact no one wanted him there. Either that or he didn't care.

'Why the request?' she asked, before realising the words had come out of her mouth.

He shrugged without pausing or looking at her.

'I have my reasons,' he said.

'Cryptic,' she offered, sarcastically.

He stopped typing and met her gaze. 'I could ask why you glance down at your satchel every few minutes without even realising it. But I won't.'

She frowned. He was right that the photo was on her mind, but she hadn't kept looking at it. Had she? But now that he mentioned it she could visualise Jessie's photo in there, staring up at her accusingly.

She'd been the one who had taken the report from the concerned parents about the teenager's whereabouts the previous day, at Sedgley. She'd been the one who had started searching the CCTV around the girl's last known locations. She was the one who had questioned the lack of urgency or interest, to be told Jessica Ryan had run away twice already and returned safely herself within a day or two. She was the one who had asked to whom the case would be handed in the face of her repatriation to her own team. The sergeant had shrugged causing her to wonder if it would be handed over at all. The assumption had been made that Jessica Ryan would turn up when she was good and ready.

At the last minute, she'd grabbed a copy of the photograph and stuffed it into her satchel.

'It's nothing,' she answered shortly.

He shrugged. 'Well, I've made contact with all the major shoe manufacturers before I crack on with NFRC, so if there's something you wanna do, I can start looking at the CCTV the boss—'

'I can do my job, thank you,' she snapped, hoping that his attention to the National Footwear Reference Collection would keep him occupied indefinitely. He could play happily in the searchable library to find a sole pattern match and quit bothering her.

A small voice whispered a reminder of the part he had played in saving her life. That he had been the one to crack the incomplete note that had led to the team finding her in the clutches of a group of despicable racist bastards. And she had been grateful. But that had been before he'd arrived to try and replace her friend.

He returned to his screen, and she focussed on hers.

Yeah, she knew his game. Offer to help and then take credit for doing all the work and get in with the boss.

Over her dead body.

CHAPTER 12

'Good morning, Inspector, and how are you today?' Keats asked, brightly.

'Suddenly suspicious,' she admitted. Keats seemed almost pleased to see her.

'Well, I've been speaking to my friend here,' he said, pointing to the sheet that was barely covering the generous girth of Gordon Cordell. 'And he seems to have quite a bit to say.'

Kim immediately understood his cheer. It was like when her interviewing technique produced a confession, or when she found a clue that gave her a fire in her belly. Keats had obviously found something of value.

She could never enter this place without remembering her first post-mortem, carried out by Keats while she'd been closely observed by her superior officer.

She had understood that she was facing some kind of initiation or test from her boss, as he had chosen an elderly male undiscovered in his sixth floor flat for ten days after death as her first post-mortem experience.

She had been determined not to reveal anything as she'd watched the man before her make the Y-shaped incision from each shoulder to the lower end of the sternum and down to the pubis.

She had stared hard as Keats used the saw to cut the ribs and remove the breastplate.

She had deliberately moved closer to get a good look at the heart, lungs, and blood vessels in the chest and had focussed her gaze as Keats had removed, weighed, and taken tissue samples from the major organs.

The stench as he'd examined the stomach contents had brought the bile to the back of her throat, and his collection of the ocular fluid had been touch and go, but a few deep swallows had forced the nausea back down.

By the time Keats had made the cut from behind one ear, over the top of the head to the other ear and peeled forward the scalp to expose the skull, she had forced herself to think less of the body as a person and more as a collection of clues.

And at the end of the whole process Kim had turned to both her sergeant and Keats and thanked them for the education but next time, she'd told them, she'd like to witness a more challenging procedure.

Her boss had looked satisfied, and Keats had stifled a smile.

She had told neither that the visions had given her nightmares for weeks.

'Don't tease me, Keats,' she said. 'Out with it.'

'And where's the fun in that?' he said, almost flirtatiously.

'Okay, now you're just freaking me out,' she admitted.

He laughed out loud. 'Then, my work here is done,' he said, grabbing his clipboard. 'I can confirm that our victim's heart had maybe five good years left without a drastic change of lifestyle. Too much grease and too little exercise had started to clog his arteries. And to prove my point his last meal was sausage, egg and chips with bread and butter.'

'How many slices?' Bryant asked, cheekily.

'Two,' Keats shot back.

Kim shook her head. Very few people understood the dark humour needed in both of their professions to get through the day.

'The rest of his organs were in reasonably good shape. He wasn't a drinker or a smoker.'

'Good to know,' she observed.

'Good things come to those that can keep their impatience on the right side of their lips, Inspector.'

'Keats,' she warned.

'I counted a total of twenty-six stab wounds to the torso, with a blade approximately five inches long. Surprisingly no major damage was done to the organs even though he was dead already; the surplus fat prevented deep penetration.'

Kim found it strange to realise that without the cut throat the same thing that was killing him could also have saved his life. The fat that threatened his heart could have been a protective layer around his organs.

'Defensive wounds?' she asked.

'No defensive wounds but you already noted the blow to the back of the head. Two glass shards were embedded in his scalp, which I have bagged and photographed.'

So far he'd offered nothing that she hadn't seen for herself the night before.

'Oh, Inspector, your patience is about to be rewarded,' he said, reaching for a round, plastic specimen dish.

'What is it?' Bryant asked, looking over her shoulder. 'It looks like a glob of blood.'

Keats frowned. 'Hmm… not exactly sure what you mean by a glob, sergeant, but yes it is congealed blood but there's something else present,' he said, sliding the dish under a microscope.

Kim took a look and saw thin sticks protruding from the mass.

'Fibres, Inspector,' Keats offered, proudly. 'Not sure of the type or composition until they've been separated and cleaned but they were present at the site of the neck wound.'

Kim took another look. 'Blue in colour?'

Keats nodded. 'Which is pretty much all I can tell you about them so far, but,' he said, looking towards the door, 'here comes the star of the show right now.'

'Hey, Mitch,' Kim said as the forensic investigator entered the room holding an evidence bag.

'We got a hair,' he said, holding up the evidence bag to the light.

'No marks for suspense building there, Mitch,' Keats grumbled.

Mitch's bearded face crumpled into a smile. 'Sorry, I'm not given to dramatics but it's a valuable find and I will explain why. The hair shaft is made up of three layers of keratin: the cortex, the middle layer, which is the largest portion of the shaft and contains hair pigment; under microscopic examination we use the pattern of air pockets and structures within to seek a match.

'The cuticle is the outer layer of cells that cover the surface of the shaft and look like fish scales or roofing tiles. Scale patterns are used to determine if the hair is human and to match one hair to another. And then there's the medulla, not always present in all hair types, but when it is it's the central core of the hair that contains cells.'

'So, what *can* you give us, Mitch?' she asked, not particularly enjoying the lesson.

'As you know, hair can supply DNA. You won't find nuclei in a single hair as that's only in the root and even with PCR amplification—'

'Mitch, what can you give us?' she asked again. She didn't need the process of cloning a DNA sequence explained to her. If it couldn't help she needed no further detail.

'I can't give you a DNA profile,' he admitted.

Damn, that's what she'd thought he was going to say.

'But, if you find a suspect and you can get a strand of his hair I can tell you if it's a match.'

That was some good news, at least.

'But...' he added, shrugging his shoulders.

'I know, any good defence lawyer would argue that the hair got on him any number of ways.'

Mitch nodded. 'We're always shedding DNA, ejecting saliva containing DNA from cheek cells. It's practically impossible to commit a crime without leaving DNA. It's finding it that's the problem.

'Clever criminals don't try and hide the crime. They don't move the body or chop off the head as it increases the risk of leaving trace evidence. They avoid any connection to the crime.

'A short trip to the shop and you become a walking trace evidence factory. Take you two,' he said, looking from her to Bryant, 'you work together for hours every day. You must be swapping so much—'

'Ugh,' she said.

'Trust me, guv,' Bryant offered, 'that thought is just as distasteful to me as it is to you.'

Keats chuckled.

'Okay, enough,' Kim said, pushing herself away from the counter. 'Cheers, guys,' she called, heading out the door at speed.

'Oh joy,' Bryant said, catching her up. 'I love it when your legs start trying to keep up with your brain. What exactly did we learn in there?'

'We learned that an experienced killer doesn't move his victim around.'

'And I'm pretty sure we already knew that,' he observed.

'We know our victim was hit with something containing glass yet there was no glass at the scene in the park, so that first assault took place somewhere else. Two sites, two opportunities to leave evidence.'

'So?'

'Also, experienced killers leave a body where DNA is near impossible to sort out, shopping centre, train station, where the sheer volume of evidence makes it impossible to isolate one single suspect. And this guy was murdered in the middle of a park. We have a hair, fibres and a boot print,' she said, feeling like Christmas was coming early.

'So, what are you saying?' he asked.

'Rookie mistakes, Bryant. I'm saying that this was our guy's first kill.'

CHAPTER 13

The Cordell house in Hartlebury was not what Kim had been expecting.

The two-storey farmhouse was an L-shaped building formed of chunky grey stone. A porch with trailing plants waiting to bloom draped over the wooden structure. Red ivy clung to the gable end wall.

She had expected something showier, more ostentatious, a status symbol reflecting his wealth and standing. She'd expected marble, pillars, a portico entrance maybe, but this place overlooking the Worcestershire countryside was both peaceful and charming and jarred with the image of Cordell in her mind.

Bryant's wrinkled forehead reflected her thoughts.

'Doesn't fit, does it?' he asked.

She shook her head as she knocked on the farmhouse door. Only one vehicle was parked in the gravel driveway.

The door was answered by what Kim would call a handsome woman. Her black hair was short and tidy and showing a generous sprinkling of grey. Her height exceeded Kim's five nine by a couple of inches.

What an imposing couple the two of them must have made, she thought.

Kim held up her identification and introduced herself.

'I thought the family liaison officer had been dispatched,' Kim said as the woman stood aside and they entered. She suspected the single car on the drive belonged to Mrs Cordell.

'I sent her away, Inspector,' she said. 'I can make my own tea, and I don't want strangers in my home. My sons are both on their way,' she stated in a manner that said that was all she needed.

Kim followed her through to a lounge that although small lacked clutter. A brick fireplace was the star of the show with recessed bookshelves either side. A curtainless window looked out onto fields of different colours. Plush fabric sofas were decorated with scatter cushions. A nook led off from the space, its walls filled with shelves of books, in front of which was a reading chair, table and lamp.

'What a lovely home it is, Mrs Cordell,' Kim said, taking a seat.

Mrs Cordell swept her hands beneath her legs when she sat as though straightening a skirt.

The woman nodded, acknowledging her words.

'May we start by saying how sorry we are for your loss,' Bryant said, taking a seat beside Kim.

Again, the nod but no words.

She sat upright with her hands in her lap and her ankles crossed.

'Mrs Cordell, we have a forensics team on their way if that's okay?'

She nodded. 'Of course, but I'm not sure what they'll find. My husband hasn't been here for weeks.'

'Oh,' Kim said, unsure of the reason.

The woman's face changed as though she'd just realised something.

'You're that detective. The one at Heathcrest. The one who said my husband had—'

'Yes, that was me,' Kim said, still peeved they'd been unable to charge him. Not that it mattered now.

'Yes, that was the day I threw him out.'

'Mrs Cordell, I didn't mean—'

'Because I knew you were right. I knew he'd done it,' she said standing. 'And now I find myself in need of a cigarette, and as I don't smoke inside you'll have to follow me to continue.'

Kim rose and followed, wondering if this woman realised that her husband was actually dead. There was no registering on the emotional Richter scale either way.

They walked through a kitchen diner formed of light wood and flagstones.

Mrs Cordell reached for a pack of smokes. She really wouldn't have pegged the woman as a smoker.

'Twenty-six-year abstinence, officer, but I think the occasion calls for it,' Lilith Cordell said as though reading her mind.

Her first admission of any feeling in any way, Kim thought, as they passed through French doors into a well-sculpted garden that was both cosy and private, with seating areas positioned to take advantage of the view.

The woman lit the cigarette, drew on it and blew out smoke.

Bryant looked longingly at the cigarette. His own four-year abstinence had been tested to its limit recently but he hadn't given in.

'So, you believed he did carry out illegal abortions?' Kim asked, continuing the conversation.

'Yes. I knew before I asked him outright. I always knew when he wasn't telling the truth. He was an over-protester when he lied. I threw him out. I was sickened. Especially…' Her words trailed away as she stared forward.

'Especially?' Kim probed.

'Because I had two miscarriages, officer. Both girls. I have strong opinions on abortion in general, never mind ones that are beyond the legal limit.'

Kim understood that the thought must have forced her to picture her own two girls that had not made it to full term.

'And that ended your marriage?' Bryant asked.

She shook her head. 'No, it was the final nail in the coffin of our marriage. Just not something I was prepared to see past. At first, I think he felt it would all blow over, that I'd let him back like

I always did, but just two days ago he seemed to realise I meant it. He reacted as I expected and threatened to take the house.'

Kim's opinion of their victim had never been high but she was now getting the impression of a spoilt, petulant child.

'And could he have?'

'Maybe,' she said, 'if he wasn't going to listen to the boys. My youngest, Luke, was going to speak to him.' She glanced around. 'I could have lost everything.'

And now she didn't have to, Kim realised.

'Mrs Cordell, you do understand that your husband's death was brutal? Someone hated him enough to actually cut his throat. Do you have any idea who could have done that?'

'Probably most people he's ever met I shouldn't wonder. Heck, even I wanted to for the last couple of—'

'Mum… Mum…' Kim heard from inside the house.

Lilith Cordell discarded the cigarette and rushed inside, straight into the arms of one of her sons.

'Oh Luke, it's awful, your father was…'

'Don't think about it, Mum,' he soothed, holding her tight. 'I'm here now. We'll get through this together.'

Kim stood outside, uncomfortable witnessing this first reunion after the news of the man's murder.

It was the first expression of emotion Kim had seen, and yet when mother and son eventually separated both were dry-eyed.

Luke seemed to notice their presence for the first time. Either his memory or his recall was sharper than that of his mother.

'You're investigating the death of my father?' he asked, incredulously.

The handsome features had turned hard.

'Yes, Mr Cordell, my name—'

'I know your name and I know what you tried to do to him. In fact, the whole world knows.'

Kim met his gaze defiantly. Regardless of the fact the man now lay in the morgue she would not apologise for doing her job. Cordell had broken the law not her.

'Are you the only police officer they have over there at West Mids?' he asked, aggressively, causing Bryant to step forward and his mother to whisper his name.

Kim didn't need protecting from anyone as she took a step closer towards the raging hostility.

'I'm the only one that matters to you, right now, because I'm going to find out who did this to your father,' she said firmly.

She wasn't sure that was the response he'd been expecting but it quietened him for long enough that she turned to his mother.

'Mrs Cordell, the forensic team should be here soon but if you think of anything else that might help…'

'I'll tell you what will help,' Mrs Cordell said, reaching for her cigarettes. 'Send your search team to his flat in Dudley, especially the bedroom. The forensic guys will have a field day in there.'

CHAPTER 14

Stacey stepped out of the taxi in front of a red-brick semi-detached property that had a small box porch on the front.

She'd lied when she'd told Penn she was heading to Sedgley to check CCTV. Although she could access and request CCTV from her own office, the Dudley Council control room was located at the rear of Sedgley station. And she was in Sedgley, almost.

His slight nod had confirmed that he'd heard but she didn't much care. She'd been desperate to escape his presence. He was an alien being in her familiarity. Like something out of place in her home or when a fly landed in her diet Coke. It was an annoyance staring her right in the face.

She adjusted her satchel and approached the door feeling guilty but unsure why. She'd been given the case in the first place, so it wasn't like she was doing anything wrong. They all worked for West Midlands Police, she reasoned, choosing to forget that she'd had to give it back and that her boss was investigating a brutal murder.

The word that came to mind for the woman who opened the door was tidy. Her petite frame was clothed in straight leg jeans and a V-neck jumper. A thin chain rested on her breastbone and a watch was the only other jewellery she wore.

'Mrs Ryan, may I come in?' Stacey asked, showing her identification, despite the fact they'd met the previous day at Sedgley.

'Have you found her?' the woman asked, answering Stacey's first question. Evidently, she had not yet come home.

Stacey quickly shook her head.

The woman deflated before her eyes.

Stacey followed her through to a spacious kitchen diner with the overwhelming stench of bleach. Stacey just about stopped herself from coughing as the smell crept into her lungs.

'She's been gone more than twenty-four hours now. I don't understand how you haven't found her. How many officers do you have out there looking for her?'

Oh, that one question prompted so many things she wasn't in a position to explain. The first being that Jessie was the third fifteen-year-old in a week to be reported missing at Sedgley, an indicator of just how many missing persons were reported to the police. Extensive resources were not available to throw at every report, especially when both of the others had been located by their parents within forty-eight hours. The same result was expected for Jessie, and so the decision to treat Jessie Ryan as a low priority case when the girl was a few days away from her sixteenth birthday and there was no evidence of foul play was not something she could reveal to the worried mother. Neither could she reveal that Jessie's two previous runaway incidents did nothing to escalate the priority. And best not to mention the fact she was no longer assigned to the case at all.

'Mrs Ryan, could you just take me through what happened again?'

'But I told you everything yesterday. I don't understand what more I can say.'

Stacey nodded as she took out her notebook. 'I know it's frustrating for you but one of the many steps we take is to revisit the information to see if there are any details you might have remembered, however small, and I promise it'll just take a minute.'

'Please, sit,' Mrs Ryan said, pointing to a round table.

Stacey did so, popping her satchel onto the ground.

'Go ahead, Mrs Ryan,' Stacey urged with the feeling she'd just dodged a bullet.

'Jessie asked after lunch if she could go to Emma's in the evening. I said yes, but Philip wanted her to clean her room first. She appeared at about seven with her coat on. She hadn't cleaned her room, so there was a bit of a row before—'

'Between Jessie and her father?' Stacey asked. She didn't recall this being mentioned the previous day.

'Philip's not her father,' Mrs Ryan reminded her. 'Although he may as well be. He's been in her life since she was six.'

Stacey's antenna reacted to this new information.

'How serious was the argument?' she asked.

'It was nothing really. Just words, things said in anger. They clash a bit but it always calms down in the end.'

'Do they argue a lot, Mrs Ryan?' Stacey asked. It could explain Jessie deciding to go to ground if she needed time to cool off.

'Sometimes,' she admitted. 'They're so alike even though there's no genetic link between them. They both have the same fiery temper.'

'And do these arguments ever get physical?' Stacey felt obliged to ask.

'What do you mean by physical?' Mrs Ryan asked, colouring.

So, the answer was yes.

'You tell me,' Stacey said.

'Pushing and shoving. A slap once, but that's been a while ago now. Jessie can be a handful at times.'

Stacey tried to stop the disapproval showing on her face.

'He's a good man,' the woman said, as though Stacey's silence had judged her.

Any man or woman laying a hand on a child of hers would have been booted out of the house with no more than the clothes on their back.

'Mrs Ryan, please be honest. Was it similar incidents to the one on Sunday that prompted Jessie's previous disappearances?'

Mrs Ryan hesitated and then nodded.

It appeared there was a great deal the couple had forgotten to mention when she'd taken their report.

'What happened next?' she asked.

'Jessie left in a huff; Philip went out for a beer to calm down. He came home about nine, and Jessie was due back at ten.'

'Did you try and phone her?' Stacey asked.

'Voicemail every time,' she answered.

'And when you came into the station yesterday morning at ten, Jessie had been missing for approximately twelve hours,' Stacey clarified.

Once she'd taken the report from Mrs Ryan the previous day, she'd only had the chance to check Jessie's social media accounts for activity before being recalled to her own team in Halesowen.

'Yes, we waited because we thought she was just in a mood, that she was cooling down after her argument with her stepdad. And we were ringing around her friends the whole time,' Mrs Ryan explained.

'And what did her friend Emma say when you spoke to her?'

'That Jessie had left at nine forty-five as normal. It's only a few streets away,' she added, defensively.

Stacey wasn't here to pass judgement on the woman's parenting skills. Right now, her only concern was Jessie Ryan's safety.

'I think that girl knows more than she's saying,' Mrs Ryan offered.

'You mean Emma Weston?'

'Yes, they've known each other since junior school but they've been best friends for a few years now. Bad influence if you ask me but Jessie won't be told.'

'"Bad influence"?' Stacey asked.

Mrs Ryan nodded. 'To be honest, Jessie changed after they started spending more time together. Started answering back and being cheeky, especially to Philip,' she explained.

'Is there any boyfriend in the picture?' Stacey asked.

Mrs Ryan shook her head. 'No, Jessie's too young for anything like that.'

Maybe a hundred years ago, Stacey thought to herself. She made a note on her pad to ask Emma the same question. In Stacey's mind there was a world of difference between just gone fifteen and almost sixteen, and if Jessie hadn't got a boyfriend in her past or present she'd be very surprised. Although not as surprised as her mother by the looks of it.

'And her father?' Stacey asked.

'Philip is her—'

'Her biological father,' Stacey clarified, although Mrs Ryan knew exactly what she was talking about. 'Does Jessie see him?'

'No. Never,' she said, vehemently.

'You're sure?' Stacey asked.

'She doesn't know him, officer. He walked out on us when she was four years old. He had no interest in being a father. Oh, it was fine when she was healthy but at the first sign of illness there were skid marks in the road. He's never made any effort to get in touch or support her in any way. As I said, Philip is her father.'

Stacey didn't push the point but she had to rule out his involvement.

'If I could just take his address before I go,' Stacey said.

'Of course but you'll get no joy there. Probably doesn't even remember he had a daughter.'

Stacey ignored the bitterness in her tone as the woman grabbed a notepad and pencil from the kitchen drawer.

'Okay, Mrs Ryan. Well, thank you for your time. If you hear anything at all from Jessie, give me a call,' she said, reaching for the piece of paper.

Mrs Ryan grabbed her hand. 'I hope you find her soon, officer,' she said, tremulously as tears began to form in her eyes. 'I don't know how much more worry I can take before I lose my mind,' she said, glancing towards a corner of the kitchen.

Stacey followed her gaze to a collection of pill bottles and medicines.

'Those are Jessie's?' Stacey asked, incredulously, wondering why the woman had not mentioned the medication the previous day.

Stacey gently pulled her hand away from the woman's grip.

Mrs Ryan dabbed at her eyes and nodded. 'That's why I'm so worried, officer. I know she's almost sixteen but she's still my baby. I can't eat, I can't sleep. I just…'

'Mrs Ryan, is your daughter's health in jeopardy?' Stacey asked.

This information put a whole new light on Jessie being just a routine runaway.

More tears forced their way from her eyelids and rolled over her cheeks.

'Absolutely, officer, without her medication, there's a good chance my daughter could die.'

CHAPTER 15

'So, what does the frightening Mrs Cordell think we're gonna find here?' Bryant asked, pulling up outside the Dudley address.

The building was an ugly, flat structure thrown up on a plot of land around twenty years ago on the edge of the Wrens Nest housing estate. Kim understood that it was occupied by a mixture of housing association and private tenants.

'Bodily fluids would be my best guess,' Kim answered.

'Ugh, nice,' he said as they waited for the landlord to arrive to let them in.

'And she's not frightening,' Kim defended. 'Not everyone is warm and cuddly with their emotions on show. Some folks are a bit more private, you know.'

'Oh, I know,' he said, meaningfully, as a male headed towards them jangling a set of keys.

He was younger than she'd expected, dressed in jeans and a dirty tee shirt.

'My dad said to ask when we can have the flat back?' he asked, as a form of greeting.

'Not until we've finished with it,' Kim answered in kind.

They followed him up the stairs silently.

He opened the door and stood aside.

'I'll be downstairs so just let me know when…'

'If you could remain at the entrance, a forensic team is already on the way, Mr?…'

'Dodds,' he answered, shaking his head. 'My dad ain't gonna like that.'

Kim shrugged. 'Then your dad should have come to tell us that himself,' she said, stepping inside.

She initially wondered if the landlord had already been inside and cleared it and then realised it was just sparsely furnished.

Mrs Cordell had revealed that her husband used the property just a few times each month when he'd been consulting at Russells Hall Hospital on a part-time basis. Being tired after a long day and all that, he'd said at the time, although the fifteen miles or so drive home to Hartlebury was hardly long distance.

Despite the fact he'd had the flat for six years there was little to show that anyone stayed there and apparently Mrs Cordell had not visited once. Kim hadn't thought to ask about his sons.

A sofa and single chair faced a television in the corner. There were no throws or rugs or ornaments. Not even a newspaper or magazine. And the guy had been living here full-time for more than a month since his wife had thrown him out.

A breakfast bar separated the space from the kitchen, which was neat and orderly except for a few items of crockery on the drainer.

She pushed open the only door from the main room and stopped dead.

'Bryant,' she called.

He came to stand behind her.

'Bloody hell,' he said.

The bedside cabinet had been tipped forward, the lamp lay on the ground.

The quilt cover was ruffled and hanging all over to the right side. It was marked with a few spots of blood, and a small pool had stained the carpet.

A suitcase had been toppled to the ground, and the occasional table beneath it had been broken. Beyond the bed she could see a smashed photo frame face down amongst a sea of shattered glass. The wardrobe door was open but the clothes hung in full view. A dirty pair of trousers and two shirts were crumpled in the corner.

'Inspector,' she heard from the hallway.

She turned.

'Wasn't expecting you, Mitch,' she said. He'd been on his way to the main residence.

'Thought there was more chance of finding something here and, looking at your face, it appears I was right.'

'In here,' she said, nodding towards the bedroom.

He came to stand beside her as two crime scene officers finally caught up with him.

'Sent a couple of guys over to Hartlebury to collect anything of interest, but I suspect anything that's gonna help you is right here,' he said, as his eyes travelled around the carnage of the room.

She nodded her agreement.

'Give me just a few minutes and you can come in,' he said, reaching into his bag for a fresh overall.

She stepped away and walked around the living room.

'Ah, here it is,' Kim said, spying a computer bag that had been hidden from view beside the single chair. She'd known Cordell had to have a laptop somewhere. One of the techies nodded that he'd seen it.

Bryant circled the room from the other direction, and they met behind the sofa.

'Sparse,' he observed. 'And definitely no blue carpet.'

She'd already noticed the cream carpet throughout the property that was no match for the fibres Keats had found. 'Certainly expected to be going back home some time soon,' she agreed. 'Bed sheets,' she said to another techie who was removing evidence bags.

'You think he was sleeping with someone here?' Bryant asked.

'His wife does,' Kim answered. 'And she seems pretty astute to me. Sex has been the motive for many a murder,' she said, glancing at the door as a thought occurred to her.

She frowned.

'How'd he get in?' she asked. There was no sign of forced entry, and the landlord's son had unlocked the door to let them in. 'Either Cordell or his attacker took the time to lock the door as they left?' she observed.

'He could have invited his attacker in,' Bryant said. 'Could have been someone he knew, but I see what you mean about locking up afterwards.'

'Okay, Inspector,' Mitch called from the bedroom.

He handed her and Bryant a pair of blue slippers.

She put them on before entering.

'Well, whoever it was, why did he invite them into his bedroom?' she asked, thinking out loud.

'Or perhaps, he was already here?' Bryant said, opening the door to the en suite.

Positioning-wise Bryant had a point. The location of the blood pool and the angle of the fallen suitcase would indicate that Cordell's back was to the en suite, so the killer could have been hiding there.

'But how did he get in?' she insisted. They were on the third floor and the locks were intact.

Bryant shrugged.

'Hey, hang on,' Kim said to Mitch as he gingerly deposited the gold frame into a bag.

He held it up so she could see the blood on the top right edge.

'No, turn it round,' she said.

Mitch did so.

Kim raised one eyebrow at her colleague.

'Okay, Bryant, why'd he take the photo?'

CHAPTER 16

Oh, Cordell, you fat, arrogant bastard, you were everything I'd dreamed of and more.

It was so easy to get a copy of your key and let myself into your flat, position myself exactly where I wanted to be and just wait.

I could have hit you so much harder with the photo frame. The muscles in my arms felt the rage in my stomach and ached to swing it harder and bash your fucking brains in. Quick. Done. But I refrained, exerted more self-control than I knew I had, given that you were right there in front of me. But it wasn't the picture in my head. I didn't want to kill you quickly, from behind, without you knowing what you'd done, the depth of pain you'd caused, you fucker.

It was important to me that you saw my face. That you knew and understood.

That first blow was only a stunner, to fell the beast temporarily.

You writhed and groaned dramatically even though it was barely a scratch. Eventually you managed to haul your bulk onto your back and that's when you saw me, recognised me as your addled brain finally caught up.

I put my boot on your chest and explained the situation so that you knew resistance was futile. This wasn't going to be a fight, you were not going to challenge me and you were going to have to make a choice.

Once you understood these things I hauled you to your feet. You were compliant and I guided you through the flat, locking the door behind us.

I drove you to the park and walked you to the spot. You tried to talk to me, to reason with me. To give you another chance. You didn't fight me. That was sensible.

I told you to drop to your knees and then I gave you the choice again, and for once you did the decent thing. You made the right decision.

I stood behind you, the knife poised at your throat and it felt good. It felt right and not one moment of regret passed through me as I dug the blade into your flesh.

For once you were a real man and sacrificed yourself given the choice that I offered.

But I hope you're up there watching and understanding that it was all for nothing.

Because there really was no choice at all.

CHAPTER 17

'Okay, guv, wanna tell me why I'm driving back out into the sticks again?' Bryant asked, as they headed through Blakedown for the third time.

'Need to find out why matey boy left Oakwood. He'd been top banana there for fifteen years.'

'You think he pissed someone off at the clinic? Enough to do this to him on top of losing his job?'

'Dunno, Bryant,' she said, staring out of the window, her signal to her colleague that she didn't want to talk any more.

The subtle, irrefutable link to Heathcrest and their last major investigation kept the shadow of Dawson right there in the back of her mind. His involvement with the school, his determination in following a lead and his eventual death in the place of a twelve-year-old boy.

She was honest enough to admit, if only to herself, that there were times she wished that hadn't been the case. And then she smothered the thought with a blanket of guilt because the boy had been saved and her colleague was a hero. But he was still dead.

She spent the rest of the journey revisiting every aspect of the case, looking for the clues, wondering where she could have prevented it.

Maybe if she'd been paying more attention to the secret societies he'd been investigating she'd have seen what was going to happen, or if she'd pulled him off the line of enquiry earlier.

And then a twelve-year-old boy would be dead, a small voice in her conscience shouted up. And if she was a better person she'd care more about that fact.

'We all miss him, guv,' Bryant said, quietly from beside her.

She didn't bother to argue. He knew her well enough by now.

'There's just one thing I wanna say,' Bryant murmured as they pulled on to the Oakland Hospital car park.

'Go on,' Kim said.

'If I'm ever hurt, I wanna come here. I don't care about the forty-minute drive. I'll take my chances.'

Kim smiled and appreciated her colleague's tact in leaving her and her thoughts alone, and in changing the subject.

Bryant eased to a stop at one of the many free car parking spaces in front of a row of planter troughs that were awash with daffodils, tulips and crocus blooms.

The four-storey red-brick building was attractive and a few planted window boxes had been added to the ground floor to further soften the exterior. Kim remembered that the ground level was for administration with a hydro pool, physiotherapy suite, restaurant, café and shop. The second floor housed the consultation rooms and the third and fourth were taken up with surgical theatres, treatment centres and en-suite rooms for patients. She could certainly understand Bryant's point.

A maintenance guy surrounded by warning barriers and a mate footing the ladder, who was changing a bulb behind the letter 'd' in the Oakland sign above the door, were closing off one of the sets of automatic doors into the building.

Kim stepped aside for a young woman guiding out a small boy with red eyes, and a colourful plaster in the crook of his arm.

Beyond the foyer the space opened up into an area with individual soft chairs in groups around coffee tables. The wheat-coloured chairs matched the oatmeal carpet and Kim wondered if she'd been swallowed by a box of cereal. She couldn't help but wonder if the interior designer had focussed his attention on just one colour card. Even the reproduction paintings had biscuity tones to be picked out.

She approached the desk, to a woman waiting with a ready smile and poised fingers.

'I don't have an appointment,' Kim said showing her identification. 'But I'd like to see the person who was Gordon Cordell's boss,' she added.

The woman's smile never faltered as she picked up the phone receiver, pressed a few keys on the phone and explained there were police officers at the front desk. All done so quietly that no one waiting in the peaceful reception area heard a thing above the gentle, non-invasive instrumental music.

Within a minute a smartly dressed male in his late fifties appeared from the corridor to the right marked for authorised personnel only.

His hair was pure white and thick atop a handsome distinguished face.

He offered a hand and a smile. 'Josh Hendon, Managing Director. How may I help?'

Kim took the cool firm grip briefly, his title reminding her that this particular healthcare facility was a profit-making business. His smile matched that of the receptionist; bright and open. She had a vision of slides being shown on initiation day. *This is how you smile at Oakland. Even if you're imparting bad news, maintain this level of smileyness.*

'We'd like to talk to you about Gordon Cordell,' she said.

Immediately his face filled with tension. He nodded and guided them through the double doors. They passed closed doors on both sides as they headed along a carpeted hallway to the office at the end, the door bearing his nameplate in brass.

And a very nice office it was too, she thought, as he stood aside for them to enter.

'Please come in, take a seat,' he said, moving to the left of the room where there was a full percolator of coffee.

'May I get either of you a drink? I can get tea if you'd prefer.'

'No, thank you,' they said together. They'd recently grabbed a cuppa and some lunch at the Little Chef in Hagley.

'Is it true?' he asked, taking a seat behind a teak-coloured desk. 'The way he died, I mean?'

'It would have been quick,' Bryant said, rather than answering the question.

'Poor bugger,' he said, shaking his head.

Kim took a seat on one of the velvet upholstered chairs and glanced at the certificates on the wall behind the man. Nothing health or medical that she could see but a whole lot of business credentials.

'May I ask where you went to school, Mr Hendon?' Kim asked.

'I started at Coldgrove Junior and Infant School in Hertford-shire before attending high school and sixth form college in Dorset and then Cambridge University for my masters in business and economics.' He met her gaze. 'I'm not from Heathcrest and I'm not in any secret society.'

'But you know of them?' she asked.

'Not personally. I don't know who the members are, at least I don't think I do; the secret clubs were mentioned in the press following the murders at Heathcrest and the death of that police officer who—'

'Dawson,' Bryant interjected. 'His name was Kevin Dawson.'

Hendon nodded. 'I was brought in six weeks ago by the board of directors to repair the damaged reputation of the clinic follow-ing unproven accusations against Doctor Cordell.'

'They weren't,' Kim said, now confident they weren't dealing with a member of the secret club.

'Weren't what?' he asked.

'Groundless accusations,' she answered. 'Doctor Cordell did perform illegal terminations. I'll rephrase. We know of at least one but there may have been others.'

'As he was not charged or found guilty of any crime I'll choose to stay on the right side of slanderous comments,' he said with a hint of humour before frowning. 'Aren't you the detective that accused him?' she heard for the third time in one day.

She briefly wondered if that's what her career would come down to. Would she be remembered for the one charge she couldn't make stick against the hundreds of charges that she had?

'I am and was just sorry that the family wouldn't confirm it. Although it's immaterial now.'

'Quite,' he said, simply.

'So, were you the person responsible for Doctor Cordell's departure?' Kim asked, wondering about new broom and all that.

'Mr Cordell was the reason for his own departure,' he said.

'How so?' she asked. The man had eked out a comfortable existence at the clinic for fifteen years.

Mr Hendon sighed. 'You met him, Inspector, so you understand that he was not the most likeable man. His manner was often brusque, dismissive and altogether unpleasant. However, he was indeed a brilliant surgeon. Countless lives have been saved because of Doctor Cordell's skill and for that reason his death is indeed a tragedy.'

'Thank you for the official speech and now I'd like to hear the "but" that was attached to it,' Kim said.

'His skill would only excuse so much bad behaviour.'

He suddenly seemed to remember himself and his earlier words. 'Not that I'm saying he was guilty. The hearing hadn't—'

'What hearing?' Kim asked.

'Doctor Cordell was the subject of an internal investigation at the time he left the clinic. He did not attend his formal interview and tendered his resignation immediately.'

Kim knew employment law well enough to understand that without that hearing taking place he was guilty of nothing.

'What had he been accused of?'

'Sexual harassment,' Hendon said, with a look of distaste.

'Any previous incidents?' she asked. Some kind of trumped up complaint was not beyond the powers of the Spades to force him out.

'I really shouldn't discuss this any further without a member of the legal—'

'Okay, Mr Hendon, I understand, but in your opinion was this complaint credible?' she asked.

'No, officer. It was no longer a single complaint. As is normally the case in these situations, one person's bravery inspires others to come forward with their story.'

She had visions of the #metoo hashtag on Twitter where women had come forward in their thousands to speak out about sexual harassment and intimidation.

'Mr Hendon, how many complaints of sexual harassment did Doctor Cordell have against him?'

'The final count was thirteen.'

CHAPTER 18

The phone was answered on the third ring but it wasn't the voice she expected to hear.

'Where's Stacey?' she asked, as the tension seeped into her jaw.

'Out following a lead,' Penn answered.

Kim tried to quell the irritation rising within her. The sooner they could catch the bastard who'd killed Cordell the sooner Penn would be reassigned. Objectively, Kim knew he was a good officer, but he wasn't right for her team.

'Bryant is gonna send over a list of names. Thirteen of them. All possible victims of sexual harassment by Cordell, and I want to know just how credible they are.'

'Okay, boss,' he answered.

'And tread gently, Penn,' she warned. 'Just background checks to start. This is a sensitive issue.'

'Will do, boss.'

'And have Stacey call me as soon as she gets back,' Kim said, ending the call. After what had happened to Dawson, if Stacey was following up a lead then she wanted to know about it.

CHAPTER 19

Although only a few streets away from Jessie Ryan's house, Emma Weston appeared to live in a whole different part of town.

Sedgley sat on the A459 nestled between Dudley and Wolverhampton and was formed of many housing estates: High Arcal, Tudor, Cotwall End, Brownswall, Giro City – so named because the majority of occupants claimed benefits.

But Stacey knew she had crossed over to the Beacon Estate, an area built of old council houses known for occupants dumping rubbish on each other's gardens, feuds and house fires. At the top of the estate lay Beacon Hill, a dumping ground for litter and stolen cars, visited by gypsies on numerous occasions.

But however grim it was it didn't compare to Hollytree, and many of the problem families had been moved from Beacon to the Brierley Hill conurbation.

The tidy lawns, shrub borders and freshly planted hanging baskets had given way to houses sitting on sludge pits with patches of grass, grimy net curtains, broken-down cars and a battered caravan in the communal parking area at the end of the road.

As she crossed the road, Stacey slid behind a decent-looking Volvo out of place in the hopeless street. Brave person leaving it unattended, she thought, traversing the uneven slabs that led to the Weston's front door.

The door was opened by a girl wearing way too much make-up over a suspicious expression.

'Who're you?' she asked before Stacey got chance to speak.

She showed her identification. 'Detective Constable Stacey Wood. I'm here about Jessie. May I come in?'

Emma Weston shook her head and placed herself more firmly in the space as though Stacey was going to barge past her and force entry to the house.

'I said all I got to say,' she said, rudely.

Stacey knew that a constable had been dispatched the previous day to take details from Emma for the report, but she'd been summoned back to Halesowen before the officer had returned to the station.

'Well if you could just say it again,' Stacey said, trying to remain pleasant in the face of the girl's rudeness.

'She came over, we listened to music, ate a pizza and she went home. Normal time. End of.'

'Was anything bothering her?' Stacey asked.

Emma shook her head.

'Did she mention an argument with her stepfather at all?'

Emma rolled her eyes. 'They was always at it. The bloke's a wan—'

'Was he physical with her?' Stacey asked, wondering if this fight had got out of hand.

'Not this time, I don't think,' she said shortly. 'But plenty other times.'

'Emma, did Jessie have a boyfriend?'

She shook her head and narrowed her eyes.

'And she's your best friend?' Stacey asked.

'Yeah,' she said defensively.

'So, you'd tell me if you knew anything further.'

'Yeah,' she repeated.

'Only you don't seem all that bothered she's missing,' Stacey observed, feeling her hackles rise at the girl's attitude. Perhaps these kids weren't as close as Mrs Ryan thought.

'I'm answering your questions, ay I?'

'You're not worried about her?'

Emma rolled her eyes. 'Jessie's nearly sixteen,' she said as though that meant she'd earned herself a wealth of experience since her fifteenth birthday. 'She's fine and she'll be back when she's cooled off. Just chill.'

'Are you so blasé because she's done this before?' Stacey asked.

Emma shrugged. 'Jessie can take care of herself. She's tougher than she seems.'

'Do you know anything about Jessie's father?' Stacey asked, reasoning that the girls had known each other for a long time.

'Why would I? She doesn't even know him really. Just his name,' she added quickly.

Stacey's senses kicked in to the sudden colour that the girl couldn't stop from rushing to her cheeks.

'Emma, is Jessie in touch with her father?'

'Dow be stupid. She ay seen him since she was a baby.'

Well, she'd be visiting him all the same to confirm that one, Stacey decided.

'Look, Emma, I'm here cos Jessie's mother is worried. She'll be seriously ill without her medicine,' Stacey advised.

'Ha, like that stupid cow—'

'Who is it, Emma?' asked a female opening the door wide.

There was no mistaking that she was now looking at Emma's mother. The dark moody eyes were the same, the heavy make-up and the scowl when she looked at Stacey's identification.

'My daughter has nothing more to say,' she said, pulling her child away from the door and closing it with a bang.

Stacey turned away, stunned at the attitude of them both. A young girl was missing and was without her medication.

Suddenly Stacey could understand why Jessie's mum wasn't all that keen on her daughter's best friend.

Firstly, she wasn't sure Emma was telling her anywhere near the truth, but more than that – as her mother had pulled her away from the door, Stacey had seen a strange look come over the child's face and if she had to name it, she would have called it triumph.

CHAPTER 20

It was almost six by the time Bryant had eked them through the rush hour traffic and on to Russells Hall Hospital car park. In her mind the miles and hours they'd spent on the road were not synonymous with the headway they were making on the case.

'What time is she here until?' Bryant asked, as he parked.

'Said she'd wait for us in the café,' Kim said, jumping out of the car. 'Until half five, which we might have made if you'd put your foot down,' she moaned.

'Yeah, damn that line of traffic that got in my way.'

Kim was feeling the frustration of not driving. Had she been in the driver's seat she'd have been ducking and diving down side streets and short cuts to reach their location on time. Bryant chose to accept that all roads would be gridlocked and resigned himself to the wait.

'If she's already gone, it'll be all your fault,' she said, striding towards the automatic doors.

'Yeah, put it on my tab,' he grumbled.

The hospital was in that manic transition phase of out-patients leaving appointments and visitors starting to arrive. Kim crossed her fingers that she didn't bump into Doctor Shah. Desk duty this definitely was not.

The café was loud and busy but Kim spotted the woman straight away. Not least because she was looking anxiously in the direction of the main entrance.

Although they'd never met Kim could see that she recognised her too.

'Mrs Wilson, thank you for waiting,' Kim said, gratefully.

Kim knew the hospital Operational Medical Director was a busy person and they were lucky to have got a few minutes of her time without a meeting.

'I'm sorry I can't give you long, I have an appointment in about ten minutes.'

Kim shot a glance at Bryant who continued past her to the coffee machine.

'I'll get straight to it,' Kim said, wondering if there were any administration posts that were nine to five any more.

Kim guessed the woman to be mid-thirties. Although the majority was still contained in a bun on the back of her head, blonde tendrils of hair had broken free throughout the day. Make-up applied first thing had long since disappeared.

'Interviews,' she explained.

'For Cordell's job?' she asked.

She nodded. 'Sorry if it seems heartless but surgeons have to be replaced immediately. Three majors and six minors cancelled already.'

Kim was guessing she meant operations. 'Not good for the figures,' Kim observed. Hospital cancellations within the NHS were a staple of every current news programme.

'Even less for the patients,' the woman replied coolly. 'Two of those majors were drastic hysterectomies.' She paused. 'Cancer.' She shook her head. 'Other surgeons are working all hours to pick up some slack, but a man down is a man down.'

Kim nodded her understanding for a person being battered by politicians, public and patients. She could appreciate someone in that position becoming jaded, but this woman appeared to have retained her humanity.

Kim felt herself warming to Vanessa Wilson.

'We understand that Doctor Cordell has consulted here for many years.'

She nodded. 'It was long before my time that he started. Way back after his wife's second miscarriage about twenty years ago. He told me Saul was seven and Luke was five but Lilith had desperately wanted a daughter. She was brought here and although we couldn't save the baby he never forgot our efforts.'

'And he became full-time just over a month ago?' Kim confirmed.

Vanessa nodded. 'When he left Oakland we snapped him up. We'd have been foolish not to,' she said glancing at her watch. 'Despite his faults he was an excellent surgeon.'

'But you knew the rumours regarding Heathcrest?' Kim asked.

'Rumours,' she scoffed. 'Take a look around, officer. We have doctors, nurses, auxiliary staff, administrators, receptionists, cleaners, volunteers. The place is like a small city. We can't afford to listen to rumours.'

'Did you contact Oakwood for a reference?'

'Of course,' she said, moving along the seating as Bryant returned.

Another check of the watch.

'They did admit that he was the subject of a disciplinary but would not divulge anything further.'

Kim understood that the woman had made a calculated decision with the information she had. Rumour and accusation elsewhere, his impeccable record here and the overwhelming priority of saving lives.

She would have done the exact same thing.

'Now, officer, I really must…'

Her words trailed away as she stood. They had run out of time.

'So, you can confirm that no complaints of any kind had been made against Doctor Cordell?' Kim asked, as the woman's phone began to ring.

She frowned. 'Absolutely not, Inspector, in fact it was the other way round,' she said, holding up her phone and striding away.

Damn it, just a few more minutes, she thought as Vanessa Wilson disappeared from view to the left.

From the right, a figure lifted his head and met her gaze.

Recognition dawned on his face as he recalled her from the previous day when she had refused his offer of a chair.

She smiled and nodded in response.

Bryant followed her gaze and then frowned at her.

'My mate, Terry,' she said, reaching for her drink.

'So, thirteen complaints back there and not one here. What are you thinking now?'

Kim took a sip of her coffee and sighed deeply. 'Honestly, Bryant. I haven't got a bloody clue.'

CHAPTER 21

'So, what you been up to today, boy?' she asked Barney as she lowered his dried food and chicken pieces to the ground.

If he could answer she was sure he'd tell her that Charlie, her neighbour, had collected him around 2 p.m., taken him for a nice long walk before taking him back to his bungalow along the street for a lazy couple of hours in the shady back garden.

The arrangement suited them all perfectly. After losing his beloved Labrador two years earlier, Charlie hadn't wanted the full-time care and responsibility of another dog at the age of seventy-six. With no family, he'd worried about what would happen if anything were to happen to him. Having been forced to give up driving he couldn't be responsible for the animal's care and vet visits. But he was a dog person, had always had dogs and missed the companionship terribly.

Her own frenetic working hours meant there was always someone she could call upon to tend to her best friend. The arrangement worked well for everyone. Not least of all Barney who got to chase the squirrels away from the bird feeders at the bottom of Charlie's garden.

She sat on the sofa with her cuppa. Within seconds Barney was by her side, nuzzling her free hand. If she remembered correctly the 'no sofa' rule when she'd brought him home had lasted two and a half minutes.

Automatically her palm rested on his head and began to stroke. He pushed his silky head against it.

'So, here's the problem, boy,' she said seriously. 'I need to go out and I'm not supposed to drive.'

He tipped his head as though listening to and considering the problem.

'Now we both know the bike is out,' she said, regretfully. 'And much as I miss it even I know that's beyond my limits and although the doctor said I wasn't even to drive a car I'm thinking it wasn't really an instruction but more an advisory recommendation. You think?'

No response.

'I mean, it's not like I'm considering mountaineering or fell walking. It's just a short ride a couple of miles, and if I take you along I won't even be on my own. So, what do you think, shall we chance it or not?'

He barked, and Kim smiled.

'That's what I thought you'd say, you bad boy.'

She stood, and Barney jumped down gazing at her expectantly.

She grabbed her car keys and jacket and opened the front door.

Barney sat beside the passenger door of the twelve-year-old Golf and wagged his tail.

'Back,' she instructed, opening the rear door. 'Now, if anything goes wrong I'm blaming you,' she advised his reflection in the rear-view mirror.

He barked as she got her legs into position. Her left was already feeling the fatigue of the day but if she took it at a reasonable speed she wouldn't have to keep jumping on and off the pedals.

She spoke to her companion throughout the five-mile trip and with relief turned up at her destination, ignoring the throbbing that was pulsing through her leg.

She got out and opened the door for Barney to follow.

He sat by her side as she knocked the familiar front door.

The occupant appeared and smiled at them both.

'Hey, Ted, unsurprisingly, I think I need your help.'

CHAPTER 22

Stacey hesitated before knocking on the man's door at 8.15 p.m. Although still light out, her mother had drummed certain rules into her as a child. She wasn't allowed to go call for her friends before 10 a.m. or after 8 p.m. Respect and decency for other people, her mum had always lectured.

But his teenage daughter is missing, she silently explained as she tapped lightly on the stained-glass panel.

The front of the house was tidy and unassuming on a road just a half mile from her own home between Netherton and Dudley.

The door was opened by a slim, attractive man in his late thirties wearing jeans and a plain tee shirt. His hair was light brown with just a hint of grey at the temples.

'Mr Dunn, Jeffrey Dunn?' she asked, holding up her ID.

He frowned and nodded.

'I'm here about Jessie,' she explained. 'Your daughter,' she added before realising that bit had been unnecessary. He knew who she was.

His face creased in concern.

'May I come in?' she asked. 'I have a few questions.'

'Of course,' he said, standing aside as though he'd completely forgotten his manners.

Stacey walked towards the kitchen looking for clues as she went. There was only one jacket hanging over the bannister. She sniffed the air, but there was no smell of perfume. The kitchen was tidy except for sandwich-making ingredients on the work surface nearest to the sink. There were no glasses, cups or plates lying around to give her a clue.

'So, what's wrong with Jessie?' he asked, disturbing her secret reconnaissance of his home.

He didn't invite her to sit, so she didn't.

'I'm afraid your daughter is missing, Mr Dunn.'

Although his back was towards her she saw the tension seep into his shoulders before he shook his head.

'I'm sure you know I've not seen her since she was four years old.'

'Not once?' she asked, moving around the kitchen to the end of the work surface so she could see his face, which was focussed hard on the sliced ham he was adding to a smattering of grated cheese.

He shook his head in response. 'Her mother wouldn't allow it once I left.'

Stacey couldn't help wondering how hard he'd tried. There were courts and procedures and people to help him with seeing his own child.

'Yes, I tried,' he said, as though reading her thoughts. 'Maybe not as hard as I should but that's not something I'm going to share with you,' he said, turning to her. 'No offence.'

Stacey was surprised to see the pain in his eyes and wondered if she had judged him harshly.

'Mr Dunn, may I ask why you left?' she asked before she could stop herself.

'I'm sure you've already had one version of that story so I won't—'

'Your ex-wife says you left when Jessie got ill,' she said, but something about his demeanour caused her to wonder.

His smile was filled with irony. 'Of course she did.'

Stacey detected little anger in his tone. More resigned acceptance.

'But you're not here for a lesson in our family history. You want to know if Jessie is here, and I can assure you she's not.'

Stacey could hear the abject sadness in his tone and felt that her very presence was bringing back painful memories for him.

'Mr Dunn, I'm sorry…'

'Take a look around,' he said, cutting the sandwich in half. 'I have nothing to hide.'

Stacey knew she would get no better invitation and, despite her regret at being the source of his pain, she quietly thanked him before leaving the room.

His openness told her that Jessie wasn't here but she had an obligation to check. Nevertheless, she trod gently as she mounted the stairs, feeling her intrusion into his memories and his home.

All doors from the landing were open. She stood in the doorway of the first, which clearly belonged to Jeffrey Dunn. A double bed, one bedside lamp, an Ian Rankin novel and an alarm clock. The other bedside cabinet was empty.

The next room held a single bed without sheets or pillows. She stepped in and opened the wardrobe; it was empty. There was no other furniture in the room.

She entered the bathroom and looked around. There were no female toiletries in the cabinet or on the side of the bath. She checked the plugholes for evidence of longer hair, but there was nothing. She checked the waste bin for anything that hinted at a female presence, but it was empty.

If Jeffrey Dunn had ever remarried there was no evidence of it now. There was no doubt that this man lived alone.

She headed down the stairs after assessing the back garden. Enclosed by fencing on both sides the rectangle was free of lawn and was half slab and half gravel. There was no garden shed or storage boxes to check.

As she reached the bottom of the stairs she saw Mr Dunn sitting in the lounge with a coffee mug in hand.

Stacey paused. 'Thank you for being so cooperative and—'

'I didn't leave because my daughter became ill,' he said, turning to face her. 'Jessie was ill from birth. I was right there with my wife, talking to doctors, specialists. Poor kid has had every test to find out what's wrong with her: blood tests, scans, MRIs, the works.'

'So why did you?…'

'When Jessie first became ill my wife and I were a team, we handled it together, kept each other strong through the fear and the worry. Little by little Kerry began to pull away from me, started handling things alone. It was like she closed her arms around Jessie and there was just no room for anyone else.' He smiled, ruefully. 'I get how self-centred that sounds but it wasn't like that. I didn't want my wife's attention. I wanted to help them both, and I couldn't get close to either of them. It crucified me and eventually I gave in.'

He paused and looked at her, the pain of his loss still evident in his eyes.

'So you see I didn't really leave – because my wife had already left.'

CHAPTER 23

Saul Cordell blended onto the M5 motorway from the M6 around West Bromwich at ten minutes past ten.

And still he didn't quite know how he felt about the death of his father.

It had been almost twenty-four hours since the call from his mother informing him of his father's brutal murder. He had felt the immediate horror at the manner of his death. He had felt the anger that some sick bastard had done this to his father, but he was still waiting for something more. For the knowledge to reach a deeper place inside him. A place that would produce tears, regret, grief.

He wondered if some part of him had gone numb. He hoped so because he'd been able to summon more genuine emotion for his patients than he could for his father.

'Don't rush,' his mother had instructed, insisting there was nothing they could do for him now.

And he hadn't.

After the phone call, he had sat in the darkness for hours waiting for some kind of reaction.

And when it hadn't arrived he had watched the sun come up and headed off to work.

He'd called his mother, who had just sent away the family liaison officer. He had smiled ruefully. Of course she had. His mother could barely tolerate family in the kitchen she'd built from scratch never mind a stranger.

He had arrived at theatre at the Queen Elizabeth University Hospital in Glasgow calm, focussed and ready to work.

The morning surgery had been a laparoscopic nephrectomy on a forty-four-year-old woman. The keyhole procedure had suffered complications when bleeding required him to revert to open surgery to remove the kidney. In the afternoon he had assisted his mentor, Doctor Flint, on the kidney transplant of a nine-year-old girl.

Neither surgery would he have missed for anything and his mother understood that. She always understood. Sometimes too much.

He knew how many times she had forgiven his father's affairs over the years to keep the family together. He didn't have the heart to tell her it had been for nothing. He had not one tangible memory from his childhood that centred on his father. He was there, of course, in the background of the slideshow but it was his mother always at the forefront.

He knew his mother hadn't necessarily stayed with his father through love. Not after the first few dalliances, he reasoned. But she had known she couldn't afford the same opportunities for her sons without him. A thought that saddened him and yet made him love her even more.

He was wondering if his brother had already reached home as bright lights shone into his rear-view mirror from behind.

'Bloody hell, mate,' he said to himself trying to block out the blinding light and concentrate on the road. He'd been driving nonstop since five o'clock and was not in the mood. The M61 had blended to the M62 onto the M6 and now the final stretch of mundane, boring concrete before he could exit at junction 3 at Halesowen.

He blinked a few times to try and remove the shards of light that seemed to have burned on to his retina.

The vehicle was almost kissing his rear bumper. Only two days ago he'd had to replace his personalised number plate after it had been stolen for the fourth time. He'd been tempted to replace it, but the registered number had been a present from his mother when he finished medical school.

He indicated and moved into the middle lane. Maybe the idiot behind was in some kind of rush.

The lights blinded him again as the car followed him into the middle lane.

Saul drove another quarter mile before switching back to the slow lane.

Immediately the car behind switched back too.

He was momentarily blinded and lost sight of the road. He gripped the wheel tightly and drove straight hoping he was following the line of the road, waiting for his vision to return.

What the hell was this guy's problem? And why had his heartbeat increased so that the blood pounded through his ears?

Although not speeding he began to ease off the pedal bringing his speed down to sixty.

Suddenly the blinding light in his rear-view mirror disappeared, disorienting him.

He briefly hoped the guy had dropped right back. He let out a breath, unaware of the tension he'd been holding inside.

Two seconds later the flash was back, the vehicle's headlights back on high beam.

'For fuck's sake,' he said, slowing to fifty miles an hour.

On, off, on, off, on, off.

His eyes couldn't adjust to the light.

He knew stopping could be dangerous. He'd read enough horror stories about that. He tried to think what to do.

On, off, on, off, on, off.

He couldn't keep his eyes on the road. His vision was seriously limited.

He couldn't dare reach towards his phone in the handset.

He felt trapped as the panic began to rise inside him.

He slowed even more as he continued to drive through the whiteout in his eyes.

The light began to fade away. He looked into the mirror to see where it had gone as it disappeared up the off-ramp of junction 2. Thank God, he thought, as the relief swept over him.

He turned his attention back to the road and the smile died on his lips.

CHAPTER 24

Kim could feel Ted's eyes boring into her from behind as she filled the kettle.

'You turn up late at night and offer to make the coffee. Hmm. It must be bad,' he said, rubbing Barney's head.

Kim reached up into the top cupboard where Ted kept the Colombian Gold pack and the cafetière, especially for her.

'It's difficult,' she admitted.

'Not your current case then?' he asked.

Her most recent request of help from Ted during the Heathcrest investigation had been her need to know about children who kill.

Once again she felt regret that she only visited Ted when she wanted help on one of her cases.

'I know what you're thinking, and I don't mind,' he said. 'I'm flattered that you come to me at all.'

How the hell did he do that? she wondered.

'So, how's your leg?' he asked.

'Getting there,' she said, carrying the tray through to the living room.

He said nothing but sat in his favourite armchair. She took the chair opposite. Barney sat at her feet.

The first time they'd visited, Barney had claimed his spot on the sofa beside her. Despite Ted's protestations she'd made him get down immediately. What was acceptable in her own home was not necessarily acceptable elsewhere.

'He loves you,' Ted said, smiling at Barney.

'I feed him, that's what he loves,' she said, stroking his head.

'What he loves is your affection. He feels it and returns it unconditionally, which in turn allows you to trust and—'

'Ted, I'm not here for owner and dog therapy,' she advised.

Ted tipped his head. 'Apparently dog walking is a very sociable activity. Helps you make new friends?' he said, posing it as a question.

'He's a dog not a bloody miracle worker,' she scoffed.

Ted smiled and looked at her hand rubbing Barney's head. 'Hmm… I think on that I'd probably disagree.'

She said nothing as Ted leaned forward and pushed down the plunger, forcing the flavour from the coffee.

'So, if it's not a current case what can I help you with?'

'In a nutshell I need you to lie,' she said, raising her chin.

'No, you don't and you'd never even ask it of me.'

He was right. She wouldn't and he wouldn't.

'Let's just say there is concern for my psychological stability—'

'It's taken them this long?' Ted asked with a glint in his eye.

She narrowed her eyes. 'Since my colleague was killed,' she clarified.

'You mean Dawson? Kevin Dawson?' he asked.

'Of course,' she said, shortly.

He raised one eyebrow. 'Strange how every other time you've been here and mentioned him it's been either Dawson or Kev. And yet now you call him your colleague. Interesting.'

'Ted…' she warned, remembering just how dangerous this man was. Every word, every inference, every tone, every gesture was analysed.

'Basically, they want to know if I'm fit for work.'

'Hmm…' he said, stroking his chin. 'I thought counselling was mandatory after such a traumatic event.'

'I was off sick, and Woody just needs to tick the box…'

'Oh, so simple…'

'By the end of the week,' she added.

He looked horrified. 'So, I'm supposed to unravel a lifetime of abuse, guilt, cruelty, neglect and declare you fit for work by Friday?'

'Other than the taking me apart bit, pretty much,' she answered. 'Because we both know that's never gonna happen.'

He nodded his understanding.

'Well, I can give you my answer and my recommendations right now and they will not change by Friday, and taking you apart would do nothing to alter it.'

'So, you already know the answer so there's no need to talk at all?' she said. 'I could just tell Woody…'

'Oh, Kim, sometimes it's like you pretend not to know me at all. Of course, we're going to talk but I'm not going to analyse your past. What matters right now is your present. And you know that as well as I do.'

'I'm actually fine,' she said. 'Totally normal and able to function.'

'Yes, you have become quite the expert at that. But, why didn't you take Woody's offer of a police psychologist, Kim? You and I both know you could run rings around any one of them. You spent the entirety of your formative years and beyond learning how to manipulate and avoid actually showing your true emotions to mental health professionals. They'd have had you signed off as fit for service in two sessions. You know that.'

'So, what are you saying?' she asked, bristling.

'I'm saying you insisted on seeing me not to satisfy Woody you're fit for duty…'

Kim said nothing.

'You came to see me because *you* want to satisfy yourself that you're fit for duty.'

CHAPTER 25

Yes, yes, yes. Two down and many more to go.

It really is so simple as long as you plan ahead.

I knew where you worked, Saul Cordell. I knew the pathetic, pretentious registration number of your car. I knew where you'd join the M5 and all I had to do was wait.

I was laughing so hard as I flashed on and off, on and off blinding you. I could imagine your panic, feel your fear. I timed my exit to perfection. Exit at junction 2, leaving you so disoriented you would never see the traffic cones, or the yellow vehicle with the flashing lights and the directional blue arrow warning you to change lane.

Splat.

Right into the back of the lorry; the sound of the impact filled the air like an explosion.

I can picture the chaos, the mayhem; everything bathed in the blue flashing lights of the emergency services. Fire, Police and Ambulance. Huddles of people rushing, planning, assessing risk, calling their superiors. All too late. Always too late.

As fun as it was it didn't come close to the satisfaction I felt at slitting your father's throat. The very action of pulling the knife across his flesh released something from inside me and for the first time in weeks I smiled.

Oh, the stupidity of the idiot Doctor Gordon Cordell when offered the choice.

Because there'd really been no choice at all.

CHAPTER 26

'Don't be ridiculous,' Kim raged. She didn't need Ted to tell her she could do her job. She knew she could.

Ted sat back and sipped his coffee.

'Why the hell would I do something so stupid, Ted? I came to you because I knew you'd help me or that I could manipulate you.'

'But why would you think that?' he asked, dumbfounded.

'Because I've always managed to do it in the past.'

'Name one time,' he challenged.

'Only one?' she said. She'd got dozens.

'We'll see,' he said, sipping his drink.

'Okay, there was that time when I told you that I was going to kick shit out of Tanya Smith if I had to spend one more minute with her in Fairview. I got back and she'd been moved for her own safety. I know it was you who sorted it,' she said smartly.

'You were ten-years-old and Tanya Smith was fifteen and had been at Fairview since she was a toddler. You had just been returned from foster home number two. I knew you weren't capable of violence for no reason and suspected she was taunting you and making your life a misery. That's why I called Fairview and told them you would benefit from a short spell on your own.'

Damn him, that's exactly what had been going on. Tanya had decided that to gain entry to her own room Kim had to pay Tanya the meagre amount of pocket money gifted to them by the state each week. Refusal had earned her a split lip. How the hell had

Ted known? Okay, he'd got lucky that time but there were plenty more examples of how she'd played him over the years.

'How about that time I told you I'd spent my last few quid to buy the new jacket you asked me about? I lied. I stole it.'

'You were thirteen and just back from your time with Erica and Keith. The minute you left I called Fairview and advised them not to let you go shopping alone for a while as you were shoplifting.'

Kim paused. Yeah, they had watched her like a hawk after that.

'So, you see, my dear, there are times you think you're pulling the wool over my eyes and you're really not. So, let's be clear.'

Kim couldn't help the smile that formed on her lips. Not many people were a match for her but even now in his late sixties he gave it a bloody good try.

He continued. 'So, you've asked for my help and this is how it's going to work. We'll talk a bit. I'll ask you a few simple questions and we'll see how much we have to work on.'

'There's really nothing to work on,' she insisted.

Barney sneezed, loudly.

'My thoughts exactly,' Ted said, smiling at the dog.

'Traitor,' she said, tapping his head lightly.

'Okay, start by telling me the things that have pissed you off today. Nothing to do with the case you're working, aside from that, what's rattled your cage?'

'Just today?' she asked.

'Yes. You have to remember I'm sixty-nine years of age. I have limited time.'

'Funny,' Kim said, narrowing her eyes. 'Okay, chronologically: being unable to drive myself to work; having a new team member foisted upon me, but he'll be gone by the end of the week so that's really not a problem. Being told that I'm not pushing my detective constable enough or encouraging her to develop. Having to apologise to my boss for doubting him on the last case. Feeling

CHAPTER 27

Austin Penn crossed the last CCTV location from his list and removed the headphones. The clock above the door told him it was almost eleven and that his first day had been a long one. But that was okay. He would put the hours in when he could and a quick call home had confirmed that today was one of those days. There would be days when he couldn't but that admission was for some other day.

In truth, he was glad when Stacey had left the office to work on whatever was calling from her satchel. Even when she hadn't been aware of it her face had been set in a scowl as though she'd been forced to eat a whole jar of marmite and the taste still lingered on her tongue.

He got it. He'd worked with this team twice before and understood how close they were; how they operated as a well-oiled machine, working without instruction, knowing and understanding their roles and skills and where they fitted into each investigation, and now one of their vital components was missing. His own team had not been quite so efficient or structured.

As if by osmosis his mobile rang. He smiled at the name that flashed on his screen.

'Hey, Lyn,' he said, knowing the smile showed in his voice. She was the other DS in his old team at West Mercia.

Her petite, elfin stature and smooth milky skin always fooled people into thinking she was younger than her thirty-one years, and so the ferocious terrier that could be unleashed on demand came as a surprise to suspects, criminals and just about anyone else who tried to take the piss out of her.

She'd been engaged to her fireman boyfriend for eleven months but still hadn't set a wedding date.

'Hey, new boy. How's your first day gone?'

He didn't mind admitting it was good to hear a familiar, friendly voice.

'You know,' he said. 'As expected.'

'It's tough fitting into a new team,' she said. 'Especially when…'

'Oh yeah,' he said. Especially when a member of that team has recently died horrifically in the line of duty, he thought, finishing the sentence in his mind.

'Missed ya,' she said lightly.

Although they'd not had specific partners in the team, the two of them had paired up on many occasions.

'And Wilma was looking for you,' she said.

Penn laughed out loud realising just how much tension he was holding in his body. Wilma was the potted plant that his old boss, Travis, had awarded daily to the teacher's pet. It was fair to say it had graced his desk the majority of the time.

'Give her my love,' he said, enjoying the easy banter between them. It had only been a day but he missed it already. More so because he knew he wouldn't be going back. He couldn't. Given the choice he would have stayed where he was. But he didn't have a choice. Not any more. But of all the things he'd been forced to leave behind, working with Lyn was probably what he'd miss most.

He clicked on his emails as Lyn carried on speaking, telling him how they'd all piled their belongings onto his old desk to prevent Travis from replacing him. A wave of homesickness coursed through him.

'So, what's the boss like?' she asked.

'Intense,' he answered, starting the process of closing down his system. His eyes passed over the most recent alerts from the internal server.

A name jumped right out the screen at him and he wondered if he'd made some kind of mistake.

'Well, I knew that,' Lyn said, referring to the joint investigation into Hate Crimes. 'But she seems like a decent—'

'Oh shit, sorry, Lyn, gotta go,' he said, ending the call.

He checked the name again.

No, there was no mistake.

CHAPTER 28

Kim arrived at the cordon to the slip road at ten minutes to eleven.

She'd received Penn's call as she'd been leaving Ted's house. She'd told him to ring Bryant and get him to meet her there.

The journey had been filled with traffic updates of closed roads and diversions.

The officers let her car through, and she drove halfway down the exit ramp of junction 2 to the mêlée of vehicles, two fire trucks, two ambulances and more squad cars than she could count.

'Right, stay and be good,' Kim told Barney as she got out of the car.

She worked hard to control the limp that was taunting her left leg. About the driving maybe the doctor had had a point.

'Adams,' she called, recognising the traffic inspector responsible for the investigation into the death of Joanne Wade from Heathcrest.

He frowned as she approached.

'You're not stalking me, are you, Inspector?' he asked with a smile.

'Yeah, cos I'd really jump out and shout your name if I was a stalker,' she said, wryly.

'So, you're here because?…'

'The name of the victim,' she said, as the sound of a generator kicked in.

Realisation dawned. 'Cordell. Is this guy related to the throat guy?'

She nodded. 'Son, I think,' she said as someone called Adams's name.

Bryant appeared as she followed the inspector towards the source of the call. It had come from a fire officer who also inclined his head in her direction, questioningly. Adams explained who she was as Bryant reached them.

'This really Cordell's son?' her colleague asked.

'Looks like it,' she said, as the fire officer moved off at speed.

'They're getting close,' Adams said, weaving through vehicles to reach the impact site.

Kim followed, and walked into a throng of people moving with a sense of urgency and anticipation.

The motorway was closed in both directions lending an eeriness to the bustle of activity amidst the silence and darkness beyond the flashing lights.

'Keep back, please,' said a fire officer placing a beefy arm in front of her.

'Fuck me,' Bryant said from beside her. His extra height gave him the advantage of looking above the fireman.

As he moved to the side Kim understood the reason for his out of character curse.

The entire front end of the Audi appeared to have disappeared, smashed against the motorway vehicle.

Kim's breath caught in her throat.

The guy hadn't stood a chance.

She could see that the firemen were pointing to the rear screen, which she was guessing they'd already smashed. She knew that they would already have tested and assessed all ways to try and retrieve the body to preserve damage.

One fireman stood poised with the cutter and nodded to his colleague. The second fireman stood back as the first positioned the claw-like blades inside the screen gap aimed up to the roof.

The sudden sound of the metal cracking apart silenced and drew the attention of everyone. Conversation of any kind was now impossible and hand movements and signs passed between the firemen in a well-rehearsed mime.

Within minutes the pincers had cut a line through the metal.

As a second fireman moved forward with the spreader, Kim could see the strategy they'd adopted. Using the natural gap left by the rear screen they were cutting and spreading open the metal to a wide enough gap to bring him out.

A third fireman approached with the ram, normally used to lift or push an obstacle out of their path.

'What the hell is gonna be left of him when they get him out?' Kim asked sadly, thinking of Mrs Cordell and her other son. This family had suffered enough.

'Hopefully enough for these guys to work on,' he said, looking anxiously to the paramedics.

Kim's head whipped around. 'You're not saying?…'

'Oh yes, Inspector, as of about seven minutes ago, Saul Cordell was still alive.'

CHAPTER 29

Kim had insisted on being the one to talk to Saul Cordell's family, who knew nothing of the accident.

Adams had made a call and halted the informing officer two miles from the front door.

She had hauled Barney out of the car and into Bryant's Astra, which he was now driving out of the cordon at the top of the slip road.

She counted backwards in her head.

Five, four, three…

'So, what were you doing driving yourself around?' he asked, on cue.

'Oh Bryant, I'm a big girl,' she protested.

'And you can look after yourself,' he mimicked, before sobering. 'I've told you to call me. I'll run you anywhere you need to go.'

'I went to see Ted,' she said, looking behind and seeing that Barney had curled up on the back seat.

'Oh… Oh,' he said as the penny dropped. 'Woody's authorised him to do your counselling?'

'Bloody hell, Bryant, you're clearly sharper at this time of night. Maybe we should consider changing your hours.'

'Ah, deflection. A defence mechanism for all occasions, but why Ted? You know he can see straight through you. I'd have thought you'd be better seeing a force appointed… aah, I think I've got it.'

'Well just make sure you keep it,' Kim said, staring out of the window. She really didn't need to be analysed by her colleague as well. And Ted had given her more than enough to think about.

CHAPTER 30

Kim took a deep breath before knocking on the door of the home they'd visited earlier that day.

'Inspector,' said Lilith Cordell with surprise.

A multitude of emotions passed over her face, concern, fear, expectation even though she couldn't have had a clue what she was here to tell them.

'Have you found him?' she asked, stepping aside as though it was perfectly normal for Kim to be knocking her door at five minutes past midnight.

'Found who?' Kim asked, momentarily taken aback.

'The murderer, Inspector. Surely that's why you're here at this time of night. I wouldn't normally be up but we're waiting for Saul, my eldest.'

'No, Mrs Cordell, that isn't why we're here,' Kim said, gently. 'Please, sit down.'

Luke appeared beside his mother dressed in grey joggers and a tee shirt. Out of his suit he looked younger but no less antagonistic than earlier.

'Inspector, I hope you have a good reason for—'

'Mrs Cordell, please sit down,' Kim said, ignoring the youngest son. 'Saul is the reason we're here.'

She simply dropped onto the couch and reached for her son's hand. He took it, his expression now every bit as anxious as his mother's.

'Is he all right?' she asked, as the last few drops of colour faded from her cheeks.

'I'm afraid he's been in an accident on the motorway.'

'Oh my God, is he… is he?…'

'Dead?' Luke finished for her.

'He was alive when we left, but barely,' Kim explained so as not to get their hopes up. 'I have to tell you that he was trapped in the car wreckage for a while. We had confirmation a few minutes ago that he was released and airlifted to Russells Hall Hospital.'

'Alive?' Mrs Cordell asked, trembling.

'Yes, but please don't get your hopes up. The accident was—'

'We must go to him,' she said, standing and turning to Luke.

'Not so fast,' Kim said, standing. This was a woman who didn't take direction well.

'We have a car waiting at the end of the drive to take you,' she said.

Luke shook his head. 'I can—'

'I insist, Mr Cordell,' she said, firmly. 'Firstly, there's the fact neither of you should be driving while in shock; secondly the squad car will get you there quicker than—'

'Inspector, what were the circumstances of my son's accident?' Mrs Cordell asked, astutely.

'We don't yet know the exact details,' she admitted. 'The priority was in releasing your son from the car.'

'You said accident,' she said.

Kim nodded. 'Until we learn otherwise. Now, the squad car will get you to the hospital and an officer will remain with you. Please, be prepared that you probably won't be able to see Saul for a while and when you do—'

'The police don't normally operate a taxi and babysitting service for the families of traffic accidents, do they?'

Kim shook her head. Damn this woman who had managed to keep her wits and composure despite the horrific news about her son.

'You think the two are related, don't you? My husband's murder and my son's accident. You think someone has it in for our family?'

Kim thought about the missing photograph from the frame at Cordell's flat.

She nodded slowly and honestly. 'Yes, Mrs Cordell, I do.'

CHAPTER 31

Kim took her coffee mug into the general office and sat on the spare desk.

'Okay, guys, thanks for coming in early, we've got a lot to get through.'

Bryant had dropped her back at the crash site just after 1 a.m. and then followed her home. He was clearly taking her doctor's advice more seriously than she was.

After her late-night walk with Barney she had crawled into bed at 2 a.m., and it was now ten minutes after seven. The maths wasn't hard to do and the vision of the crumpled metal was still at the forefront of her mind.

'So, you all know about Saul Cordell's accident. Thank you for flagging that up, Penn,' she said, nodding in his direction.

He nodded.

'You all know we're getting nowhere near that case. Traffic will handle it whether it was accidental or intentional. They only allowed me to inform the family because I'd already spoken to them about Gordon Cordell. We're not going to be able to prove any link to our case that isn't perceived as coincidental, though Adams has agreed to keep us in the loop on all the findings.'

Kim paused as a voice in her head said, *they really gonna say the two cases aren't linked?* The words didn't come but they had sounded very much like Dawson. He had always had the knack of sharing her same levels of incredulity. He would have argued that they needed to take the case from the collision investigation team, finding the coincidence too dry a mouthful to swallow. And she would have had to remind him that they couldn't control everything. But the room was quiet and the conversation was happening only in her head.

'Stacey, you're the contact for Adams, so feel free to call him every few hours and ask for updates, okay?'

'Yeah, boss,' she answered, making a note.

Kim was unsure if it was her imagination or if the constable was looking particularly pensive.

'How is he?' Penn asked. 'Saul Cordell, I mean.'

'Critical,' she answered. 'Doctors are still trying to identify all his injuries. He's been put into an induced coma to give his body a chance to adjust. We know there are countless broken bones, internal bleeding and possible brain damage.'

Kim had called the hospital the moment she'd got out of bed. The nurse had explained the coma had been induced to protect his brain from swelling. She understood that the controlled dose of anaesthetic caused a lack of feeling or awareness and that Saul could not be woken by stimulation, including pain. Given the extent of his injuries she suspected it was the only way to try and save his life, so even if she could sneak in without Traffic knowing she wouldn't be speaking to him any time soon. The report from the constable with Mrs Cordell and her younger son had confirmed they had spent the night by his bedside. Kim couldn't even imagine what they were going through.

'Jesus,' Stacey said, shaking her head.

'Prognosis isn't great but his mother and brother are by his side, which is fine by me,' she answered. Short of locking them away until they knew what they were dealing with, the hospital was a safe place to be. Another constable had taken over the babysitting and had been advised to keep a respectful distance. She knew a third shift wouldn't be authorised, so they had to come up with something today or the two of them would be left vulnerable.

'You think they're in danger?' Penn asked.

'I think we have to explore the possibility of a vendetta against the whole family because of Gordon Cordell's murder and the brutality of the crime. This was not a functional kill.'

'Could be any one of them, boss,' Penn continued. 'Maybe just started with the dad but it could be something to do with the sons.'

He had a point. Daddy Cordell might have been first because he was the easiest or closest.

'Get into it, Penn,' she said, realising they couldn't just assume it was Cordell senior because he was an unlikeable bastard. Luke Cordell appeared to have been cut from the same cloth, but about Saul she had no information at all.

'Anything back on the shoe print?' she asked.

Penn shook his head. 'Still going through the database and sent all the main manufacturers reminders last night. I'm hoping for something later today.'

She nodded. There was nothing they could do on the fibres until Mitch had more detail to offer them.

'How about the sexual harassment complaints?'

'I've established that not one of the women who made a complaint still work at the clinic. All ex- employees and all seemingly good character.'

'Dead end, then?' she asked, feeling the doubt that so many genuine complaints had been forthcoming at the same time.

'Not sure, boss,' Penn said, mirroring her reservations. 'May be a bit too tidy. I'd like to give it another shot to make sure.'

She nodded her agreement.

'You still think the Spades are behind Cordell's murder, guv?' Bryant asked her.

She shook her head. 'Not any more.'

'Why not?' he asked.

'Basically, because I'm still alive,' she said. 'Woody assures me he passed on the message, and he's received no backlash or instruction for me to stop, so I'm pretty sure they have nothing to hide on this one.'

She turned back to Penn. 'I'd still like to know if those sexual harassment complaints are genuine.'

'Got it, boss.'

She turned to the constable who was looking increasingly uneasy. 'CCTV, Stace?'

'Oops, sorry, Stacey, I borrowed your notes earlier,' Penn said, reaching across and pushing a single piece of paper towards her.

Stacey's eyes fell to the desk.

'Err... umm... traffic cameras on Mucklow Hill are out of order. Nothing showing from the petrol station. B&Q at the island have a PTZ facing that's been vandalised. Camera at Shenstone Island showed 196 cars going past in the time frame. The hardware shop opposite the park has turned his camera on the yard to uncover petty theft. The three cameras from the town centre are—'

'Stace, I don't need your work record,' Kim said, frowning. Stacey didn't do blow-by-blow accounts. 'Is there anything of interest?'

The constable finished reading her notes and shook her head.

'Okay, work with Penn for now. Bryant and I will be going back to the hospital to find out more about Cordell. I'd like to speak to some of the folks that worked with him.'

Kim caught an accusing glance from Stacey to Penn. She had no clue why but she had an idea how to find out. Stacey was not a secret keeper.

'Bryant, get some names of people we can speak to.'

'Okay, guv.'

*

Kim headed into The Bowl and pretended to shuffle some papers on her desk until she heard the polite cough she'd hoped for.

'Boss, can I have a word?' Stacey asked.

Kim nodded towards the door.

Stacey closed it and sat down.

'Gotta tell the truth, boss. Penn just covered for me in there. I didn't do the CCTV checking. He did and then tried to get me off the hook.'

Which is why it had sounded as though Stacey was reading the information from a list instead of retrieving it from her own brain.

'What's going on, Stace?' Kim asked.

'I was gonna come in early boss and catch up, but then you called an early briefing so I didn't get chance.'

'But why didn't you do the CCTV checks yourself?' Kim asked with concern.

'Boss, while you were gone, my time at Sedgley was spent doing mainly grunt work but just before I came back I took a report on something and it kinda stuck to me.'

'What kind of something?' Kim asked, folding her arms.

'Missing girl, Jessie… Jessica Ryan, fifteen years old. Possible runaway. No one really gave a shit cos she's a few days away from hitting her sixteenth birthday and she's pulled this kind of caper twice before.'

'Okay,' Kim said, waiting for more. Police resources dictated that priorities had to be made. A hard fact of life but a fact all the same. And a fact that Stacey knew well in the face of a murder investigation.

'I just didn't want to abandon her,' Stacey said. 'And now, I've found out that she's on a lot of medication and could be at risk if she doesn't take her stuff. There was violence involved with her stepfather, and her best friend is as cagey as anything. Doesn't feel right to me,' she said.

'You want to carry on working it despite the fact it's not ours?' Kim asked.

'I do, boss. I wanna know what's happened to this girl.'

Kim was suddenly revisited by Woody's words, like the shadowy ghost of Christmas past. *You've got to bring her on*, it said, before she sighed it away.

'Okay, Stace, follow it and see where it goes, but working on the Cordell case comes first, and I want to know exactly where you are and what you're doing at all times. Got it?'

The last time Stacey had investigated alone she had almost lost her life at the hands of a bunch of vicious, despicable racist bastards.

Stacey beamed. 'Thank you, boss,' she said, heading out the door.

Kim looked after her, knowing she'd done the right thing in giving Stacey the green light to go this one alone.

So, why the hell did she feel so shitty?

CHAPTER 32

'There was no need to do that,' Stacey said, once the boss and Bryant had left the room.

Penn shrugged but said nothing as he continued to tap away on his computer.

'I don't need anyone to do my job for me,' she said, resenting the fact he'd thought she needed help. And that she'd actually be grateful it had come from him. This was her office and her team. Not his.

'Cool,' he said, reading something on his computer.

'So, don't expect me to thank you or anything,' she growled.

'You're welcome,' he said, without looking at her.

'You had no place—'

'Sorry, I thought I heard you say thank you. My mistake.'

'Look, Penn, I'm not sure how things worked in your last team but here we don't lie to the boss. Me and Kev…'

'I'm not Kev,' he said, quietly but firmly.

'Too bloody right you're not,' she snapped, feeling the rage of that one single truth clutching at her stomach. 'And actually, that's what I'm going to call you from now on "Not Kev".'

'Cool,' he said, again. 'Now, I've got an idea for getting to the bottom of this sexual harassment thing but I'm gonna need your help.'

Stacey felt her jaws lock together at the calm, neutral tone of his voice, as though she'd never spoken. His complete lack of reaction was becoming pretty annoying.

She'd had no choice but to come clean with the boss. Every minute she'd spent on the case the previous day without her boss's permission or knowledge had eaten away at everything she valued in being part of this team. She'd expected impatience, anger, disapproval and a refusal to allow her to take the case forward. Instead the boss had listened, understood and sanctioned. With conditions.

And one of those conditions was that work on the case of the murder of Gordon Cordell came before anything else. Even her growing disgust at the man sitting opposite.

'Okay, you've got me for the next ten minutes. Use it well.'

CHAPTER 33

'You do know there's a bit of a problem developing back there?' Bryant asked as they headed towards the car.

The early morning mist through which she'd driven to work had now been burned away by a watery sun.

'It'll sort itself out,' she replied.

'You sure?' he pushed.

'What do you expect, Bryant? How do you expect m… her to feel? Stacey and Dawson were a great team and they were better friends than even they knew.'

'It's not Penn's fault,' he offered. 'And you might need to step in is all I'm saying. Penn might not take too well to being treated—'

'Bryant, I get that it's been a while but name your worst time joining a new team.'

He thought. 'Probably having my locker door glued shut as a PC. Got in all kinds of shit for breaking it open.'

'Good for you if that was your worst,' she replied. 'When I joined CID I walked around for half a day with a sign on my back saying "tea bitch". Now do you see any glued lockers or malicious signs?'

'We both know it can take many forms, guv,' he said, seriously, but Kim wasn't in the mood to listen and was prepared to drive home her point.

'You've just spent a few weeks at Brierley Hill. They bake you a cake? Crack open the welcome bunting? Take you for a pint down the local after a shift?'

Bryant took a deep breath. 'That was a temporary secondment due to—'

'And so is this,' she said, firmly. 'One case and then he's gone.'

'Even so,' Bryant persisted. 'You know Stacey is being more than a little stand-offish with him, and it's almost like you're deliberately allowing it. My dad used to say "why have a dog and bark yourself" which is what you're—'

'Bryant, I have no idea what you're talking about.'

'You really want something on her record about bullying and—'

'Don't you dare use that word in connection with Stacey,' she raged. 'You know that girl as well as I do and she is not a bully. Not even close. For fuck's sake, she's a black, bisexual female in the police force. You really want to talk to her about bullying?'

Bryant refused to back down. 'Firstly, that would give her no excuse to pay it forward; secondly, I'm not saying she's a bully. I am saying isolation lives in the same family and you may have to manage the situation before it gets out of hand.'

'Oh how I love when you tell me how to manage my team,' she growled. 'You really think I'm gonna let anyone get bullied right in front of my eyes, even if they're temporary? I can see that Stacey is being cool towards Penn but I can't make her like him. Providing she remains polite and professional I'll let them sort it out themselves.'

'If this case goes on longer than…'

'Bryant,' she said, turning to face him as he put the key into the ignition. 'You're an anecdote man. You have a never-ending supply and one to suit every occasion. So, here's one for you.'

He turned off the engine and looked her way.

'When I was ten years old at Fairview there were four of us in one room. Two sets of bunk beds. The two girls opposite were best mates, Zoe and Liz, both fourteen and in Fairview since they were nippers. Neither of them was going anywhere. Talked all night about the flat they were going to get together when they were old enough.

'One day Zoe's aunt came and got her after agreeing to give it a try. Bye, Bye, Zoe. Two days later a seven-year-old kid was given the bottom bunk beneath Liz. Obviously, Liz made her life a misery, nicking what few things she liked and breaking what she didn't. One time she spooned a whole tin of sardines onto the girl's mattress. We had the smell for weeks.'

'So, what did you do?' Bryant asked.

'Absolutely nothing,' she said. 'The kid had to find her own breaking point, the limit at which she'd fight her own corner. Sticking up for her and fighting her battles wouldn't have helped her in the long run. She had to do it for herself.'

'And did she?' Bryant said, starting the car.

Kim shrugged and glanced up at the window realising that she had outright lied in her story about Liz and Zoe.

Because that wasn't what she'd done at all.

CHAPTER 34

'So, let me get this straight?' Stacey asked, incredulously. 'You want me to ring one of the sexual harassment victims, pretend I'm a victim and get her to open up to me?'

'Yes,' he said, simply. 'I'd do it myself if I could.'

'And if she works out that I never even worked at Oakwood?'

'Why would she? If we choose the one that's been away longest she won't have a clue of the names behind the other complaints. Just don't use your real name.'

She'd heard better plans and, to be fair, she'd heard worse. And it was probably something she would have done herself.

'Okay, give me the number,' she said. 'And what's her name?'

'Cheryl Hawkins.'

Stacey keyed in the number as Penn read it off to her.

The phone was answered after the second ring.

'Hello, is that Cheryl?' Stacey asked.

'It is,' the female voice said, warily.

'Hi Cheryl, my name is Stacey Penn and I'm sorry to bother you but I overheard your name and...' she paused for drama. 'I'm one of Cordell's victims too and—'

'How did you get this number?' she asked, sharply.

'I just want to talk to someone about what happened. I mean I'm having trouble with—'

'Look, whoever you are just leave me the hell alone.'

The line went dead in her ear.

'Well, that worked,' she grumbled.

Penn raised one eyebrow. 'Didn't realise when I asked for your help it meant we were gonna get married but—'

'What now?' she asked.

'Well, there's the honeymoon to book…'

'Grow up,' she snapped.

'Try another,' he said. 'We've got a few to go at. We only want to know if they're genuine complaints. It only takes one.'

'Okay, next,' she said.

'Pippa Round,' he said, and then read out the number.

This one answered immediately.

The hello was rushed against a wall of background noise.

'Hi Pippa, sorry to call, you don't know me. My name is Stacey and I worked at Oakland too.'

'So?' she said, impatiently.

'I worked closely with Doctor Cordell a few months ago. I'm another one of his victims.'

'And?'

Jesus she'd caught a real conversationalist here. This was going nowhere.

'I just… I'm not sure what we do?' she said, trying to think of something to say.

'About what?'

'Well, I mean the man's dead and—'

'Listen, if you'll take my advice you'll do what the rest of us are doing,' she hissed.

'What?' Stacey asked. 'What should I do?'

'Spend the money and keep your mouth shut like everyone else.'

The line went dead in Stacey's hand.

'Well, Notkev, I think we just got our answer.'

CHAPTER 35

Kim spotted a familiar face amongst the early morning bustle of Russells Hall Hospital.

'Hey, Terry,' she said to the volunteer in the red tee shirt. 'Where might I find the office of the Operational Medical Director, Vanessa Wilson?'

He started pointing and explaining and then stopped and smiled. 'It'll be far easier if I just take you.'

'Thanks,' she said, falling into step beside him.

'How's the leg?' he asked, pleasantly.

'Bearing up,' she answered. 'And thank you for your kindness the other day.'

'You're welcome, that's what we're here for. Assisting visitors and the odd errand now and again.'

'Did you know Doctor Cordell?' she asked, imagining that the talk around the place was of little else. Kim understood this was a large community of workers, numbering in the thousands but she was guessing every other conversation in the entire place centred around the murder.

'Not really. That's to say I knew of him. Saw him pass through, saw him when I dropped off files or post to his office a few times, but I've only been here a few weeks,' he said, turning a corner away from the main corridor.

She glanced at him questioningly. She guessed him to be mid-thirties, shaved head, slightly overweight but appearing to be fit and healthy. Most volunteers seemed much older.

'Forced period of unemployment, officer. I'm a jobseeker and apparently it looks good on your CV if you've done voluntary work. Shows willing.'

'Fair play to you,' she said.

He stopped walking. 'Down there, second on the left,' he said, pointing down the corridor.

Kim thanked him and headed towards the office, realising they had completely left behind the hubbub of the hospital.

'Not gonna get bothered down here too much, eh?' Bryant said as she knocked on the door.

'Come in,' Vanessa Wilson called out.

Despite her surprise at their impromptu visit she beckoned them in and then pointed to the phone at her ear.

'Look, can you just pick her up from school and take her to my mum's? I'll call later,' she said, facing the window.

'Yeah, you too,' she said, with less stress in her voice.

'Sorry about that,' she said. 'Six-year-old has developed sickness and diarrhoea in the half hour since I dropped her off.'

'Yep, been there many years ago,' Bryant sympathised.

She reached for her diary looking genuinely concerned. 'Sorry, did I miss?…'

'No, Mrs Wilson, we just happened by for a quick word.'

She looked relieved.

'Okay, but please call me Vanessa. Now, how may I help you?' she asked, finally sitting down.

They had caught this woman at the end of the day and now at the start of the day. Right now the hair was held back tightly, the make-up was flawless and there were no telltale crease marks across her midriff.

'Mrs… sorry, Vanessa, are you aware that Gordon Cordell's eldest son was brought here late last night?'

'Saul?' she asked.

'You know him?' Kim asked, surprised.

She nodded. 'Vaguely. He's been to the odd function with his father. He's a surgeon too. I've not yet had chance to read the nightlies. What's wrong with him?'

Kim guessed that the nightlies was some kind of overnight briefing. 'Car crash on the motorway last night. He's in ICU, in an induced coma. It was pretty bad,' Kim said. 'It was nothing short of a miracle he survived, and no one expected him to live through the extraction from his vehicle.'

'Bloody hell,' she said, her eyes wide. 'I must go down and see him. That poor family.'

'Yes,' Kim agreed. 'But we're back because of something you said yesterday when we mentioned complaints against Doctor Cordell. You said something about it being the other way round.'

'Oh, it's nothing,' she said. 'Just an internal matter.'

'Let us be the judge of that, please, Vanessa. It might be important.'

'Okay, Doctor Cordell made a complaint against a member of cleaning staff, Angelo Mancini, who has been a cleaner here for eleven years. Doctor Cordell caught him attempting to steal equipment from Theatre 3, I should add allegedly, and reported him for attempted theft.'

'To you?'

Vanessa shook her head. 'No, he went directly to the police, but I assured them I would deal with it. So, it's now an internal investigation with a disciplinary hearing at the end of this week.' She paused. 'You don't think?...' She clamped her hand over her mouth. 'Oh my goodness... no... it couldn't... he wouldn't...'

'What?' Kim asked, as she could see the sums being done in the woman's head.

'Mr Mancini didn't react well to being suspended from duty. He promised he would "get" Cordell and he would "get him good", but I'm sure he didn't mean anything…'

Kim felt the excitement churn at her stomach.

'Vanessa, I think you'd better let us have Angelo Mancini's address.'

CHAPTER 36

Stacey stepped out of the taxi outside Emma Weston's house. She didn't feel the teenager had been truthful with her the day before but there was no point trying to speak to her again until she had something to ask. She hadn't got a particularly good vibe from the mother either.

She had returned wondering if the neighbours had seen or heard anything. She looked up and down the street but no property looked exceptionally inviting.

She thought about the house that had a nice Volvo parked the day before. They were directly opposite. She crossed the road and began walking and then stopped before she got there, right next to a white transit van.

She looked at the property. Dishwater-grey net curtains hung at the upstairs window with a dark-coloured roller blind behind. Four slabs with huge gaps in between formed a makeshift path to the front door over a quagmire of grass tufts and mud.

She took long steps and hit the glass in the absence of a knocker. A few cigarette butts were piling up beneath the front room window.

There was no answer and no movement. She knocked again. Harder. It definitely looked as though the white transit belonged to this house. There had to be someone home.

She heard the sound of cursing, and footsteps thundering down the stairs.

'What the fucking?...'

The man's words stopped dead as he laid eyes on her.

Stacey was aware that the bearded bear of a man was hardly dressed and was covered only in a black tee shirt and a pair of yellow shorts. Bird tattoos covered his meaty arms.

'Sir, I'm really sorry to disturb you but is that a dashcam in your transit?'

'That'd be funny if I hadn't just worked a bloody long night shift. Now, what the?…'

His words trailed away as she held up her identification.

'I ain't broke no laws,' he protested, shaking his head. 'Little bastards keep slashing my tyres, and you lot won't do anything without evidence.'

'Sir, you're not in any trouble. I'll start again. I'm Detective Constable Stacey Wood investigating the case of a missing fifteen-year-old girl and I'd really like your help.'

Sleep-deprived or not she saw the anger seep out of him. He scratched at a spot on his chest that was just to the right of a toothpaste stain.

'Well, put like that, how can I refuse?' he said, standing aside.

Stacey stepped into a dated residence full of swirls and twirls but much tidier than she'd expected. There was no television or radio playing and that was because this was his night time.

'Sir, was your van parked there on Sunday night?'

'For a while, why?'

'Could I see the footage?' she asked.

'It's not Emma Weston who's gone cos I saw her this morning,' he said, reaching for his phone from the telephone table in the hall.

'No, her friend, Jessie, blonde, pretty, fifteen years old.'

'I think I know who you mean,' he said, pressing an app on his phone. He tapped in the details surprisingly quickly with his meaty fingers.

The screen sprang into life. He passed her the phone. 'Here, have a look while I go and put some clothes on.'

'Not on my account,' she said, appreciating the offer. 'I'll let you get back to bed as soon as I can.'

She keyed in the date she wanted and entered '10.30' but the screen came back blank. She rolled backwards until she caught a movement. She stopped it and watched. A few people walked past. Three kids on bikes rode up and down the pavement a couple of times, and a small Jack Russell terrier appeared from nowhere, took a dump and disappeared again. She kept watching, and at 8.35 p.m. both girls exited Emma Weston's house. The footage caught them walking down the path talking animatedly. Emma was waving her hands around in what looked like frustration. Jessie seemed to be walking away.

Stacey couldn't take her eyes off Jessie, seeing her in the flesh instead of staring at her photo. Just as her mother described, wearing black leggings, a long tee shirt and a denim jacket.

Emma stopped walking at the end of the path, and they faced each other. Emma was still gesticulating, and Jessie crossed her arms. Then for a few seconds neither of them seemed to speak. Stacey half expected them to begin that game of tic-tac-toe, a staple of the playground, then Jessie said something. Emma's right hand came up and slapped Jessie round the face.

'She's a feisty one,' said the guy from behind her. For a big guy she hadn't heard him approach.

Stacey continued to watch and could feel the stunned silence that fell between the two friends as though neither could believe what had just happened.

Suddenly, Jessie turned and started to walk away. Emma began to follow when the screen suddenly went blank.

'What happened?' Stacey asked, wanting to watch the soap opera continue before her.

'I switched it off cos I was on my way out. I went to work.'

'And you never saw either of them when you left?'

He shook his head, slowly.

'No, officer, I never saw a thing.'

CHAPTER 37

Kim realised that there were very few cases she worked that didn't bring her back to Hollytree in some form or another.

Any concessions to spring disappeared as they drove on to the sprawling estate, as though nothing would dare to burgeon in this place.

Kim had visited many council estates where efforts had been made in the planning stages to inject some colour with occasional flower beds, borders or trees, patches of grass to soften the landscape.

Not Hollytree.

The view was harsh and functional, formed of concrete, tarmac and paving slabs. There were no front gardens, just identical maisonette blocks circling the thirteen-storey tower blocks at the centre.

Bryant parked next to the bins at the side of a maisonette block sporting a giant spray-painted penis.

As they got out of the car a hunched, hooded youth passed them, flicked a cigarette end on the ground close to Bryant's feet and snorted derisively.

'Original,' Kim observed as the youth turned and spat to his left.

'Bloody trilobites,' Bryant said, shaking his head.

'Huh?' Kim asked.

'Trilobites, otherwise known as Dudley Locust, inhabited the borough way before humans. Often compared to the woodlouse. Died out about 400 million years ago when the coal swamps were formed, though I reckon a few got left behind.'

As the kid turned and gave them the finger, Kim had no choice but to agree with her colleague.

'Second one along,' Bryant said, as they both swatted the air around their faces as a few bluebottles left the overflowing bins and headed straight for them.

They dodged a pushchair and two bikes to get to the target property. Loud music met their ears as they knocked the door.

Another door opened to the left and a young woman stepped out, already snarling.

'If he answers the door tell him to turn that fucking racket down. I've got kids in 'ere,' she roared.

Who can probably hold their own in the noise department, Kim thought, if their mother's volume level was anything to go by. Proving her point, a piercing squeal travelled through the open door.

'We'll advise him,' Bryant said, knocking again.

She folded her arms across a vest top.

'You'll need to knock harder than that. He'll think it's me and just ignore yer.'

Bryant thanked her and knocked again.

The woman shook her head and went back inside, slamming the door behind her.

'Okay, let's thunder it,' Kim said, realising the neighbour was right.

They both knocked at the same time continuously. The music stopped, but they did not until the door opened.

The man before her was younger than she'd expected. In his mid-twenties, the tee shirt he wore displayed rippling muscles in his arms and shoulders with black hair tied back in a ponytail.

His battle-ready face creased in confusion. Kim guessed he was primed ready to give his neighbour a mouthful.

Bryant held up his identification.

He looked to his right. 'I thought it was the biatch from next door,' he said.

'Mr Mancini?' Kim asked.

He nodded as his frown deepened.

'Angelo Mancini?' she checked.

He shook his head. 'Giovanni. It's my dad you want. He's in bed.'

Not asleep, Kim thought, with the volume of that music.

He turned and called his father from the bottom of the stairs.

Angelo appeared and headed down the stairs as Giovanni ushered them in. Suddenly all four of them were in the dark, cramped hallway.

'Please come through,' Angelo said, heading into a small lounge just past the kitchen. Kim detected a faint trace of accent in the older man but nothing in his son, which told her they'd lived in the UK for a long time.

As she followed him into the lounge Kim noted this was a man's space only. The area was tidy and free of clutter and ornaments. She couldn't count the burn circles on the coffee table caused by hot mugs being placed straight onto the wood. A car magazine and a fitness leaflet lay on the arms of two sofas both pointing at the television. The music centre sat on a glass table against the wall adjoining the neighbour's property. A variety of remote controls took centre stage on a sideboard beside an incongruously placed pot plant with a busy pink flower.

Kim took a moment to appraise the two men who had sat on opposite sofas leaving herself and Bryant no choice but to sit beside either one of them. Looking at them both she could easily visualise what Giovanni might look like later in life. Both blessed with olive complexions and dark eyes beneath generous eyebrows, the similarities seemed to end there. Angelo's dark hair was cut short with an unruly wave at the centre of his forehead. His son was a good foot taller with added muscle.

'How may we help you?' Mr Mancini senior asked.

'We're here about Doctor Gordon Cordell. We understand there was some kind of incident between the two of you.'

His face tightened but he shook his head. 'It's in the past, officer,' he said. 'The man is dead.'

'Yes, he is,' Kim said. 'But we need to understand what happened. He reported you to the police?'

Younger Mancini had sat forward, his elbows on his knees. He awaited his father's response.

Angelo nodded. 'He did but it's over now. It was a misunderstanding.'

Kim felt her frustration begin to grow.

'But it's not over, is it?' she pushed. 'We understand that the OMD, Vanessa Wilson, called off the police investigation, but you still have a case to answer internally.'

'My dad is not a thief,' Giovanni said, angrily.

Kim acknowledged his statement in defence of his father. It was to be expected.

'Doctor Cordell accused you of stealing hospital equipment?' she said, returning her attention to the older man.

Angelo nodded. 'It will be all over when I have my meeting. I will clear it all away,' he said, wringing his hands.

'You seem very sure of yourself, Mr Mancini,' she said.

'Because they cannot find me guilty,' he said, simply.

'You mean because the only witness is dead?'

He shook his head. 'No, because I didn't do it.'

Kim paused. Either this man was stupid, naive or overconfident. Maybe he'd watched too many episodes of *Law & Order* and believed that his declaration of 'I didn't do it' would suffice.

She could visit every prison in the UK and hear that same proclamation from ninety per cent of the population.

'My colleagues know I didn't do it,' he said, nodding towards the sad excuse for a plant on the sideboard. 'And have said they will speak up for me.'

Kim opened her mouth to explain that unless they were right there when it happened testaments to his good character would do him very little good indeed.

She was prevented from speaking as Giovanni reached to the side of the chair and pulled out a pair of long-lipped Reeboks.

'Sorry, I've got to go. I'll be late for work.'

'That's fine, we only need your father,' she explained, turning back to Mancini senior.

'Mr Mancini, where were you on Monday evening at around 6 p.m.?' she asked.

'Don't answer, Dad,' Giovanni said, standing up.

'I have nothing to hide. I was here, watching TV,' he answered.

'And I was here with him,' Giovanni added.

Kim wondered if there was any way they could prove or disprove that fact.

'And why would you ask him that?' Giovanni cried. 'Look at the size of him to that fat bastard.'

Kim ignored the younger man. 'Mr Mancini, we understand that you threatened Doctor Cordell. You told him you'd get him good. Is that correct?'

Giovanni moved towards his father. Bryant stood and blocked him.

'Easy, son. Let your dad answer the question if he wants to.'

Angelo slowly began to nod his head.

'I said it, but I didn't mean it like that. I meant…'

His words trailed away as he decided not to clarify.

'What did you mean?' Kim asked, already forming an arrest warrant in her head.

'Tell 'em, Dad,' Giovanni said.

Angelo shook his head. 'They cannot find me guilty if I didn't do it,' he repeated.

Kim briefly wondered if he meant theft or murder. Or both.

'Why won't you tell them?' Giovanni said, holding his hands up to Bryant to signal he did not need to be held back.

'The man is dead. His family…'

'What about his family?' Kim asked sharply. The man's son was in hospital fighting for his life.

'Nothing,' he said. 'It helps no one.'

'Why are you doing this, Dad?' Giovanni raged. 'He was a selfish, arrogant bastard who cared for no one but himself. He insulted you, humiliated you in front of everyone, reported you to the police, almost lost you your job, your reputation, and yet you refuse to tell them. I'm glad the bastard is dead after what—'

'Look, both of you,' Kim said sharply. 'I'm gonna be honest. Doctor Cordell was brutally murdered by someone who was raging, and although he wasn't a very personable kind of guy, I only have one person who issued him with a direct threat.'

She could see the fear in the old man's eyes but he shook his head.

'For fuck's sake, Dad,' Giovanni cried.

Kim stood and reached for her back pocket.

'Okay, Mr Mancini, you leave me with no choice…'

'Okay, okay,' he said, looking to the hand he was expecting to hold cuffs.

Oldest trick in the book.

She sat back down.

He sighed. 'Okay, I'll tell you what really happened.'

CHAPTER 38

Stacey was waiting outside Cornbow High School when the dinner bell rang at 12.30 p.m.

It had taken her less than ten minutes to find the smoking spot just outside the school gates, evidenced by the collection of nub ends smoked and dumped before heading into school.

Oh, how she remembered this spot at her own high school. All the cool girls had gathered each lunchtime to either smoke or pretend to in order to be in with the popular girls. She would have liked to say she cared nothing for such social acceptance, but she had indeed stood amongst them, holding a cigarette and copying the other girls. One taste had been enough and she hadn't gone back again.

As expected she saw Emma Weston heading towards her.

Stacey watched carefully the fifteen-year-old girl that hadn't yet learned to master her face. And the first emotion Stacey saw was fear.

'What are you doing here?' she asked, taking a pack of smokes from her pocket.

'Just wanted a word about Jessie,' Stacey said, moving a few feet away as more kids began to congregate and light cigarettes. A sudden mushroom cloud of smoke rose from the group.

'So, you lied to me yesterday,' Stacey said.

'Nah, I never,' Emma said, narrowing her eyes.

'Yeah, you did. You told me Jessie left your house normal time, alone, and that was the last time you saw her.'

'That's right,' she said, stubbornly.

'Emma, you were lying. You both left the house around eight thirty.'

'Nah, we never,' she said, drawing on the cigarette.

Stacey could see the girl was going to need more detail to freshen her memory.

'You were arguing, Emma,' Stacey said.

Emma shook her head as she blew out a stream of smoke. 'Nah, we don't argue. She's my bestie. Whoever told you that is lying.'

'I saw you,' Stacey said.

'Don't be stupid,' she said, a vein of doubt creeping into her voice.

'That really how you talk to a police officer and an adult?' Stacey snapped, tiring of the girl's attitude. 'Wind it back a notch or we'll be doing this down the station, got it?'

Emma offered her a face puckered with annoyance but she nodded.

'So, I saw you walk down the path together and you were arguing. Jessie said something you didn't like and you slapped her.'

Emma's face reddened, but she said nothing.

'What was it about, Emma?'

The girl shrugged and looked away. 'Don't remember. We're mates. We argue.'

'You slap all your friends?' Stacey asked.

'Only the ones who won't listen,' Emma bit back, giving herself away.

'And what wouldn't Jessie listen to?' Stacey asked, realising she'd hit a nerve.

'Can't remember,' she said, shaking her head.

'Emma, try harder. It could be important. Your bestie has now been missing for more than forty-eight hours and you don't seem all that fussed, which is beginning to annoy the hell out of me not to mention making me suspicious of your—'

'She said she wanted to go to Dale's house, and I didn't want her to go. That's it. Happy now?'

'Ecstatic. Is Dale her boyfriend?' Stacey asked.

Emma nodded. 'S'posed to be.'

'Do her parents know?' Stacey asked. Her mother had insisted there was no boyfriend.

'You're kidding. They'd throw her in a tower or dungeon or something.'

'And you never thought to mention this Dale kid to anyone until now?' Stacey asked, trying to keep hold of her temper. The girl had been spoken to twice and this was the first time she'd heard his name. 'Or that she was headed to his house the last time she was seen?'

She shrugged and looked away.

Stacey shook her head in wonder and counted to ten. She had to remember she was questioning a minor without consent of an adult. She couldn't go in hard. What she really wanted to do was grab the kid by the shoulders and shake some understanding into her.

'Emma, you do get the gravity of this situation, don't you?'

''Course I do. She's my buddy.'

'So, why didn't you want her to go to Dale's house?' Stacey asked.

'Just didn't,' she said, kicking at something on the floor.

'You went after her?' Stacey asked.

'Yeah, to tell her I was sorry, but she wouldn't listen, so I let her go and do whatever she wanted, and that was the last time I saw her. I swear.'

CHAPTER 39

Thankfully, younger Mancini had decided his dad could be left alone now he'd decided to talk and had finally left for work.

Kim could feel the release of tension that left the house with him. She had given Bryant the signal to offer to make coffee, feeling that Mancini senior would open up more one-on-one.

'Your son is a very angry young man,' Kim observed, as the front door closed behind him.

'Protective of me as I am of him. It's only ever been the two of us. His mother died when he was only a year old. He doesn't remember her.'

'I get it,' she said, wondering why there had been no second wife. Single-parent families often tended to become a small team depending primarily on each other, especially when no step-parent had entered the picture. If you hurt one, you hurt the other.

'So, Cordell accused you of theft and humiliated you?' Kim asked.

He nodded but waved it away.

'He thought I was going to say something.'

'About what?'

'What I saw in Theatre 3,' he said.

'That's the place he accused you of stealing medical equipment from. He said he walked in on you,' she clarified as her phone began to ring.

She took it from her pocket. It was Keats. She pressed ignore. Any lab results could wait.

'He didn't walk in on me, officer. I walked in on him.'

'In Theatre 3?' she asked as her phone rang again.

'Yes,' Angelo answered.

'And what was he doing?' she asked, silencing the phone once more.

'Sex, Inspector. Doctor Cordell and a nurse were having sex.'

Kim held up her hand to pause Mancini, even though she was desperate to hear more of Mancini's counter-accusation.

She moved into the hallway as Bryant popped his head out of the kitchen doorway.

'Damn it, Keats, what's up?' she snapped when her phone rang for the third time.

'Cedars Retirement Home, now,' he said, before the line went dead.

CHAPTER 40

Dale Jones answered the door with a game controller in his hand.

Stacey had to wonder at the level of addiction that meant he couldn't allow it out of his grasp for the time it took him to scowl at anyone who knocked the door. As he was doing to her right now.

'Dale Jones?' she asked, holding up her warrant card.

His eyes widened in surprise. 'Jeez, what's the five-o want with me?'

Objectively Stacey could see what Jessie might see in this kid. Already sixteen and out of school, she must have been flattered by the attention of a boy one year older. A year counted for a lot when you were fifteen.

His lower half was clad in skintight jeans, and his black tee shirt was a multicoloured skull. His fair hair was clean but untidy. No piercings or body mods she could see.

'I'm here to talk about Jessie,' she said.

'You find her?'

She shook her head.

'What time did she get here on Sunday night?'

He looked from side to side as though playing to an audience. 'She didn't come here.'

Stacey felt her gut begin to react. It was a ten-minute walk from Emma's house to Dale's place.

'I swear,' he said.

'She didn't text, phone, anything to say she was coming over?'

'Nada. Saw her a few days before. We went to Maccie's and she was a bit off. Wouldn't say why, and that was the last time I seen her.'

'You don't seem very bothered by her disappearance,' Stacey observed.

He shrugged. 'It wasn't serious or anything. She was only fifteen. Not even old enough to…'

'You didn't have sex with her?' Stacey asked before she realised how personal a question that was.

He smirked. 'Nah, had a mate done for statutory rape. I'll learn from his mistakes. Look, she was a nice girl and all but we'd only been hanging out a few weeks, so…'

His words trailed away as though he had nothing else to give.

'Do you have any idea where Jessie may have gone, because Emma is convinced Jessie was on her way to see you.'

His face darkened. 'Don't believe a word that little bitch says.'

Stacey was taken aback by the venom in his voice.

'You don't like her?'

'She's a lying, nasty slut and I wouldn't piss on her if she was on fire,' he spat. 'Now, sorry but I gotta get back.'

Stacey stood there, stunned, as he closed the door in her face.

She had a sudden wave of sympathy for Jessie Ryan. She seemed to have been stuck between a rock and a hard place.

Two of the most important people in her life appeared to hate each other's guts. And yet neither of them seemed to care that she hadn't been seen in days.

CHAPTER 41

'So, what are you thinking about our Italian stallions?' Bryant asked.

'Not sure,' she answered as he took a shortcut to bypass Brierley Hill High Street. The lunchtime traffic would slow them down on their way to Cedars Retirement Home and Keats had been clear. Short and sharp but definitely clear.

She had tried to call him back, but the call had gone straight to voicemail, so she had no clue what they were heading towards or what connection it had to their current case. It was a retirement home; people died.

'You think he did it?'

She shrugged. 'Junior is angry on his dad's behalf, and yet Angelo is surprisingly calm. He doesn't know the name of the nurse, and we have no way of proving or disproving his story.'

'You think Angelo made it up?' Bryant asked.

'Could have, just to deflect the attention of the initial complaint. Vanessa made no mention of a counter complaint, and if there are no other witnesses we may never know. What I do know is that we have two members of the same family involved in horrific incidents in the space of twenty-four hours, and one person who issued a direct threat. Let's be honest, Angelo Mancini wouldn't be the first person to try and steal stuff from a hospital.'

'But he'd never done anything before,' Bryant offered.

'That they know of,' she said. 'He may not have been caught.'

'Well, his colleagues seem to support him. That was a good-looking weed in that plant pot,' he observed, drily.

'Yeah, no expense spared to bring him a token of their affection. Who'd he piss off to receive that?'

'You did seem to take an instant dislike to Angelo Mancini,' Bryant said.

'Did you just get here?' she queried. 'I take an instant dislike to everyone I meet.'

'True. Okay, let's rephrase and say you seem to be unwilling to give him the benefit of the doubt.'

Kim opened her mouth and closed it again. Yes, she had to admit there was something about the man she didn't like. He was too calm about the situation, showing no emotion at all, and yet she knew him to be capable of high emotion after issuing a direct threat in the first place.

She put it out of her mind as Bryant pulled into the grounds of Cedars Retirement Home in Tividale, an area at the north-west corner of Rowley Regis, nestled between Oldbury and Dudley.

The facility was a purpose-built red-brick building not far from Rattlechain Lagoon. Kim remembered asking Keith and Erica to take her to Rattlechain Lagoon after hearing mention of it at school. It had sounded so exotic and adventurous.

Keith had explained to her that the nickname came from the Rattlechain Brickworks, where in the 1890s, a marl hole, a clay pit, was created which had subsequently been used as a disposal site by local factories. For thirty-two years, industrial waste like white phosphorus and other toxic chemicals had been tipped unregulated and unrecorded into the lagoon, leading to its status as a hazardous waste site.

Kim hadn't wanted to visit after that, and she guessed Sandwell Council had snapped up the land for the care home at a very reasonable price, enabling them to erect a brand new building.

Kim idly observed that the yards of net curtain negated the point of having such expansive windows. Surely designed for the residents to look out.

Inside the front door was a square space with a glass partition on the right-hand side.

Kim held up her badge to the young, flustered woman behind the desk.

The buzzing of the door lock sounded, and she pushed through.

A green-clad carer was waiting on the other side.

'Follow me, please,' she said, quietly walking through a large, bright, airy room to the left and passing a dining room that was being set for lunch. The aroma of tomato and garlic wafted through towards her, and a short line of eager diners was already forming.

The chatter stopped as they traversed the distance. Even the less interested residents appeared to be following their every move. And if they knew nothing they knew as much as she did. She still had no clue what she was doing here.

The carer stood at the patio doors and pointed.

'I've been told not to step—'

'It's okay,' Kim said, opening the door. Whatever it was, Keats wouldn't want unnecessary people in the area.

The garden stretched the entire length of the building and was a mixture of patio areas, trees, shrubs, planters and a brick path.

Kim followed the path around a raised vegetable garden and saw Keats standing behind a bench that looked onto a collection of bird feeders.

'Keats,' she said from a few feet away.

He didn't turn.

'Keats,' she repeated.

No response, even though he wasn't currently engaged in conversation with anyone else.

'Keats, what the hell is going?…'

'Oh, sorry, Stone, I thought we were only answering each other on the third time of trying,' he said, referring to his attempts to call her.

'I was interviewing a witness,' she snapped.

'Who I presume is alive and well, unlike this poor soul who is not and requires your urgent attention.'

Kim walked to the front of the bench and placed her hands on her hips.

The woman appeared to be mid- to late-seventies, average build, wearing a flower-covered dress and a cardigan. Her left wrist held a delicate gold watch, and a locket hung around her neck. She wore tan-coloured tights in flat comfortable shoes.

Her head lolled to the side, and her eyes stared out straight in front of her.

'Okay, Keats, give me a clue why I'm here,' she said.

'Her name is Phyllis Mansell. She's seventy-six years old. She rises at 7 a.m. every day to swim for half an hour in the on-site pool. She spends most of her day chatting to other residents and makes cups of tea for the staff. She organises coach trips to the seaside and calls the bingo numbers on a Saturday night. She's never smoked, is not a heavy drinker and comes outside every day at 12 to feed and watch the birds.'

'Blimey, Keats, you her pen pal or something?' Kim asked, still unsure why he'd called them.

'This lady had no serious health issues, was fit and sprightly and yet here she is. Dead.'

'But you've not even examined her yet to determine cause of death,' Kim noted.

'I know, are you impressed right now?'

'Not sure *impressed* sums up how I'm feeling about you right this—'

'Oh, and these little blighters here might have given me a clue,' he said, taking an evidence bag from his jacket pocket.

She took what appeared to be an empty bag from his hand.

'Looks like they got away,' she said, turning it over.

He passed her his glasses. 'Look closer.'

She put them on and held the bag up to the light.

'Fibres?' she asked.

'At least half a dozen of them, found on her lips.'

Kim glanced back at the body. The fibres on her lips were blue, matching nothing on her person but potentially similar to the ones found around the neck wound of Cordell.

Kim now understood the reason for the call and the absence of staff outside.

'You think she was murdered and that it was someone here? That this is linked to the murder of Doctor Cordell?'

'That's your job, not mine but the gardens appear to be enclosed.'

'Okay, Bryant, tell the manager no one leaves and we want access to their CCTV. Now.'

CHAPTER 42

Stacey stepped back into the office just after 2 p.m. carrying a large cup of diet Coke.

'Hey, I'd have got you one but didn't know what you liked,' Stacey said, although to be fair she hadn't given him a thought at all.

'No probs, fairy cake?' he asked, offering her the Tupperware container.

Stacey shook her head. 'You trying out for *Bake Off* or something?'

He shrugged and put the tub behind him next to the printer.

'So, what we working on?' Stacey asked. She'd devoted enough time to Jessie Ryan for one day, and although she'd have liked more time, she'd promised the boss this case would come first.

'Boss wants some background on these guys,' he said, pushing a yellow Post-it note towards her.

She read the names. 'I'm guessing Italian.'

'Maybe,' he said, deadpan.

'What's the boss after?' she asked. 'Unless it's some kind of secret.'

'Father and son. Senior is Angelo. Works at the hospital. Cordell made a complaint against Angelo for trying to steal stuff. Angelo threatened Cordell, and now Angelo says he caught Cordell having sex with a nurse and the surgeon was trying to silence him. Hence, the reason for the complaint.'

'Jesus, slow down. So, what exactly am I looking for?' she asked.

He shrugged. 'Boss didn't specify.'

Stacey sighed. She'd guess the priority was Angelo Mancini as he had issued the threat. She needed to get cracking on some work for the boss so she could investigate Jessie's friends in more detail.

There was bad blood between Emma Weston and Dale Jones and she wanted to find out what it was.

CHAPTER 43

'But I've got staff that are finishing their shifts,' Maura Birch said, wringing her hands. As the manager of Cedars she had let them into the CCTV room as Kim had repeated her instruction that no one was to leave.

'We can't physically restrain them,' Kim said as the word 'unfortunately' flew through her head. 'But we will want to speak to every member of staff, so they can either wait or come down to the station.'

'Okay, I'll pass that on,' she said, scurrying away.

'New building, old system,' Bryant moaned as he pressed the button to rewind the VHS tape; meaning at best they were only going to get snatched time-lapse images. She hadn't seen such an antiquated system in years. Most CCTV systems recorded straight to hard drive and could be copied to disc within seconds.

Maura Birch had already confirmed that Phyllis Mansell had gone into the garden at 12 p.m. and had been found at 1.15 when she hadn't come back in for lunch.

She had also confirmed that the CCTV coverage outside was limited.

'Is that it?' Kim asked.

'Yep, just the one fixed camera pointing at the patio area closest to the back door.'

'Our Maura wasn't joking when she said it was limited,' Kim observed. 'But at least we get to see who came out the door,' she said.

Bryant nodded as he tweaked the timing.

'There she is,' he said, hitting the pause button.

There was something eerie about watching the figure on the screen and knowing that right this minute that same body was being placed into Keats's van.

Bryant pressed play. They got three further snatches of her before she went out of view.

'Looked perfectly healthy, guv,' Bryant observed.

'Oh yeah,' Kim said, concentrating on the screen. Why would anyone want to hurt the woman? Apparently, she was friendly, helpful, popular and good with the staff.

And why would any staff member do such a thing knowing full well there was a camera right there? More importantly, what the hell did this have to do with the murder of Gordon Cordell?

'We're not going to find anything,' she said.

'Jesus, guv, we're only ten minutes in.'

'There are no cameras in the bedrooms, bathrooms, and shower room, so why would someone do it out here where they have to pass a fixed camera?'

'People forget about cameras, guv. They see through them. And what if it wasn't staff? What if it was a visitor? They wouldn't know there was a camera right there.'

'But why, Bryant?' she asked in frustration 'Why would anyone want to kill her?'

'Well, we gotta watch the tape until—'

'You watch,' she said, standing up. 'I want to look at something else.'

Kim headed out of the CCTV room. She saw the collection of staff congregating around the reception with cardigans and handbags. She narrowly avoided the daggers being thrown in her direction as she stepped back out into the garden and a stream of hazard tape.

'Hey, Mitch,' she said as the techie came towards her.

'This connected to the doctor?' he asked, doubtfully.

She shrugged. 'Keats found blue fibres on her lips and called me to take a look. Not seeing any connection yet but I wanna check something.'

'Need any help?' he asked.

'No, but I'll shout if I do.'

He nodded and headed back to the crime scene.

*

She strode to the west side of the garden. A gate was padlocked with a fire escape on the other side. The gate was seven feet high and not easy to climb. Kim ruled it out as an access point.

Adjoining the gate was a stump wall which was less than a foot away from the next property, an equipment hire shop specialising in garden tools. Kim had noted that their customer parking area was directly on the other side of that wall. Also ruled out as someone standing on a car roof to scale a wall wouldn't have gone unnoticed.

She walked the length of the brick boundary looking for any weakness or irregularities.

The hire shop stretched beyond the end of the garden wall, so there was definitely no access point on the west side.

She knew that the east side of the garden was flanked by road, so anyone climbing a wall would have been noticed within seconds. That left only the back wall.

Conifers and shrubs lined the wall that stretched about seventy metres, and there was nothing available to stand on.

'Hey, Mitch, got a sec?' she called.

'Yep, wassup?' he asked, pushing his face mask on to his head.

She looked to the wall. 'I kinda need to get up there.'

His eyes widened. 'You want me to lift?…'

'Do I look like a bloody ballerina?' she asked, shaking her head. 'Cup your hands.'

He looked relieved as he followed her instruction.

She put her left foot into his hand and pushed up with her right while grabbing hold of a tree branch for support.

A sharp pain shot through her left leg as she used her other hand to grab the top of the wall.

'Hold me steady,' she called down.

'Got you,' he replied. 'It's like tossing a caber,' he said as she put both hands on to the wall and heaved herself forward so her stomach was over the top of the wall, her upper half hanging forward and her behind sticking up in the air.

'Jeez, the things you see when you haven't got your gun,' Bryant said from behind her.

'Hold me steady,' she barked to her colleague. His hands closed around her ankles so she shuffled further forward to get a better look.

The entire rear of the property was a patch of waste land. An area of concrete slab was surrounded by clutches of tall grass. Around the outside was a bike race track with a couple of cones marking out the route. A single bench looked on, telling Kim she was looking at an old park area.

'Shit,' she said, realising someone could very easily have remained unnoticed back here.

'Hold tight,' Kim said as she moved forward a little further to look along the base of the wall. Her gaze passed over weeds and tall grass until it reached an upside-down milk crate that had flattened the grass around it. Recently.

'Ah, damn it,' she called. 'Mitch, are you still here?'

She couldn't ask Bryant to loosen her ankles and go take a look.

'Oh yeah, I ain't missing this floor show,' he said.

'About halfway along the wall, right by the yellow conifer, see it?' she asked.

'Hang on, just heading towards,' he called.

'Take your bloody time' she called as the brick dug deeper into her stomach and her leg throbbed with pain.

'Okay, marking it now,' he said.

Logic told her the killer had used the milk crate and the conifer to get over the wall and back again. Who knew what he'd left behind. If it was there, Mitch would find it.

'Okay, Bryant, now you gotta help me down.'

'Err… guv, that's a request too far, I'm afraid. There's no way I'm touching your…'

'Fine, I'll just stay up here until my arse drops off and you can help me, shall I?' she asked, shimmying herself backwards.

'It's just… well…'

Over the course of their working relationship she had seen him touch dead bodies riddled with maggots and bacteria. She'd seen him assist Keats with moving a young man covered in his own vomit and yet he sounded positively traumatised at the prospect of touching her behind.

'Get out of the way and I'll jump down,' she snapped, trying to brace her left leg for impact.

'No, no, it's okay. I can do this,' he said as though he was trying to psyche himself up to jump the space between two skyscrapers.

'Today would be good,' she growled.

'Okay, okay,' he said, putting his hands on her upper buttocks and easing her down.

'Thanks, buddy,' she said, sarcastically as she brushed the brick dust and gravel from her hands.

'You were right about the tape,' he said.

'So, we know how he got in but we don't know why,' she said, heading back towards the building.

She stopped walking and turned to her colleague.

'You know what's weird?'

'Many things today,' he said, looking back to the wall. 'But what in particular?'

'It wasn't robbery; she was still wearing her jewellery. It wasn't even violent but it was personal. She was the target. He came in, killed her and left. Even though she was in her twilight years she was fit, healthy, outgoing and popular, yet he came into the garden, quietly snuffed out her life and left again. What kind of person would do that and—'

'And you want to know why,' Bryant interrupted.

'Yeah but more than that. How did he know exactly where she'd be at exactly what time?'

Bryant shrugged and continued walking.

*

She followed him into the building and approached a nervous-looking Maura Birch.

'Okay, let 'em go,' she said, nodding towards the staff members eager to be on their way, dead resident or not.

Kim pulled Maura away from the other staff members.

'Miss Birch, forensics will need the area kept clear. Another team will be arriving to take statements and continue with the investigation. They'll need access to your staff, possibly the residents and it might be worth you starting to think of any reason, anything at all, to explain why someone would want to hurt Phyllis Mansell.'

Her skittering eyes widened. 'There's no one that disliked the woman, officer, at worst she got told to shut up now and again. She was a bit of a bragger, you see,' the woman whispered.

'About herself?' Kim asked.

'Oh no, that wouldn't have been so bad. It was always about her daughter and sometimes she'd go on about it a bit.'

'And her daughter is?'

'Her name is Nat Mansell. She's a nurse, a surgical nurse, at Russells Hall Hospital.'

CHAPTER 44

'So, what's your gut doing?' Bryant asked, as they got back into the car.

'Bloody cartwheels at the minute,' she admitted.

'You know I'm going to disagree,' Bryant said, reversing the car. 'Just because the victim's daughter works at the hospital doesn't mean it's the same killer as Cordell. Vanessa said they have thousands of employees. Most folks know someone who works at the hospital. I just don't think it means as much as you think.'

'Good job you don't mind being wrong, then,' she said. 'And even if you're right, we have to at least give the theory some air time. Two deaths linked to the hospital in two days is not something we can afford to ignore.'

'But it's not really linked to the hospital, is it?' he said. 'Phyllis Mansell is the mother of a nurse at Russells Hall Hospital.'

'Who was murdered earlier today for no good reason we can see.'

He shook his head, stubbornly.

She took out her phone and scrolled down. 'I'll get Dawson to…'

Her words trailed away as his name came into view on her screen.

She breathed in and looked out of the window. How many times over the years had she so absently scrolled to his number and called, never imagining there would come a time when he was no longer there to take her call.

She knew full well that his phone had been handed in, well what was left of it after his fall, and yet she couldn't bring herself to delete his contact information from her contact list. Because then it would be gone.

'Yeah, I think he's still out there too,' Bryant said, quietly.

She swallowed. 'I'll get Inspector Plant over to Cedars to get some statements. I suspect everyone was busy tending to lunch and that anyone who saw anything would already have come forward, but it won't hurt to check,' she said, changing the subject.

'Get Penn to deal with Plant,' Bryant said.

She shook her head. Giving Penn tasks she would normally have given Dawson did not sit well with her.

'No, thanks, I'm happy to do it myself.'

CHAPTER 45

'Hmm… not a lot to shout about for Mancini senior,' Stacey said, looking at her notes.

'You speaking to me?' Penn asked, looking around his screen.

'Not really but feel free to listen.'

He shrugged and returned to his screen.

'A conviction for petty theft almost twenty years ago and a complaint about a brick through his kitchen window.'

Penn's head appeared again. 'It really sounds like you're speaking to me.'

'I mean, does that sound like the murdering kind?'

'Now that was an actual question?' Penn remarked.

'Okay, just forget it,' Stacey snapped.

Penn regarded her for a second. 'But what exactly is the murdering type?' he asked. 'If all killers stuck to a formula, we'd have much easier jobs. Not all killers evolve through a training programme of broken homes, childhood abuse or a traumatic event. Some people snap and kill in the heat of the moment through passion, jealousy, rejection.'

'But is it enough?' Stacey asked. 'Being accused of theft and facing humiliation, is it enough to inspire such a brutal act?'

The boss often talked of proportionate response and this didn't strike her as proportionate.

'In 2012 Billy Clay Payne and Billie Jean Haysworth were shot for unfriending Jennelle Potter on social media. Roger Wilkes, a homeless guy in St Louis, was stabbed for not sharing his bag of

Cheetos. Shaakira Dorsey was beaten to death for making fun of a girl for farting, and a guy in South Africa was beaten and stabbed by his own family for changing the TV station.'

'You have to be joking,' Stacey said, narrowing her eyes.

He shook his head. 'Look 'em up. Not what you'd call proportionate, except the remote control one. That one I get,' he joked. 'But see beyond the theft itself,' Penn continued. 'If the hospital found him guilty, it would be pinned to every reference request, and for a guy in his fifties that pretty much seals the deal. He's been through this before when he was younger and there were more jobs around. So, no job, no wage, humiliation, possible loss of his home. It's no longer about just an accusation. It's more about what he has to lose.'

'But if the disciplinary never went ahead they'd have no legal reason not to let him back to work and he keeps everything?' she mused, still wondering where those random murder facts had come from.

'Exactly,' he said. 'Want me to take junior?' he asked.

'No, thanks,' she said, curtly. 'And FYI, it's not cool to sound like you're quoting a page from Wikipedia to prove your point. You just look like a know-it-all.'

'Okey dokey,' he said, breezily. 'Sure you don't want me to look at junior? I need a break from shoe prints but if there's nothing else you'd rather…'

'Okay, take him,' she said. If he was so keen to do it, she could start looking at something else.

'And it's full by the way, seeing as you cared to ask.'

'Huh?' she said, frowning.

'Full Coke,' he explained. 'That's what I like to drink. No diet, no zero just good old-fashioned Coke.'

'Ah good to know,' she said, typing a name into the computer.

But he was wrong in what he'd said, because she really hadn't cared at all.

CHAPTER 46

'How the hell can it be closed?' Kim asked the hospital security guard who was ushering them away from the administration block. For once Bryant had actually put his foot down while driving them from the Cedars to Russells Hall so they could catch the OMD before she left.

This time she'd found the office without the help of Terry but couldn't get past the key coded door that had been open the previous day.

She guessed her constant banging on it had caught the attention of whoever was monitoring the camera in the corner.

'It's the admin block. They normally leave around five.'

She turned to face the tall, lean security guard with smooth, dark skin and peered at his name badge.

'Look, Tyrone, I reckon Vanessa Wilson is still back there working, so if you could just let us through.'

They had established yesterday that she wasn't the clock-watching type.

'She's not. Problem with a poorly kid or something,' he said, shrugging. 'Left a couple of hours ago.'

'There must be someone we can talk to?' she raged. Who finished work at this time of day?

He shrugged again. 'Sorry, you'll have to come back tomorrow.'

'And I'm sorry but that's not...' her words trailed away as a movement to her left caught her attention. 'Okay, thanks,' Kim said.

Bryant glanced at her questioningly. He had leaned against the wall, settled in for the long haul. She didn't normally give in so easily.

'We'll find our way back from here,' she assured the guard.

He shrugged and looked around before moving away.

'Jesus, guv, you accepting no for an answer?' Bryant said as she walked slowly behind the guard back to the main corridor. 'And his name wasn't Tyrone,' Bryant observed.

'Yeah it was. His name badge said—'

'And the SIA licence on his arm said otherwise.'

Kim narrowed her eyes at her colleague. Trust him to notice the detail of the man's security industry identification.

'Some people in front-facing jobs don't like to use their real name, especially where they might meet conflict or live locally, so they use a middle name to make themselves less identifiable.'

'Oh, got it.'

The security guard not named Tyrone turned once to make sure they were still behind before he turned the corner.

Kim immediately stopped walking and turned the other way.

'Follow me,' she said, heading for the stairwell at speed.

Once through the door she took the stairs two at a time. She heard a door squeak above her.

'Guv, what are we?...'

'Just keep up, Bryant,' she hissed as she pushed open the heavy fire door back onto the corridor.

She looked both ways and swore.

'I thought I saw someone I recognised,' she said as her phone dinged receipt of a message.

She took out her phone and read it. Surprised at the sender and the contents, she read it again.

'What's up,' Bryant asked.

She shook her head. 'Never mind,' she answered, looking up and down the corridor. 'I swear I just saw—'

She stopped speaking as the double doors to the medical assessment ward swung open.

A white-clad orderly was backing out of the ward, guiding a hospital bed. She stood back against the wall and turned her head to look at the noticeboard.

'It's just an X-ray, Mr Braithwaite,' he said. 'We'll have you back in no time.'

'Bloody hell, he kept that quiet. We had no idea he worked here as well,' Bryant observed, following her gaze.

The man they were watching was Giovanni Mancini.

CHAPTER 47

Eeny, meeny, miny, moe! The phrase used by children for selection, making a choice. Isn't that how it goes when you point at something and decide which one you want?

Children sometimes take a moment or two when making an important decision. They weigh up the long- and short-term gains, the instant or lasting gratification.

But not you.

The decision was swift, immediate and without hesitation. For me it was anti-climactical. Disappointing.

I expected more from you. I wanted indecision, pain, suffering in your plight. I wanted you to feel the suffocation of being trapped in a nightmare that makes no sense, that is so breathtakingly painful you wonder if your heart will suddenly stop beating right that second. I wanted to see you so consumed by fear and grief that you would break right there in front of me. But you didn't.

Oh, you were a cold bitch.

You made your choice so quickly. You asked me once to reconsider. It seemed half-hearted, insincere. I refused and you accepted. How do you know that I wouldn't have relented and let you both live?

As if.

That's not how this game works.

That's not how real life works.

But you didn't even try.

You told me everything. Spilled the information like a knocked-over cup. You gave me everything I needed. I knew exactly where she'd be at the exact time. Watching the birds out in the garden. The information tumbled out of you as though it caused you no hardship at all.

But you will suffer. You will feel pain. You will feel despair. If you couldn't feel it for the loss of someone you love then you will feel it for yourself.

Because you made your choice but it really wasn't a choice at all.

CHAPTER 48

'They've both done time,' Penn said, peering around his computer.

'Huh?' Stacey asked. She'd completely forgotten he was in the room.

'Giovanni Mancini,' Penn said, taking off his headphones. 'Got a few months custodial for an assault in his late teens.'

Stacey had moved on. Her own investigation had uncovered a police witness statement for Dale Jones, who had been a character witness for a friend accused of statutory rape, as he had already mentioned to her. The sixteen-year-old had had no involvement with the police either before or since.

'And although it was a long time ago, senior Mancini was put away for a month for that petty theft twenty years ago. So, they've both done time.'

'Anything else?' Stacey said, trying to sound interested. Basically, he'd found nothing.

'Nope,' he said, reaching for his empty Tupperware box. 'Except, it's almost seven and I'm going home.'

'Okay, see yer,' Stacey said, without looking up.

She waited until he was out of the room and let out a long breath. The tension immediately left her body.

When Penn was around it made it harder to pretend. To pretend that Dawson was coming back.

She stared past the blurring of her eyes, willing the emotion to subside.

She knew she had to be patient with herself, the therapist had told her that. Not to expect too much. His death was a loss to her. Yeah, she knew that too.

She also knew that although her head had accepted that her friend was dead she was waiting for her heart to catch up.

'Pull yourself together, woman,' she chided herself.

She blinked away the tears and focussed on the screen.

She had established Jessie Ryan's boyfriend was clean. He'd committed no crime or he just hadn't been caught.

And now she turned her attention to Emma Weston. Stacey could not rid herself of the image of the girl slapping her best friend around the face, right before they disappeared from view and Jessie disappeared altogether.

She typed in Emma's name and address and took a sip of her drink.

She paused mid slurp as data filled the screen.

'Jesus,' Stacey said, placing down her drink.

For a fifteen-year-old kid she'd been busy.

Emma Weston had been arrested for violence.

And it had happened more than once.

CHAPTER 49

It was almost nine when Kim stepped into the Lyttelton Arms in Hagley. She'd been home after a frustrating day at work to get a bite and take Barney for a walk.

The venue had been her suggestion, falling around halfway between their locations and because there was something about the place she liked and admired.

The pub was originally the eighteenth-century former home of Lord Lyttelton and had reinvented itself countless times over the years. In the late nineties it had been a traditional ale drinkers' pub like hundreds of others in the area. And like many of its contemporaries it had faced closure following the smoking ban and the eruption of cheap beer chain establishments in every high street.

In the early noughties it had saved itself from extinction by becoming a Harvester but was now a trendy gastro pub catering to people who wanted a quiet drink after work as well as those seeking an evening of lively entertainment.

In Kim's mind it was the little pub that could.

He'd said eight thirty but she'd known he'd wait. He'd texted her for a reason.

Her eyes searched the space that was not overly busy on a Wednesday night.

He sat at a window seat and nodded in her direction.

His salt-and-pepper hair had been recently cut showing off a healthy complexion that did nothing to hide the tiredness around his eyes. And now she understood the slump of his shoulders weighed down by hopelessness.

She detoured to the bar and asked for a coffee, before taking a seat opposite.

'You drinking, Travis?' she asked, glancing at his glass.

'A couple of pints,' he answered.

'You driving?' she asked, frowning, as a waitress passed her carrying plates of spit-roasted chicken, and sea bass.

He shook his head. 'Taxi.'

'So, what's this about?' she asked, as the guy from behind the bar placed her coffee in front of her before rushing back to a group of four who had just entered.

'How's the leg?' Travis asked, taking a sip of his drink.

She frowned at him. He had not asked to meet her for a welfare check.

'How's things at home?' she asked.

He smiled showing the ghost of a twinkle in the piercing blue eyes. They had never talked about personal stuff and they wouldn't start now despite what they'd learned of each other.

To say their history was chequered was an understatement.

They had worked together as DSs for a couple of years, had worked well together before she made DI ahead of him. Around the same time, he had punched a suspect in the face and she had covered it up. Along with the fact that when she'd questioned him about it he had struck her too. He had immediately requested a transfer to West Mercia and made DI not long afterwards.

Bitterness and animosity had grown between them in the years since as they had fought over bodies and crime scenes, their friendship long forgotten.

And then they'd been forced to work together on a Hate Crimes case that had straddled their neighbouring forces of West Midlands and West Mercia. Only then had she learned that his actions back in the past had been due to his forty-three-year-old wife's diagnosis of early onset dementia. She also knew that he was in love with a woman that he'd never allow himself to have.

The knowledge had helped her understand his actions, and their two teams had worked together to uncover a bunch of mindless racist pigs and save the life of Stacey Wood. And that was how she'd met Detective Sergeant Austin Penn.

'I got your card,' she said, taking a sip of her drink.

'Least I could do. He was a bright lad.'

She nodded her agreement but said nothing.

'So, how's my boy doing?' he asked.

Ah, so that's what this was about.

'You can ask him yourself when he comes back after this case is finished,' she said.

'He won't be coming back to West Mercia,' Travis stated.

'How the hell do you know?' she asked. 'He moves police force like he's playing musical chairs,' she said. 'West Mids, West Mercia and now West Mids again. Seems to be going for some kind of record.'

'He has his reasons, Kim,' he said.

She shook her head. 'They don't concern me.'

'I thought you liked Penn,' he said.

'I did when he was one of yours. I like him a lot less as one of mine.'

'He's a good officer. He multitasks well, equally as good out in the field as he is with data mining and—'

'I know he's a good officer but I'm not keeping him, Tom,' she said, resolutely. 'He doesn't fit. I've made it clear to Woody that once this case is finished I want him gone.'

'Didn't you say that about Dawson once, in the early days?'

She shrugged in response. She didn't remember.

'He wasn't your cup of tea but you stuck with him. You gave him a chance. You coached him, you taught him, you corrected him and he was a much better officer because of it.'

She tipped her head. 'Tom, don't blow smoke up my—'

'Yeah, cos I'd really do that with you. It's true. I saw how you worked with him. He looked up to you, respected—'

'Enough, Tom,' she said, holding up her hand. For some reason she couldn't hear this right now.

He sighed, heavily. 'Penn's a good officer if you give him a chance. I know he's not the easiest person to warm to but he's a decent guy whose had his fair share of…'

'Like what, Tom?' she asked. 'And why do you care so much? You've always kept your distance from your officers, so why the concern for Penn? What's his story?'

Travis opened his mouth to say something and then appeared to change his mind and say something else.

'Let's just say I've grown to understand him. And I think he deserves a shot at being part of your team.'

She shook her head, unmoved.

'It's not happening, Tom. I appreciate you inviting me here to tell me absolutely nothing that would convince me to change my mind but—'

'Do you remember Holly Baxter?'

Kim groaned and nodded.

'Came into the station with a black eye, said her neighbour had assaulted her in the hallway for no reason. We brought him in for questioning. I felt there was something not right. The female PC who interviewed Holly Baxter felt something was off. But you wouldn't have it. You questioned the neighbour for hours trying to get a confession. Even when the woman admitted she'd done it herself to get a rest from his loud music for one night, you still wouldn't have it and demanded to see the coffee mug she'd used to injure herself.'

'And?…' She'd believed she was being thorough.

'There's a difference between stubbornness and sheer bloody-mindedness. Look, all I'm saying is he's a good officer. He could

CHAPTER 50

'Okay, guys, new day new energy,' Kim said, looking at the board that had changed very little from the day before. Cordell had been murdered on Monday and it was now Thursday and two clear days of space without any real development were mocking her. Only last night she'd heard a phrase on the TV about 'trudging through molasses' and although she wasn't exactly sure what molasses were it sounded about right to her.

'Just to recap, we spoke yesterday to the only people known to have a grudge against Doctor Cordell, being Angelo and Giovanni Mancini, who both state they were home on Monday night. Angelo Mancini claims he caught Cordell having sex with a nurse in Theatre 3 and that Cordell's accusation of theft was designed to shut him up and get him out of the way, allegedly. We only have Angelo's word on that.'

'And the nurse?' Stacey asked.

Kim shrugged. 'We're hoping to find out today from Vanessa Wilson if there's anyone in particular that Cordell spent time with, especially Natalie Mansell, the daughter of the woman murdered at Cedars Retirement Home yesterday. She had blue fibres on her lips that may or may not match the fibres found around Gordon Cordell's wound.'

'To complicate matters further,' Bryant added. 'We learned last night that Giovanni Mancini also works at the hospital as a porter, so both were in the same vicinity as Cordell.'

'Checked them both out,' Penn offered. 'Senior Mancini has form for theft but not for almost twenty years. Nothing since he's been working at the hospital. And junior spent a few months away for grievous bodily harm in his late teens. Again, nothing since.'

Kim sighed heavily. Nothing there to hang her hat on.

'Stace, any progress on your missing girl?' she asked. Under her instruction Stacey had produced a summary document and circulated it to the team to bring everyone up to speed.

Stacey shrugged. 'Appears to have just disappeared into thin air. She left her best friend's house after an argument but never made it to her boyfriend's a few streets away. Her stepfather was out looking for her and never found her.'

'Mobile phone?' Bryant queried.

'No activity since Sunday night and now the battery has been removed by the looks of it. Can't locate it.'

'What are you thinking?' Kim asked.

'I've got reservations about the friend,' Stacey admitted. 'She's got form for violence and she was definitely unhappy with Jessie enough to smack her one.'

'What about the boyfriend?'

'Seems clean. For him the relationship isn't serious. I'd like to get into Emma's house. She's hiding something but I have nothing for a search warrant,' she said, as though the jig was up and she could take it no further.

'Correct,' Kim said. 'But you really gonna give up so easily, Stace?' she asked. 'Use your imagination and use your resources.'

Kim turned back to them all. 'Come on, guys. There's something out there just waiting to be found. I want fresh energy, fresh ideas, enthusiasm and a burst of energy. Got it?'

'Yes, boss,' they all shouted back.

'So, I want more digging on Cordell. I want someone liaising with Forensics for updates on both Cordell and Phyllis Mansell.

I want someone liaising with Traffic for any update on Saul Cordell's accident.'

She looked from Stacey to Penn. 'And how you divide that workload is completely up to you,' she said as her phone began to ring.

She answered the phone and listened to Woody.

'Damn it,' she said, hanging up the phone. She turned to her colleagues.

'Extra emphasis on Traffic. Saul Cordell just died.'

CHAPTER 51

'So, what do you want, Forensics or Traffic?' Penn asked, once the boss and Bryant had left the room.

'I'll take Traffic,' Stacey said, 'because I'm sure you want to get back to your footprint.'

'It'll wait, and what you sounding so snarky about?'

'I'm not snarky,' she said in a tone that kind of proved his point.

'It's Jessie, isn't it?' he asked, taking his headphones from his bag.

Yes, it was. She had barely slept thinking of the girl having spent her fourth night out there somewhere away from her parents and her home, her stuff, and all that was familiar to her.

Last night she had pored over the girl's social media accounts looking for any sign of activity, but everything had just stalled. Jessie's last post on Facebook had been a share of a cutie puppies video on Sunday afternoon. Her last tweet had been two days before she disappeared, and her Instagram pictured a Chinese takeaway on Saturday night, a full twenty-four hours before she'd gone missing. Every one of Jessie's accounts remained exactly as it had been when she'd checked them on Monday morning, except for posts on her timeline from friends asking where she was.

Stacey had also spent a few minutes checking the social media of Emma Weston, which had only one post since Sunday. On Monday evening the girl had posted a photo of Jessie and an appeal for anyone who had seen her to make contact. Over a hundred people had commented on the post but none had offered any information. Good wishes, memes, GIFs, hugs but no sightings.

'She doesn't have her medication,' Stacey said, quietly, answering Penn's question.

Penn frowned as he reached into the Tupperware box for what appeared to be a rock cake.

'What's the medication for anyway?' he asked.

Stacey opened her mouth to respond, and then closed it again.

She wasn't going to admit to Penn, because she could barely believe she was admitting it to herself; stupidly, she had never even thought to ask.

CHAPTER 52

'So, who was texting you last night?' Bryant asked as they pulled off the station car park.

'None of your business, Dad,' she said.

'Which would be true if you had any kind of personal life, but as you don't, I'm guessing it was work related and I'd just like to be kept in the loop.'

He had a point.

'Travis checking up on Penn.'

'Nice of him. Did you explain to him that you've covered your eyes and put your fingers in your ears until the kid goes away?'

'I can manage until this case is over,' she stated.

'And then he'll be gone?'

'Yep.'

'You're sure?' Bryant pushed.

'Oh yeah,' she insisted.

'And what about the next?' he asked, negotiating a traffic island.

'Next what?'

'Replacement,' he answered. 'Woody is not gonna let us stay as a team of three for long.'

She shrugged. 'Cross that bridge when we come to it,' she said.

'Yeah but maybe we should just give it a go,' he said.

'You think we should keep Penn?' she asked, horrified. The name Judas hovered around her lips.

'I'm saying the fact he is so different to Dawson may be a good thing.'

'Bryant, you stopping talking would be a great idea right now.'

'Look, guv, I'm just—'

'I mean it,' she snapped.

Bryant blew air out of his nose but, sensibly, closed his mouth and remained that way until he parked on the hospital car park.

'Okay, I won't mention it again,' he said. 'Your team is your call.'

'Too fucking right it is,' she said, slamming the car door.

As she headed towards the entrance she tried to analyse her growing rage towards her colleague. Bryant had always pushed her harder and farther than anyone else but he always showed correct judgement in stopping short of her tolerance limit. But right now either his judgement or her tolerance was broken and she wasn't quite sure which.

'Reckon she's in yet?' Bryant asked, as they strolled past the café and the smell of toast and bacon.

'Of course,' she replied, shortly, still swallowing down her irritation.

She was surprised that Terry wasn't perched at his usual spot but then she supposed it wasn't even eight yet.

Despite the early hour Kim felt sure Vanessa Wilson would be at her desk. They had established the woman didn't work normal hours and had left early the previous day due to a sick child, and Kim was guessing that fact would have ensured she was at her desk all the earlier the next day. Vanessa Wilson had not managed to secure the role of Operational Medical Director at the age of thirty-five by working eight-hour days.

As expected the door to the admin block opened when she pushed.

Three doors down she knocked and received an immediate instruction to enter.

Kim pushed open the door and paused.

Yes, she had expected to see Vanessa Wilson sitting at her desk bright and early. What she hadn't expected was to see a small person sitting on a mat surrounded by toys on the floor.

'My daughter, Mia,' Vanessa explained, looking over the top of the desk. 'Can't go to school, childminder won't take her because she's ill, my mum's busy and my husband is away until Saturday.'

Kim smiled down at the little girl who was looking up at them questioningly.

'Hi, Mia,' she said, giving her a little wave.

'My Little Pony,' she said, holding forward a plastic pony with a long purple mane.

'Oh, that's lovely,' Kim said, exhausting the limits of her ability to communicate with children.

Bryant stepped forward and bent down to the child's level.

'You don't have children, then, Inspector?' Vanessa asked, with a smile in her voice.

'That obvious?' Kim asked, taking a seat opposite the woman.

'It's a learned behaviour,' Vanessa said. 'Well, it certainly was for me. When I first had Mia I couldn't understand why my sound reasoning at 2 a.m. about the fact she was crying for no reason had no effect on her at all. I could sit in a room with medical personnel, lawyers and government officials and get my point across and yet one tiny human destroyed my entire self-image.'

'And did it work the other way?' Kim asked as Bryant's pony noises elicited squeals of delight from the little girl.

How the hell did he do that? she wondered, finally forgiving him their earlier altercation.

'You mean did I try and spoon-feed my colleagues while making "choo choo" noises once I returned from maternity leave?'

'Something like that,' Kim said.

'Not quite that bad but I did clap excitedly after one of my colleagues burped during a lunch meeting if that's what you mean.'

Kim couldn't help the smile that teased at her lips.

'So, my security brief tells me you were trying to bang down my door after I'd left last night. What was so urgent?'

'I needed to speak to you about a surgical nurse here at the hospital,' Kim answered.

Vanessa reached into her drawer and took out a business card. 'All my numbers are on there in case it happens again.'

Kim took it. 'Her name is Mansell. Her mother was murdered at Cedars Retirement Home yesterday afternoon.'

'Oh my god, how absolutely terrible. Does Nat know?'

Kim shrugged. 'The address they have at the retirement home is an old one, and her phone keeps ringing out.'

'Oh no, let me get you everything you need,' she said, reaching for the phone.

'Before you do, Mrs Wilson…'

'Vanessa, please,' she said. 'Over this last week I've seen more of you than I have my husband.'

'Vanessa, is there any link between Natalie Mansell and Doctor Gordon Cordell?'

As the colour began to leave her face Vanessa nodded.

'Yes, Inspector. She was a witness for Doctor Cordell in his complaint against Angelo Mancini.'

CHAPTER 53

'Bloody hell,' Stacey said, loud enough for Penn to hear.

He ignored her.

'Oi, Notkev, look at this,' she said, turning her screen.

Her first call to the Practice Manager of Wychley Medical Practice had not been fruitful. She had refused Stacey access to Jessie's medical records based on the absence of consent from the patient, and no matter how many times she'd tried to explain that the patient was missing, the woman had not budged. Stacey had requested an urgent call from Jessie's GP, Doctor Bristow, who had called her back ten minutes ago. After quoting Section 29 of the Data Protection Act 1998, the doctor had correctly explained that he was not compelled to allow access, but after listening to her had agreed that the need to disclose the patient's records outweighed the patient's interest in keeping the information confidential.

She had just signed into their system on the temporary credentials he had given her and her mouth had fallen open at what she'd seen.

Penn's eyes widened as they quickly ran across all the entries.

She scrolled down to show the extent of what she'd found.

She scrolled back to the top.

'The poor kid has been in and out of hospital since she was born. Started with feeding problems when she was just seven months old. She's had apnoea, diarrhoea, seizures, cyanosis, fevers, asthma; the list just goes on and on. It's like a bloody medical journal,' she said, as the fear for the girl's safety grew in her stomach.

Penn was trying to keep up as she scrolled. 'Let's see again,' he said.

She went back and used the cursors to move through the screen slower.

His eyes whizzed across the page as his fair eyebrows drew together. 'Go back to 2013,' he said, coming around to stand beside her.

'Why?' she asked, as she began to scroll down.

'There,' he said, pointing at the screen.

She looked at what he'd noticed.

'A three-year gap,' she said. 'From 2013 to 2016 there was hardly anything. Just a couple of chest infections.'

'Yeah, but look at the problems afterwards,' Penn said. She could hear the puzzlement in his tone.

'She's been in and out almost every month for the last couple of years.'

'She's been having ECGs, chest X-rays, MRIs, CT scans and... bloody hell...'

'What?' Stacey asked.

'Five months ago she had transesophageal echocardiogram,' he said.

'Let's pretend I was off sick the day the police gave us medical training,' she snapped.

Penn ignored her tone and explained. 'Patient is sedated to ease the discomfort and decrease the gag reflex while an ultrasound probe is passed through the oesophagus. It's invasive but shows all areas of the heart including aorta, pulmonary artery, valves, atria, everything.'

'How do you even... never mind. I don't even care,' Stacey said. 'But Jesus, this kid's been through it.'

'Results were inconclusive and Mrs Ryan demanded a second opinion,' Penn said. 'Insisting that the symptoms had not decreased.'

Stacey reached the end of the list and read the final entry.

'Which would explain that,' Stacey said, quietly.

'Oh yeah,' he answered.

Staring at her was a signed admission form.

'She's due to go into hospital tomorrow for an angiogram.'

'My dad had that done,' Penn said. 'He had anaesthetic pumped into his wrist for his radial artery. They slid a narrow plastic tube up the artery to his heart and injected dye so the arteries would show up under an X-ray. He was sixty-seven and shitting himself.'

And Jessie Ryan was due to have this procedure tomorrow.

'What's the purpose of it?' Stacey asked. She'd heard the term on medical programmes but had no clue what it meant.

'In my dad's case it was to detect narrowing of the arteries but it was pretty much after all other tests had been exhausted.'

'Like Jessie?' Stacey asked.

He nodded, and Stacey didn't feel the need to state the obvious.

With all the health problems this teenage girl had, if they didn't find her soon, Jessie Ryan could die.

CHAPTER 54

'Bryant, you could always try your luck going over thirty miles an hour,' she groaned, feeling her right foot pushing down on the imaginary accelerator at her feet.

'It's ten to nine, guv, and kids run out of side streets,' he said, patiently.

'You did hear Vanessa, didn't you, or were you too busy combing the mane of the pony?'

'To be fair it was quite therapeutic but yes I did hear.'

'So, you know Nat Mansell has not been at work since Monday and could be lying dead in her own home right now?'

'Then there's no need to rush, is there?' he asked, smartly.

She fought the urge to reach over and grab the steering wheel. He was enjoying having control of the car a little too much for her liking. She had the feeling this case would be solved much quicker if Bryant would learn to put his foot down.

She remained silent as he drove through Gornal Wood which was located on the western boundary of the Dudley Metropolitan Borough and had been the epicentre of the 2002 earthquake that had been felt as far away as North Yorkshire.

'Love that place,' Bryant said, nodding towards the Crooked House pub where the left-hand side was approximately four feet lower than the right due to mining subsidence.

'Aah, it's this one,' he said, coming to a sudden stop as he'd turned into Wilde Street.

The narrow road separated identical fifties semi-detached houses facing each other. Each home had a small drive and a patch of garden in front of the house.

Bryant pulled on to the empty drive. Kim noticed a four-course-high brick wall that separated the nurse's small garden from the one next door.

Nat Mansell's lawn was cut short with a one-foot border that appeared to have been recently dug over ready for plants. A small bucket holding a pair of gloves and some hand tools sat in the corner underneath the front window.

'So, we know she lives alone, divorced seven years ago, with no kids and doesn't drive,' Kim said as they approached the porch door.

'You know, this could be completely coincidental,' Bryant said.

'Jesus, you have been on holiday,' Kim said, waiting for her colleague to wake up and smell the coffee. 'Not sure how they do things at Brierley Hill but here we find clues and put them together until we find the bad person.'

Bryant ignored her and knocked on the door.

'She hasn't been to work since the day Cordell was murdered, she hasn't called in sick, she was linked to the complaint against Mancini and her mother was murdered yesterday afternoon.'

'Well, since you put it like that...' he said, knocking again but harder.

She bent down to listen at the letterbox.

'Nothing.'

Bryant stepped to the left as she stepped to the right.

'I'll see if there's anything open around the...'

'I've got a better idea,' she said, grabbing a glove and hand shovel from the bucket.

She put on the glove, turned the spade and used the handle to smash the glass. She reached inside and turned the lock. If they continued to run this investigation on Bryant time their killer would have died of old age before they caught him.

'We're in,' she said, stepping over the broken glass.

The box porch was tidy with a fern overflowing its pot in the corner. A pair of dirty gardening shoes sat on a rubber mat and a couple of coats and a scarf hung from a brass coat hook. On the box shelf in front of the window was an oversized teacup and saucer holding a collection of cactus plants.

Kim pushed open the door to the living room and stopped dead.

'Oh shit, Bryant, come take a look at this.'

CHAPTER 55

The living room stretched the front of the house with wooden stairs attached to the adjoining wall. Aside from that the entire room was carnage.

Every cushion was on the floor. Lamps had been smashed and occasional tables upended. Porcelain figurines lay in shards along the mantelpiece. The phone was on the floor in the middle of the room, the cord disconnected.

'Either a bloody good struggle or Nat Mansell had some kind of manic episode,' Bryant said, stepping into the room behind her.

Kim trod carefully across the carpet and gingerly opened the door to the kitchen diner at the back of the house, her heartbeat already increasing at the thought of what she might find.

She sighed with relief at two rooms that appeared to be all in order

'Check upstairs,' she called over her shoulder.

She assessed the two rooms. The neat orderliness of the rear of the property and the chaos at the front.

She checked the patio door that led out to a small, lawned garden. It was locked.

Everything had happened in the front room.

She could hear Bryant's footsteps above as he moved from room to room. Every second that passed without a distress call from above slowed her heart down.

She breathed out as his footsteps thundered down the stairs.

Thank God he had found no body.

Kim stepped back into the lounge and looked more closely at the chaos. Amongst the debris in front of the mantelpiece were two photo frames face down. She carefully lifted one which contained a photo of a man in his seventies smiling from beneath a Christmas cracker paper crown. Kim guessed it was Nat Mansell's father, who had died seven months earlier, according to Vanessa Wilson.

Kim placed it back down and picked up the other.

It was empty.

She showed it to Bryant. 'Any guesses who might have been in here?'

'Phyllis Mansell?' he said as they faced each other across the chaos of whatever had happened in this house.

'Why take the photo, Bryant? Surely if he wanted to kill the woman he knew what she looked like.'

Bryant shook his head. It made no sense to him either.

'I think she let him in,' Kim said, looking around.

Their killer had not forced himself into the house. Nothing in the porch had been disturbed.

Kim remembered the staff photo Vanessa had shown them and visualised the petite brunette walking back into the lounge and closing the door behind her. A struggle had followed and yet there was no blood, no sign of injury, so where the hell was she?

'He's got her,' Bryant said. 'It's exactly like Cordell. He's taken her somewhere to—'

'Handbag,' Kim suddenly said.

'Gucci's normally my first choice,' Bryant joked.

'Where is it?' Kim asked, ignoring him and looking around. There was no purse, no house keys, no bus pass.

'Maybe the killer took it or she grabbed...'

'Yeah, she must have asked him to delay his plan to brutally cut her throat while she gathered up her things,' she said, incredulously. 'But if those things aren't scattered around then they're normally all together in a handbag.'

'Which isn't here,' Bryant agreed.

'He didn't hurt her, Bryant,' she said, looking around. 'No sign of forced entry, obvious struggle but both doors locked.'

'Guv, like many other things in this case, it makes no sense.'

Sense or not, those were the facts.

'She let him in, maybe to talk about something, things got physical but she left of her own accord, with her handbag and whatever else, and locked the door securely behind her. Just like with Cordell.'

'But she didn't tidy up so that means...'

'She's scared, Bryant. The woman must be terrified.'

'But where the hell is she?' he asked.

Kim crossed the room at speed.

'Follow me, Bryant. I think I might have the answer.'

CHAPTER 56

'Have you found her?' Mrs Ryan asked, as she opened the door.

Stacey shook her head quickly, extinguishing the hope and excitement from her eyes. Stacey wished she was here with better news.

'Please, please, come in,' she said, stepping aside. 'Philip went back to work this morning but I couldn't,' she explained. 'He can't stand sitting around not knowing where to look next, and I can't bear the thought of leaving the house in case she comes back and I'm not here.'

The tears filled her eyes as she sat in the same spot as the other day. And then she stood again. 'I'm sorry, can I get you?...'

'I'm fine, Mrs Ryan, please sit down,' Stacey said, quietly trying to calm the woman's nervous energy. 'I just wanted to let you know where we're at.'

Mrs Ryan sat down and nodded.

'We've spoken to Emma, who had a fight with Jessie on Sunday night.'

'A fight?' she asked, dumbfounded. 'It got physical?'

Stacey decided she deserved the truth.

'Yes, Mrs Ryan. There is footage of Emma slapping Jessie.'

'She hit my daughter?' the woman asked, enraged.

Stacey nodded.

Mrs Ryan stood. 'That little slutty bitch actually struck my child?' she asked.

Stacey hid her surprise at the venom spewing out of the woman's mouth. Bad enough were the names she was calling a fifteen-year-old girl but the vitriol attached to the names was disturbing.

'I'm sure it was nothing more than a spat, Mrs Ryan. She—'

'What did she do to my child? Did the little cow punch her or?…'

'It was a single slap,' Stacey explained wondering why she was feeling the need to defend Emma Weston. 'Just an argument that got heated. All best friends have them,' she said.

'Friends don't hit each other,' Mrs Ryan said, pacing. 'And this coincidentally happened on the night my child disappeared.'

'Yes, coincidentally,' Stacey agreed.

'And what did she have to say for herself?' Mrs Ryan asked.

'That she was trying to stop Jessie from going round to her boyfriend's house.'

The woman's face turned ashen.

'B-boyfriend?'

'Yes, Mrs Ryan, Jessie did have a boyfriend, named Dale Jones,' Stacey said. 'Seems like a decent kid. A year older than Jessie but it wasn't anything serious.'

Mrs Ryan's eyes held a question.

Stacey shook her head. 'He says they didn't have sex, and I believe him.'

The relief on her face was short-lived. 'So, did he see her Sunday night? Was he the last?…'

'I don't think Jessie ever got there. They hadn't planned to meet and he insists he never saw her.'

'And you believe him?' she asked, incredulously.

Stacey thought about the kid standing on the doorstep with the game controller in his hand. Her copper's instinct had not reacted to him at all.

'Yes, I do.'

Mrs Ryan frowned, 'So, where did Jessie go?'

'That's exactly what we're trying to find out. She left Emma's house but never arrived at Dale's and unfortunately there's not a lot of CCTV in between.'

'So, how are you?...'

'We've circulated Jessie's photo, which will be shown at every possible briefing until we find her. I promise you she will not be forgotten.'

'Thank you,' Mrs Ryan said, reaching across and touching her hand.

'Now, Mrs Ryan, can we talk about Jessie's health. I need to know just how poorly she is.'

Mrs Ryan nodded and took a deep breath. 'Where do I start? My poor daughter has been through so much. Her problems started when she was just a couple of months old.' She smiled, sadly. 'Just like any new mum I would sit and watch her for hours, marvelling at the miracle she was. I would count the seconds between her breaths to make sure they were regular and even. And then one night her chest just didn't rise. I thought I was imagining it but I was right. I called an ambulance and luckily I knew how to do CPR.

'She was breathing by the time they arrived. They were wonderful. Took us to the hospital so Jessie could be checked over.

'The doctors found nothing wrong, which was both a huge relief as well as terrifying. I was so grateful there was nothing wrong with her and just one of those things, but terrified that without a diagnosis and treatment it would happen again. And, of course it did.'

'How many times?' Stacey asked, wondering what this woman had gone through every time her child had stopped breathing.

'Too many to count,' she said. 'Jessie seemed to grow out of it by the time she was around 18 months. I crossed each night off the calendar without an episode until we reached two months, then three months and eventually six months. I was ecstatic. I actually felt I could breathe properly. Enjoy my life again. And then the stomach cramps started. Agonising pains that doubled her over. Back to the hospital we went for more tests.'

Tears filled her eyes.

'She never had the childhood I'd hoped for. We were bounced from hospital to doctor to specialist with contradictory diagnoses. More tests. Sometimes it seems that her whole life has been lived in a hospital room. I knew most of the staff by their first name. They were wonderful, always making sure I was okay when it wasn't even me that was ill.'

'But there were a few years when her health seemed to improve,' Stacey observed.

'I stopped taking her,' Mrs Ryan admitted. 'Seeing the constant fear on her face almost killed me, so I tried holistic methods and put her on an additive-free organic diet, and her health began to improve. She put on weight and had a growth spurt. It was unbelievable how she blossomed. And then two years ago our world came crashing down when Justin, Jessie's younger brother, died…'

'Oh, my goodness, I'm so sorry,' Stacey said, sincerely.

She wiped away the tears before continuing, though more formed immediately. 'Thank you,' she said. 'And then soon afterwards Jessie began to complain of chest pains and I couldn't ignore that. They've done all kinds of tests, which have been inconclusive, and Jessie keeps begging me to let her be, but I can tell when she's having trouble, and how can I ignore chest pains? She's my child. I have to do what's best for her.'

The woman was openly crying now, the tears spilling out of her eyes and over her cheeks.

She looked so lost, forlorn sitting in the middle of the sofa, terrified.

Stacey couldn't help the compassion that surged through her.

She took a seat beside the woman and took her hand. 'Everything will be okay, Mrs Ryan,' she said tapping her palm.

'I can't lose another one,' she sobbed, turning to Stacey for comfort.

Stacey's arms went around her.

'Please bring her back. Promise me that you will.'

Tears stung her own eyes. 'I will, Mrs Ryan, I promise.'

Mrs Ryan cried out, a strangled sound drenched with desperation, and Stacey simply held her while she wept.

'That's why I can't stand the thought of that no good little bitch striking my child,' she explained, through sobs. 'My girl has been through enough.'

'I understand, I really—' Stacey's words were cut off by the sudden sound of forceful knocking on the front door.

'Let me get that,' she said, using the opportunity to extricate herself from the distraught woman.

The door had barely opened an inch when a woman started trying to barge in the door.

'Okay, Kerry, this is what—'

Stacey's instinct had been to block access with her arm across the doorway.

The woman eyed her suspiciously. 'Who are you?'

Stacey was prevented from answering as Mrs Ryan appeared at her side. 'It's okay, officer. This is my neighbour, Cath.'

Stacey stood aside as the woman entered, her pudgy arms clutching a folder to her bosom.

She walked straight over to the dining table and began to lay out her papers.

'Okay, Shaz at number ten is working up a Facebook page to send out an appeal. She's already done a twittering page and started tagging local groups, whatever that means,' she said, shrugging. 'The twins at number six are setting up a story on Instasomething, and I've printed off some photos for shop windows. Lewis and

Denny from twenty-seven are gonna hang around Merry Hill and see if she turns up there and—'

A single sob broke free from Mrs Ryan as a look of gratitude and almost pleasure washed over her face. One more sniff and the tears were gone.

'Oh, Cath...' Mrs Ryan said as the neighbour ambled towards her.

Right now, Stacey realised, they were both grateful for Cath's arrival.

Stacey began to step away as Cath enfolded Mrs Ryan in a hug.

'We'll find her, Kerry. I promise,' she said.

With nothing further to add, Stacey slipped unnoticed from the house.

CHAPTER 57

'Stop the car,' Kim screamed.

'Guv, it's a main bloody road,' Bryant said.

She began opening the passenger door.

'For God's sake,' he cried, slamming on the brakes. Horns sounded on the main road that ran to the east side of Cedars Retirement Home, drawing attention from everyone around, including the petite brunette on the single wooden bench.

Kim had guessed Nat Mansell would want to be close to where her mother had been. She was running scared, which always led you to seek out the people that made you feel safe. Except Nat Mansell's mother had been murdered on the other side of that wall.

Kim dodged the people on the pavement as Bryant drove away to find somewhere to park the car.

The woman on the bench had risen and was looking in her direction. Her posture appeared startled and wary.

'Please, wait,' Kim called as the woman reached for her handbag. Why was Nat Mansell avoiding her if she'd done nothing wrong?

Kim guessed there were about fifty metres between them, and she prayed that the woman stayed where she was.

Nat looked around and then began hurrying away at speed.

Kim quickened her pace as stabbing pains shot through her shin. She couldn't remember all of the bone doctor's instructions but she was pretty sure no running was a given.

'Miss Mansell, wait, please,' Kim called, breaking into a trot.

She had hoped Bryant was coming from another angle to try and cut her off, but his car was still at the end of the road, stuck on a red light.

Damn it, she cursed as the woman's steps took her ever nearer to the housing estate at the edge of the grass.

Kim forced her legs to pick up speed focussing on the power in her thighs instead of the agony in her shin.

'Wait,' she called, having made ground on the distance between them.

'Leave me alone,' Nat called out before picking up speed.

'I just want to talk,' Kim called, matching her speed so the distance between them didn't widen.

She didn't respond.

'Miss Mansell, Nat, just give me a minute,' Kim called. 'I need to talk to you about Cordell.'

'Just leave me alone,' she repeated, and Kim could now hear the emotion in her voice.

This woman was scared.

'I'm a police officer. I can help,' Kim said, having taken a few metres out of the space.

'No one can help me,' she cried.

Kim felt the pain turn to lightning strikes shooting down to her ankle and right up to her thigh but she had to push past it.

She needed to talk to this woman. Now.

Seeing that she was almost at the road that would take her beyond Kim's reach, she stopped and turned. She held up her hand.

'Don't come any closer or I'll run, I swear.'

Kim stopped running, and cried out at the agony thundering through her bone.

She swallowed away the stars that threatened her vision.

'Were you having an affair with Cordell?' Kim called out.

She nodded. 'We were in love,' she called back.

Lilith Cordell hinted her husband was a serial adulterer but it appeared this fling had been more serious.

'You know who killed him, don't you, Miss Mansell?'

She shook her head, looking stricken.

'Is it the same person who killed your mother?' Kim asked, trying to remain upright.

'You're hurt,' the woman said, as Kim felt herself buckling to the ground. Her left leg muscles screamed and it felt like they were detaching themselves from the bone.

Kim could see the indecision all over her face. The woman was a nurse.

'Please,' Kim shouted. 'Tell me…'

'I can't, I'm sorry,' she called out, backing away. 'I can't help you. I'm so sorry but I made a choice and now I've got to live with it.'

And suddenly she was gone but Kim had no idea where as a black veil of darkness lowered and covered her eyes.

CHAPTER 58

'Guv, guv, wake up. Guv, come on,' Kim heard before she opened her eyes.

It took her a moment to realise where she was. The discomfort of the damp grass beneath her was trumped by the knife being run up and down her left leg. She groaned as she tried to sit up.

'Stay there,' Bryant said, steadying her and putting his jacket around her shoulders.

The April morning sun was warm on her face but her body was shivering uncontrollably.

'It's the shock, guv,' Bryant said. 'You've pushed your leg too hard. You need to be checked—'

'Bryant, tell me that siren in the distance isn't for me?' she said, looking around for the blue lights.

'I may have accidentally called it in.'

'What, you fell over and landed on the 999 button?' she asked, cuttingly.

'Yeah, that was exactly it,' he said as a first responder pulled off the main road and onto the grass.

'Now, if you'd tried that manoeuvre, Bryant, I might have c-caught her,' she said as a violent shudder coursed through her.

'Whatever,' he said as the first responder approached.

An ambulance pulled up behind the responder's vehicle. Two paramedics jumped out with a stretcher.

'Hell, no,' she raged and then looked at her colleague. 'Bloody hell, Bryant.'

'I don't decide who comes. I just made the call,' he said as his phone rang. 'Woody,' he said taking a step away.

'You called the boss?' she asked, incredulously.

'Yeah, got bored waiting for you to wake up,' he said, answering the call.

'What's your name?' asked the paramedic as he kneeled on the grass.

'Well, it ain't Usain Bolt, is it?' she snapped.

He raised an eyebrow.

'Kim Stone,' she answered.

'And where are you?' he asked, pulling on a pair of latex gloves.

'Sitting on a field in the middle of bloody Tividale being gawped at like a circus animal,' she said, nodding towards the onlookers gathering around the edge of the field.

'Did you hit your head?' he asked.

'No.'

'So, what exactly happened?'

'Stupid mistake, moved too fast, leg gave way, passed out but I'm fine now. Plaster came off a few days ago,' she explained, pointing to her left leg.

He frowned before moving around to her left-hand side. 'Did the doctor not explain?…'

'Yes, he did,' she said, holding up her hand. 'I am solely responsible for this level of stupidity,' she said.

'Yes, she is,' Bryant confirmed after ending the call. 'And Woody wants you either at the hospital or back at the station. Preferably the hospital but…'

'Actually, you can blame him for some of it. If he'd got the car closer…'

'This may hurt a bit,' said the paramedic as he placed both hands at the top of her knee.

She looked at him questioningly.

'Just checking everything is where it should be,' he said, flatly, as the two guys with the stretcher arrived.

'Thanks guys, but I won't be needing—'

'They're staying,' said the first responder.

'Seriously, go help some sick person,' she protested, deeply disturbed by the resources being used because she'd tried to run.

They made no move to retreat and stood behind the first responder.

'Bryant, tell 'em I'm fine.'

'They won't listen to either of you,' said the first responder as his gloved hands moved down her leg.

'I'm sure there are people that need their... aargh...' she cried out as his hands squeezed around her shin.

'I did mention it might hurt,' he said, without flinching.

As his hands moved away from the break spot she breathed a sigh of relief. He took a pupilometer from his medical bag and shone it in both of her eyes. She was reminded of the scenes from the film *Men in Black*.

'Okay, I've forgotten everything. I never saw a thing. You can let me go now,' she joked in an effort to show him she was fine.

'She's Perrl,' he said, over his shoulder.

'I'm what?' she asked.

'Pupils are equal, round and reactive to light,' he answered, placing his pen light back in his bag.

'Sounds like I'm good to go,' she said, pushing herself forward.

'Any headaches, nausea?...'

'Seriously, I'm fine,' she said, shaking her head.

'I don't think you've done any permanent damage but I'd like you to go to hospital for an X-ray to make sure.'

'Nah, I'm good, thanks,' Kim said, holding out her hand to Bryant to help her up.

The paramedic took off the gloves. 'I can't force you to go but it is my best advice.'

'Hospital or station, guv,' Bryant reminded her.

'At least let me see you walk a couple of steps,' the paramedic said, stepping back.

Kim lowered her left foot to the ground and put her weight through it. She hid the pain behind an 'I told you I'm fine' smile.

'Grimacing on the inside, eh?' he asked with a half smile.

The second step was less painful than the first. The next one was less tentative as the vision of the bone snapping in half disappeared from her mind.

'A few more steps,' he said, turning to Bryant. 'You going to be with her for the rest of the day?'

'Due to sins in a past life, I'd imagine so,' Bryant replied drily.

'Keep an eye out for any signs of concussion from the fall: throwing up, balance issues, complaints of blurred vision, confusion, saying things that don't make sense…'

'Yeah, some of those are gonna be difficult to isolate from normal—'

'Bryant,' she warned, sending him daggers. She didn't need him giving them any excuse to hassle her further.

She'd taken two more steps when her phone started to ring. It was the squad room.

'Stace,' she answered before she heard the voice. 'Oh, Penn,' she corrected, feeling the tension seep into her jaw.

She listened as he spoke.

'What?' she said.

He continued.

'You are kidding?' she asked.

He finished speaking, and she ended the call.

She smiled at the trio of technicians. 'Sorry, guys, looks like I'm going to the station after all,' she said.

'We are?' Bryant asked.

'Oh yes, but first we have to pick up something on the way.'

CHAPTER 59

Stacey tapped twice on Emma Weston's door as another shower started depositing thick raindrops onto her head. She moved closer to the building for shelter as a few spots found their way past her jacket collar and down the back of her neck.

The door was opened by a frazzled-looking Mrs Weston.

Her face instantly hardened.

'Emma's at school,' she said, placing herself firmly in the doorway. 'And she told me about you turning up there yesterday. I should complain,' she said, stepping back and moving to close the door. 'This is harassment of a minor, and she's told you everything—'

Stacey was ready and put her hand out to stop the door closing in her face.

'I'm here to see you,' Stacey said, pleasantly but firmly. 'And to stop your daughter getting herself into any deeper trouble than she already is.'

The woman hesitated. 'What kind of trouble?'

'Lying to a police officer, obstructing an investigation. It really is in your interest to give me a minute of your time, Mrs Weston.'

Fear crossed her face but she frowned it away and opened the door. 'Okay, but be quick, I've got to get to work.'

Stacey followed her into a small kitchen off the hallway. The sink was full of sudsy water, and plates and cups littered the work surface.

'Thank you, Mrs Weston, I just need—'

'Susan, call me Susan,' she said, lowering the glasses first into the water. 'When you use my last name you just keep reminding me of the bastard that left me.'

As she hadn't been invited to sit, Stacey remained standing by the fridge freezer.

'I've just come from Jessie's house,' Stacey said.

'Good for you,' she said, without turning.

'I get the feeling you don't care for the Ryan family all that much,' Stacey said, still hoping to appeal to the woman's maternal instinct.

'Not my kind of people,' she said.

'But your daughters are allegedly best friends,' she said.

'Allegedly?' she asked, glancing sideways. 'Emma would do anything for Jessie. Anything. Despite the fact Jessie's parents have tried to keep them apart since the day they met.'

'It hasn't worked though, has it?' Stacey asked. 'But does Emma understand the complexity of Jessie's health issues?'

'Of course she understands. They've known each other for years and been best friends for the last few years.'

'So, as a mother you can understand how Mrs Ryan is feeling right now?'

'I'm sure she's very worried but there's nothing more I can tell you. Jessie left here to go see her boyfriend and that's the last time we saw her. End of.'

'And Emma knows she's due to go into hospital tomorrow afternoon for an angiogram?'

Susan swallowed. 'Of course.'

Stacey knew that this wasn't working. She could still feel Mrs Ryan sobbing against her chest as though her heart would break. Stacey was unsure Susan Weston would be moved by that even if she told her.

'I'm guessing life's not always easy with Emma?' Stacey asked.

Susan gave her a cutting look. 'What do you mean by that?'

'She's found herself in a spot of trouble, hasn't she? More than once?' Stacey said.

'What teenager hasn't?' she said, reaching for a tea towel.

'Three episodes of violence. One GBH?'

'She took her punishment, officer, now if you don't mind...'

'Did Emma tell you that they fought on Sunday night?' Stacey asked.

Susan's hand paused inside the glass she was wiping.

'F-fought?' she asked.

'At the end of the path,' Stacey explained. 'When they both left the house. They were arguing and Emma slapped Jessie.'

Susan continued to wipe the glass that was now bone dry.

'Just teenage stuff,' she said. 'All best friends fight.'

'But Emma was the last person to see Jessie before she disappeared, and she has a history of violence. I'm trying to keep her out of trouble, Susan, but if you don't start helping me...'

'What do you need?' she asked, drying her hands.

'To take a look in Emma's room.'

Susan looked doubtful.

'The minute I apply for a search warrant it's gonna...'

'Go on,' she said, nodding towards the stairs. 'First on the left and don't make a mess. I know what you lot are like.'

Stacey turned and headed up the stairs. She hadn't lied about the search warrant, except to say that she didn't have a hope in hell of getting one.

But she knew that Emma Weston was hiding something and she wanted to find out what.

CHAPTER 60

'I'm not sure Woody would agree that the Hollytree estate is on the way to the station,' Bryant observed as they pulled up next to the wheelie bins that now had a pile of black bags three deep surrounding them.

'I told you what Penn said and you know full well we don't have enough for a search warrant, so we need the element of surprise on our side,' she said, getting out of the car.

'Guv, less than half an hour ago you were lying on your back, unconscious, in the middle of a grass patch. We could have uniforms...'

'Needs to be us, Bryant, now get out of the car,' she said, closing the passenger door.

The car ride had served to stiffen her leg once more, but after a few tentative steps she slowly began to test it with her weight.

'Stop looking so bloody worried,' she said, as Bryant knocked the door. His sideways glances were beginning to freak her out.

'Mr Mancini, may we come in?' Kim asked, barging past the senior man of the house.

She continued her journey to the living room, where Giovanni sat with damp hair and a towel around his midriff, messing with his mobile phone.

He stood and looked behind for his father.

'Sorry to barge in like this,' she said once they were all in the same room. 'But we'd like you to accompany us to the station to answer a couple of questions, Mr Mancini,' she said, turning to the younger of the men and looking down at the side of the sofa.

'And we'd like you to bring those Reeboks with you.'

CHAPTER 61

Stacey sat down on the bed, disheartened. She'd searched every-where; every drawer, every cupboard, every corner, underneath things, on top of things, behind, in front and she wasn't feeling particularly proud of herself right now.

She'd waded uninvited through the personal possessions of a fifteen-year-old girl not only without her knowledge but also without her consent. And she'd found nothing. She sighed heavily as she tried to picture the two of them that night, before the argument, sitting here on Emma's bed; talking, whispering, messing around on the laptop, watching TV listening to music, talking about make-up, boys.

What had they been listening to? she wondered, glancing at the music centre at the back of the dressing table. Most kids used their phones and earphones or portable speakers, not the tall clunky ones taking up unnecessary space in a small room.

Stacey frowned as she stood and moved back towards the dresser.

Why indeed were the huge speakers taking up valuable space when even her clothes had spilled out of the small wardrobe onto a nearby chair?

She looked from one to the other. One had a thin film of dust coating its shiny blackness. The other did not.

She picked up the dusty one and placed it back. She picked up the other and felt the weight difference immediately.

Emma was a girl who was used to having her possessions searched and needed to find inventive new places to store her secrets.

Stacey lifted the speaker away easily. It wasn't even plugged in. She took it to the bed and felt around the edging of the mesh frontage. She pulled along the top edge. The speaker came apart. In front of her was a pack of cigarettes, a disposable lighter, a card for a family planning clinic in Walsall and a scrunched-up supermarket carrier bag.

Stacey tentatively opened the bag around what appeared to be a collection of items.

As she took them out one by one her breath caught high in her chest.

A battery, a sim card and a carcass with a sequinned union jack exactly like the one described on the missing person's report form.

A figure appeared in the doorway.

Susan's horrified gaze saw what she was holding.

'Mrs Weston, can you please explain why your daughter has Jessica Ryan's phone?'

CHAPTER 62

'Sir, I'm fine,' Kim said, for the third time. And it was almost the truth, if she ignored the pounding sensation from her shin bone right down to her ankle. Not a detail she needed to share with her boss.

Jack, the Custody Sergeant, had made it perfectly clear when she'd entered the station that Woody wanted to see her. Bryant had taken Giovanni Mancini to an interview room as she'd headed up the stairs. So far, Woody had lectured her, told her off and asked her repeatedly if she was okay.

'Now can we talk about Giovanni?...'

'Stone, you were unconscious on the ground in the middle of a field.'

'Only briefly, sir,' she said, wondering if that would make a difference.

His raised eyebrow said not.

'You know you should have gone to the hospital for an X-ray and a check-up to make sure...'

'Sir, I have a suspect downstairs for the murder of Doctor Cordell and possibly Phyllis Mansell, but I need to take a good look at his shoes.'

'He's here voluntarily?'

She nodded.

'You don't have enough to arrest?'

She shook her head. Working at the same hospital as the victim along with a few thousand other people and wearing the same mass market brand of trainers as hundreds of thousands of fellow consumers were not reasonable grounds to arrest. And that was all she had. She couldn't even link Giovanni directly to the complaint from Cordell. If they'd been talking about the father, she might have had a chance. But the father wasn't wearing the Reebok trainers.

'Then you can't touch them as you well know.'

'But, couldn't I just get them off him, take some photos, send them to Mitch and?...'

'Stone, we'll both forget you just asked me if you could do something that would get the case thrown out of court and both of us joining the unemployment line.'

'Not really sure there is a line any more, sir, to be honest,' she replied.

'For clarity, Stone, the answer is categorically no. If those shoes leave his feet for even a second, you and I will have a very serious problem. Are we clear?'

'Of course, sir,' she said, as if there was never any doubt.

He calmed quickly and changed the subject. 'And the counselling sessions are progressing well?' he asked.

'Absolutely,' she answered, edging closer to the door. 'You gave me a time limit for the report and you shall have it by the end of the week.'

He thought for a second. 'Yes, I'm realising that you do appear to perform better when working to an exact time frame.'

His expression told her that he'd just had some kind of light bulb moment. It wasn't so much smug. Woody didn't really do smug. But it was damned close.

'So, with that in mind, I'd like an updated X-ray of your left leg on my desk by the end of the day.'

She balked. 'Sir, I can't get that... I have too much to...'

'Then, I suggest you get on and interview your witness, Stone, and I repeat once more, his shoes stay on.'

CHAPTER 63

'So, what would you like?' Bryant asked as they stood outside interview room one.

'What I'd like is to get my hands on those Reeboks and see if they match the boot print on Cordell's jacket. And then I'd like to check 'em for blood.'

Penn's call had informed her the print was a match for the exact type of shoe he was wearing, but to confirm a match she needed the actual pair of shoes used to make the print.

'Yeah, dream on. I meant good cop, bad cop. What're we doing?'

'Policing in the twenty-first century would be a good one,' she said, raising an eyebrow, before entering the room.

'Thank you for your patience, Mr Mancini,' Kim said, pleasantly, as she took a seat opposite him.

'As you know, you're here voluntarily just to answer a few questions. You're free to leave at any time, do you understand?'

He visibly relaxed at her tone.

'Sir, you understand we're investigating the murder of Doctor Gordon Cordell and your family appears to have a recent grievance against his actions.'

'He had a grievance against us, but we didn't fucking—'

'Mr Mancini, you were very agitated yesterday on your father's behalf.'

'Too bloody right.'

'Can you explain why you were so angry at Doctor Cordell?'

'Not so much him. He was an arrogant, conceited wanker and got exactly what he deserved to be honest. He lied about my father who had discovered his filthy little secret and tried to destroy him just so he wouldn't get found out. But I'm more angry with that fucking Medical Director woman for just tossing out my dad like that without even listening to him. Thing is, my dad wasn't gonna say anything anyway. He's seen all sorts of stuff but just keeps quiet, goes about his business and cleans up people's shit.'

'I think Vanessa Wilson has procedures to follow,' she explained.

'I don't give a fuck about procedures,' he spat. 'My dad left that place feeling like a liar and a thief and he doesn't bloody deserve that.'

'Okay, Mr Mancini,' Kim said, calmly. He was a passionate man, quick to temper and she didn't want him walking out yet. Not before she'd got those shoes.

'She's a tight-assed bitch who treated my dad like shit.'

He lurched forward, taking her by surprise. 'Do you have any idea how many times he's worked a double shift because someone called in sick? Oh, can't mention that because it's illegal. How many times he stayed late because some new kid hadn't been able to stick to the schedule. And he never complained once. You know why? Because he was grateful. He was so thankful to have a job he just kept his mouth shut and got on with it. And they all called him a fucking thief,' he said, shaking his head.

'All?' Kim probed gently.

'Yeah, Cordell, his whore and the fucking director bitch. They're all as bad as each other.'

'And your father was definitely with you on Monday evening?' Kim asked.

The shift in questions caused a momentary lapse in concentration. He seemed to hesitate before nodding.

'We were together at home, watching telly.'

'Okay, Mr Mancini, and where were you both yesterday afternoon?'

He frowned at her. His dark eyebrows within touching distance. 'I'm sorry, but I'm not going to answer that.'

'But surely you can recall where you were this time yesterday?'

'I didn't say I *couldn't* answer it, I said I *wouldn't*, now I think it's time—'

'Okay, sir, no problem,' Kim said, reassuringly. 'At present, I only have one more question to ask, okay?'

He nodded his agreement.

'Giovanni, may I please borrow your Reeboks?'

His face darkened even further as he began to shake his head.

'No, officer. I'm afraid you may not.'

CHAPTER 64

'You can't say I didn't ask nicely,' Kim raged back out in the corridor.

'Oh yeah, you asked him very nicely and in a roundabout way if either him or his father is a cold-blooded killer, so I'm not that surprised he wouldn't let you have his Reeboks,' Bryant said.

'You honestly think it's just a coincidence that he's wearing the exact type of shoe that we're looking for?' Kim asked but didn't wait for an answer. 'Penn confirmed it on the database and with the manufacturer.'

'He also confirmed that those shoes are their second biggest selling pair of trainers and have been on the market for seven years now, meaning that there's... a lot of them out there.'

She couldn't disagree with that.

'And why would he wear them so openly if he'd used them while committing a murder?' Bryant asked. 'They might still have blood on them.'

'His dad is a cleaner. He could easily sort them out. Pretty sure they have stuff to attack bloodstains in a hospital,' she observed.

'Except Mancini senior isn't at work right now. He's on paid suspension. How'd he get the stuff to clean the shoes?'

'Oh, so we should disregard completely that one of our key witnesses in this case is wearing the exact same make of trainer found imprinted on the jacket of our dead body? Yeah, that makes sense. Feel free to nip upstairs and tell Penn he's wasted about thirty hours of his life finding evidence that we're gonna choose to ignore.'

Bryant ignored her frustration and continued. 'Mancini is here under his own steam. He can leave any time, and I think you're just going to have to accept those things are staying right where they are: on his feet.'

Kim opened her mouth to retort and then closed it again.

'Do me a favour, Bryant. Ring Stace and ask her to get Mitch here. Now, I'm going for coffee and when I get back I am so done being nice.'

CHAPTER 65

Stacey put down the phone. 'Strange. Boss wants Mitch here. Don't think we've ever done that before.'

'And Mitch is?' Penn asked.

'Forensics guy. Normally leads the teams of crime scene folks.'

Stacey found his number and put in the call. He asked if it was urgent, and she said yes, not really knowing but assuming her boss wouldn't have made the request otherwise.

'So, what are you doing now you've found the paw print?' Stacey asked.

'I've been chasing up Forensics for anything more on Phyllis Mansell, but the lab experts on the blue fibres are on a half-day training course about advances in polymers... or something,' he said.

'So, you've got nothing to—'

'So, I started going through the three dozen or so witness statements to Saul Cordell's accident and there's one here that's bothering me.' he said.

'Just one?' she asked, sarcastically. Out of thirty-six statements that all said the same thing he was focussed on the one that said something different.

She still needed to have a good look at Jessie's phone and decide on her next move, but the boss had been clear on the case priority.

'So, what's the story with this statement?' she asked.

'Young guy says he saw something a bit dodgy going on around junction 2 of the M5 around the time of the accident.'

'Dodgy?' Stacey asked.

'He told the officer he'd be better off chasing the idiot who was flashing his lights a few miles back.'

'And Traffic say?'

'That he was just trying to detract attention from himself because he was caught doing 119 miles per hour, but the kid got a ticket anyway, so what did he have to gain?'

When thirty-five statements said the exact same thing and one said something different common sense dictated a majority rule. Except in police work that got trumped by instinct and Stacey could understand why it was giving Penn pause for thought.

In all honesty she wanted to focus all her attention on Jessie Ryan's disappearance, but for now that would have to wait.

'If there's even the slightest possibility that Saul Cordell's death was not an accident we've gotta dig as deep as we can,' she said, grudgingly.

He nodded his agreement.

'Okay, you call the kid, and I'll get started on the CCTV.'

CHAPTER 66

'Okay, Giovanni, I'm gonna give it to you straight,' Kim said, setting her coffee down on the table. 'A man is dead and so is an elderly lady and I'm wondering if you had something to do with it.'

His face paled as he began to shake his head.

'I have evidence building that I think is going to point towards either you, your dad or both of you, so I think you should—'

'Am I under arrest?' he asked, looking from her to Bryant.

'Did you hear me read you your Miranda rights?'

He shook his head.

'I'm just being honest with you because I think you're hiding something.'

'But I—'

'Don't say anything right now. Just listen.'

'But I wouldn't hurt someone because—'

'Thing is, Giovanni. You were very angry at the way your dad was treated by both the hospital and Doctor Cordell. It's understandable you'd want to protect his honour, defend him.'

'But I honestly—'

'I want you to know that we understand. We get it,' she said, glancing at Bryant, who had a firm set to his jaw and she knew why. He'd get over it. The guy wasn't even under caution.

'So, I'm wondering if a situation just got out of your control, that you didn't intend to hurt—'

'I wouldn't… I swear,' he said, looking to Bryant, who nudged her leg beneath the table.

She ignored him.

'See the thing is to hurt someone just because you feel like it or to defend your family is almost like two different crimes, and I don't think you'd just hurt someone for no reason. Even a judge would understand feeling strongly about—'

'A minute outside, guv?' Bryant said, breaking the tension she'd deliberately built between them.

She smiled tightly and left the room. She waited for Bryant to close the door.

'What the hell are you doing?' she hissed.

'I could ask you the same question,' he snapped. 'The bloody Reid technique?' he asked. 'I was counting the steps with you. Textbook, and even in the correct order. Lead suspect, shift blame, discourage denial, reinforce sincerity, offer alternatives, give a more socially acceptable motive like the defence of one's family,' he said, eyes flashing.

'It's an effective method,' she defended.

The whole programme was a three-step process. Fact Analysis followed by a Behaviour Analysis Interview and then the nine steps of Interrogation.

'Yeah, but you skipped straight to third base and hammered the guy with a monologue rather than a question and answer session which—'

'Bryant, I want some answers and the technique can be—'

'It's guilt presumptive and you know it. It's confrontational, psychologically manipulative with the single purpose of getting a confession, but more than anything, guv, it's beneath you. That guy is here voluntarily, without a brief, and he hasn't even been arrested.'

Her own frustration churned at her stomach, compounded by the truth of his words.

The force directive was to apply the principles of the PEACE model. Preparation and Planning, Engage and Explain, Account,

Closure and Evaluate which encouraged more of a dialogue between investigator and suspect.

And she did. Normally. But right now she wanted results.

She met her colleague's gaze. 'Okay,' she said, knowing he had a point.

'Don't humour me,' he spat.

'I'm not. You're right. I shouldn't have questioned him like that. I just know he's hiding something and—'

'We'll find it the legal, ethical way but not at any cost,' he answered.

'People are dying, Bryant, in case you've forgotten that.'

'And we're the good guys, guv, in case you've forgotten that.'

Almost. Sometimes. But not with her colleague's integrity working right alongside them.

A constable approached and nodded in her direction.

'Marm, Mitch Allen is waiting for you in reception.'

Kim smiled at Bryant's puzzled expression.

'Great timing,' she said, looking along to the foyer. 'Would you be kind enough to send him back here?'

CHAPTER 67

Susan Weston was waiting when her daughter opened the front door. The four hours at work and the three hours wearing a line in the kitchen lino had done nothing to dampen her anger.

Susan had lost count of the times her daughter had brought the police to her door but this time was different. This time was serious.

'Hey Mum, what?…'

'What the hell did you think you were doing, Emma?' she cried out as her daughter entered the kitchen.

Emma visibly paled. 'What-what's happened?'

'And where have you been?' Susan exploded. 'You finished school an hour ago.'

'I just went to check—'

'Are you actually trying to get us caught?' Susan cried, banging her hand down on the breakfast bar.

'No… no… I just wanted to make sure…'

'What if she's watching you, eh? What if that copper or someone else is keeping an eye on you and watching where you go? Do you have any idea, any idea at all what could happen to us?'

'Mum, I'm sorry,' Emma said, moving towards her.

Susan backed away. She wasn't done shouting yet.

Rarely had she lost her temper with her only child. Since Emma's father had left seven years before they had become a team, unbreakable. They had grown even closer as they'd tried to make sense of their smaller family unit. And as she'd held her weeping daughter and explained that Daddy wasn't coming home she'd vowed that she would protect her daughter for the rest of her days. And she had tried every day to keep that promise. And if that had shaped their relationship more as friends than parent and child she was paying the price now.

Because right now she was angry, frightened and more than a little disappointed, especially with what she had to say next.

'And that copper saw you hit Jessie?'

Emma coloured, showing Susan that the police officer had been telling the truth.

'Jesus Christ, Emma, what the hell were you thinking? Someone's got it on camera. Why didn't you tell me… before?…'

'It'll be okay, Mum, I promise,' Emma said, taking her hand.

'No, it won't, Em,' Susan said, as the fear clutched at her stomach. 'You kept the damn phone. Why did you keep it in the house?'

'Where is it?' Emma asked, as panic widened her eyes.

'That officer has it.'

'You let her take it?' Emma asked.

'How the hell was I supposed to stop her?' Susan screamed.

'If she didn't have no warrant she had no—'

'Emma,' Susan snapped. 'It's a bit late for that now. Is there anything on there that could hurt us?'

Emma thought for a minute and shook her head.

Susan thanked God for small mercies.

Her daughter pulled her chair closer. 'Mum, it'll be okay. It'll all blow over and everything will be fine.'

Susan felt the rage seep out of her at the sheer naiveté of her fifteen-year-old daughter. So much older and yet so young too.

How the hell had she got involved in this in the first place? How had it come to this?

Emma looked at her, her eyes full of reassurance for her benefit and her mouth turned down in fear.

And that was why, she remembered.

Her daughter hadn't known what to do and had asked for her help. And she'd said yes.

Susan took a deep and cleansing breath. What was done was done. There was no way back for either of them now.

'That copper knows something is going on, Em. She's gonna come back and when she does we'd better have our damn stories straight about what happened to Jessie on Sunday night.'

CHAPTER 68

'Okay, Mr Mancini, thank you for your time,' Kim said, from the doorway. 'You've been a great help and now we'll take you home.'

The relief was evident on his face.

Mitch reached them as they piled out into the corridor.

She nodded in his direction, appeared to have a sudden thought and spoke loudly enough that Giovanni Mancini could hear her.

'Actually, Bryant, take him out to your car the back way. I don't want people seeing him here. He's a witness not a suspect and I don't want anyone getting the wrong idea.'

Bryant pulled a face. 'Bloody hell, guv, that's…'

His words trailed away as he glanced at Mitch and a smile began to pull at the corners of his mouth.

'I *really* don't want people to get the wrong idea,' she said, as they all headed to the rear exit.

She offered a bewildered Mitch a look that said all would become clear shortly.

'Yeah, sorry about this, pal,' Bryant said. 'But the boss has got a point. You don't need folks asking what you're doing coming out of the nick, do you? My car's just over there.'

And the only thing between them and Bryant's car was tarmac, a kerb, and a raised bed of soil awaiting a few summer plants.

Bryant stepped on to the dirt, and Mancini followed. Three strides later Bryant and Mancini were beside Bryant's car.

'Cast it, Mitch,' she said, nodding towards the deep and clear footprints in the fresh soil.

He laughed, shook his head and opened his bag of tricks.
There had been no other way.
She needed that bloody shoe print.

CHAPTER 69

'So, what now?' Bryant asked as they watched Mancini close the door behind himself.

'We gotta wait,' she said. 'My gut is telling me those bloody shoes mean something. It was a perfect print on Cordell's back, and I reckon those prints in the dirt are going to tie our guy to the crime.'

'But didn't Nat Mansell say something about a choice?' Bryant asked. 'What the hell does that have to do with these guys?'

'I don't know,' she said, trying to fit the pieces together in her head.

'And these guys both have alibis for Monday night. They were both here, together.'

'Yes, they were, weren't they?' Kim said, opening the car door.

'Oh, great, what now?' he said, already knowing that whatever it was had been prompted by something he'd said.

She strode purposefully past the door to the Mancini home and knocked on the next.

The woman who had abused them the previous day appeared wearing the same vest top and a toddler on her hip.

'What?' she asked.

'You got a minute?' Kim asked.

'I've got two hungry kids under the age of three, whadda you think?'

'We'll be quick,' Kim said.

She adjusted the child on her hip and waited.

'Were you at home on Monday night, say from five or six o'clock?'

She nodded. 'I'm always here from six o'clock,' she added, wryly.

'Do you remember if the Mancinis next door…'

Kim's words trailed away as the thumping music started up.

'No, they weren't here,' she said. 'At least, he wasn't,' she said, nodding towards the wall.

Kim felt the excitement in her stomach. They had alibied each other, so either one or both were lying.

'How can you be sure?' she asked, feeling that one day was probably like another for this girl.

'Cos if he's home, this is what I get. Any time of the day or night.'

'But not Monday?' Kim asked.

She shook her head. 'I took this one to the doctors, coughing like a good un. Got back to peace and quiet around quarter to six and—'

'And you're sure this was Monday?' Kim asked.

'Fuck me, love, you want me to write it in blood? I know when I took my kid to the quack.'

'Thank you. You've been a great help,' Kim said.

The woman offered a rare smile before closing the door.

Kim headed back to the car but paused.

'Guv, it's not our fight,' he said, as she knocked loudly on the door.

'We're the police, Bryant. Everything's our fight.'

'Fair point,' he said as he joined her in banging on the glass.

Giovanni Mancini opened the door and rolled his eyes.

'Yeah, guys, this is now harassment.'

'No, this is harassment,' she shouted above the music that was blaring down the hallway.

'Constant loud noise is intimidating, threatening and aggressive behaviour which makes it our—'

'I can do as I please in my own home,' he challenged.

'Technically yes, realistically no. And is it worth losing your home over?'

'Why are you sticking your nose?…'

'And not just you,' she clarified, ignoring him. 'Once we get you in court on an ASBO the council will get involved and they'll just throw you out. You've got a job so you can find somewhere else to live and the woman next door trying to raise two kids will finally get some peace. Hope your new place has got room for your dad who may or may not have a job very soon.'

She paused. 'Or, you could just turn your music down and show her some fucking consideration,' she said.

He swallowed.

She headed back to the car. The music had died down before she got there.

Bryant shook his head. 'I swear, if that guy doesn't make a formal complaint—' He stopped speaking as her phone rang.

'Keats,' she said, pressing the answer button. 'Please tell me you have something useful for me,' she said.

'Where are you?' he asked.

She looked around. 'The depths of hell.'

'If you mean Hollytree, that's perfect. Come around to the shops. I have someone here I think you're going to recognise.'

'Shit,' Kim said, getting into the car.

She'd wanted Keats to give her something but another body wasn't what she'd had in mind.

CHAPTER 70

'Someone really should have listened to that kid,' Penn said, putting down the phone.

'Well, you more than made up for it. You've been gassing to him for half an hour.'

'Yeah, well, he wanted me to know how unjustified his speeding ticket was but just look at this, Stacey,' he said, getting Route Planner on the screen.

'Todd Marsh came on the motorway here, at junction 1, drove for about three miles. He saw a vehicle up ahead, flashing lights and changing lanes. He slowed down thinking it was a police vehicle pulling someone over, which was kinda prophetic in a way, then continued to hang back in the fast lane. The vehicle behind then turned off all its lights cos our guy said the brake lights went out, so he knew it wasn't police. He sped up and passed them. Got the feeling it was some kind of road rage thing and didn't want to get involved. Thought the van had been cut up somewhere and was making a point.'

'Van?' she queried.

'Red transit,' Penn said. 'And even better, partial plate. Ends in ZZ5. He thought it was funny and reminded him of sleep.'

'So, you think this guy in the van was actually trying to kill Saul Cordell?' she asked, doubtfully. A part of her still pictured him driving home late at night to see his family after learning about his father's death. Tired, emotional, not concentrating as much as he should have been. Didn't see the cones or the motorway vehicle until it was too late.

'Or it could even be that speedy boy had it right first time and it was some kind of road rage incident and nothing to do with the case,' she offered.

'Bringing us back to the theory of coincidence in which neither of us believe. And even if that was the case…'

'Someone should be trying to find the van,' she finished for him.

He shrugged. 'Let's try tracking this guy down and find out,' he said.

Stacey stared at the screen. 'He ploughed into the motorway vehicle just past junction 2, didn't he?'

'Yep,' Penn answered.

'So, there's a good chance our guy exited there, yeah?'

'Makes sense,' Penn agreed.

They both started tapping away furiously focussing all efforts on CCTV in that area.

If they were dealing with a third murder, the boss needed to know. Now.

CHAPTER 71

'Yes, it's definitely her,' Kim said, looking down into the ashen face of Nat Mansell.

Despite circulating the woman's photo to every constable, sergeant and PC she could reach, someone else had found her first, murdered her and dumped her behind a row of abandoned shops, amongst rotting rubbish that had been putrefying for weeks.

She had already assessed that CCTV wouldn't help them on this one. Of the six properties behind which they stood only two were not boarded up. One was a newsagent who had no coverage as he paid handsomely for the protection of the gang that ran Hollytree, and the other was the part-time community centre that opened a few hours a couple of times each week. They had one camera on the front door but nothing around the back.

Kim shook her head, sadly. Only a few hours ago she had been chasing this woman for answers across a patch of grass. And now she was dead. If only she'd stopped and talked, Kim knew she could have protected her.

'She wasn't killed here,' Keats observed. 'Not nearly enough blood.'

'Any significance in this place being the dump site?' Bryant asked.

'Maybe it's a statement,' Kim said, looking around 'Places don't come much grimmer than this. Even after death he's telling us how he feels about her. A final insult. Or it was just the easiest, quickest place to dump her body,' she concluded.

'Multiple stab wounds,' Keats said, lifting up her slashed shirt to reveal a torso bloodied and slashed.

'Jesus, he hated her,' Kim said. Lines of blood had seeped from the minor wounds before death and trailed around her sides to her back.

'Why the rookie moves?' she asked, turning to Bryant. 'Why risk unnecessary contamination with the body by moving it if the sites mean nothing to him? Why take Cordell all the way to the park instead of killing him right there in his flat?'

Bryant shrugged. 'Either knows exactly what he's doing and is sure he's leaving nothing of himself behind, or is a complete novice who doesn't understand the Locard principle of leaving something of yourself at every crime scene.'

'But he is leaving stuff behind, isn't he?' she said. 'So far we have a boot print, a hair and fibres, so he's actually proving that Locard was on the money,' she said, turning to Keats. 'Time of death?' she asked.

'I'd estimate five to six hours,' he said.

She turned to Bryant. 'Fuck. Within an hour or two of us spotting her at the retirement home,' Kim growled as a shudder ran through her. They had been so close to saving the woman's life and her damn leg had let her down. On a normal day she could have caught Nat Mansell and wrestled her to the ground if necessary. Anything to keep her safe.

Her brain followed the chronology of the day. 'And right before we turned up to find a damp Mancini clad in bath towels,' she observed.

'You're convicting the guy because he took a shower?' Bryant asked.

'Would have got pretty bloody from this, don't you think?' she asked.

'Yeah, let's round up everyone who took a shower around that time, or even a bath or a quick wash in—'

'Mitch is after you,' Keats said to her across the body. 'Wants to show you something at the lab.'

She nodded and began to walk away. She frowned and turned back.

'Keats, lift up her top for me again,' she said, only just register-ing what she thought she'd seen.

He did so carefully.

She studied the picture before her for a moment. 'Okay, Keats, thanks,' she said, turning and heading for the car.

'Didn't get your fill the first time, eh, guv?' Bryant asked.

Kim shot him a look and took a few steps to the side. Away from listening ears. He followed.

'Bryant, I'd like to apologise,' she said, through gritted teeth.

He looked genuinely perplexed. 'For what?'

'Whatever it is I did that made you think I'd put up with these small digs indefinitely. Clearly it's my mistake, so I apologise and you knock it on the head right now.'

His eyes blazed with whatever bee was buzzing in his bonnet but whatever it was now was not the time. And he knew that. 'Got it, guv,' he said, moving back towards the body. 'So, what are you thinking?'

Kim followed. Whatever was brewing between them hadn't been put to bed, but it was at least having a nap.

'Potentially almost thirty stab wounds to her body,' Kim said, thoughtfully. 'And seventy per cent of those were aimed at the woman's stomach.'

'You think that means something?' he asked, doubtfully.

'You already know my answer to that, Bryant. Everything means something.'

CHAPTER 72

'Boss says leave it for tonight,' Penn said, putting down the phone.

Stacey had just heard him update her on the lead they were following. They'd got nowhere so far on the CCTV but they'd identified sixty-three vehicles with a number plate ending in ZZ5 Looked like they were going to be busy on the phones tomorrow.

Penn reached for his Tupperware container and put it into his man-bag.

'Listen, Stacey, before I go I want to mention something that's been bothering me,' he said, peering down at her.

Oh, here it comes, she thought, bracing herself. He was going to tell her he was upset about the way she'd treated him. He was going to go above her head and complain about her attitude, claim that he couldn't work with her because she was a bitch. Explain that he'd tried countless times to bridge the gap, even blame her for any mistakes on the case. He'd probably already written a letter of complaint and mentioned the nickname she'd given him on top of everything else.

Tomorrow she'd be called in to the boss's office and reprimanded for not making friends with the new guy. It wasn't something she relished and it wouldn't change how she felt about him. She'd just have to learn to hide it better. Maybe she could have tried a little harder but it was too late now. The damage was done.

'Go on,' she said, sticking out her chin.

'That three-year gap,' he said, scratching his bandana.

'Huh?' Stacey asked.

'In Jessie's health records. How does the kid go from so many health problems to practically nothing for three whole years? Doesn't make sense.'

Well, that wasn't what she'd been expecting at all.

CHAPTER 73

'What you got?' Kim asked, entering Mitch's makeshift lab down the hall from Keats's office.

The small space didn't compare to the state-of-the-art laboratory at Ridgepoint House in Birmingham which counted as the West Midlands Police Forensic Headquarters but it was used by a couple of the senior techies when basic, urgent analysis was required.

Kim had only visited Ridgepoint House once and was thankful for the tour guide who directed them around a labyrinth of interlocking rooms set out with lasers, lamps, microscopes and cameras. She had felt like a lab rat herself as she'd wandered through the maze of sterile white walls.

She remembered the fingerprint lab where they were told that the team had lifted prints from more than 25,000 separate exhibits including firearms, mobile phones, documents, broom handles, car doors, windowpanes, handcuffs, sex toys and fruit.

Mitch had been stationed several floors above the fingerprint lab, as part of an elite team of experienced investigators and crime scene coordinators, the faces of the team that liaised with detectives to oversee the forensics on major crimes such as murder, rape, and arson.

And Mitch was as thorough as they came.

She had no idea of the state of his private life but she did know his work ethic often matched her own.

She remembered one of her first cases as a DI. The victim, an elderly woman, had been smothered by a pillow in her bed. Her son had claimed to be out shopping for his imminent holiday, something they could not disprove. Mitch had worked from seven in the morning until eleven that night when he'd called her with a DNA match from droplets of saliva on the pillow that had come from the victim's son. They had arrested him two minutes before he boarded a plane to Spain and, judging by his luggage, he'd not been planning a return flight any time soon.

Without Mitch's determination and skill, Mr Longton would now be languishing in Mallorca instead of Winson Green prison.

'Please tell me it's my footprint,' she said, hopefully.

He shook his head. 'Tomorrow, hopefully, but in the meantime, take a look at these little beauties,' he said, moving away from the microscope.

'Sounds like the best offer we've had all day,' Bryant quipped.

She sat down in Mitch's seat and took a look.

'That's a fibre?' she asked, doubtfully. Mitch had magnified the fibre so she could see that it was constructed like a pie that had been cut and the pieces spaced out as opposed to the clean smooth surface of fibres she'd seen before.

He nodded.

'Okay,' she said.

He replaced the slide with another.

She looked again.

'Same?' she asked.

'Identical. First batch were the ones taken from the lips of Phyllis Mansell. Second batch were a bit harder to distinguish from the blood found around the wound of Doctor Cordell, which is what I was trying to do when I received a request earlier today from some crazy police officer.'

She turned to her colleague. 'Bryant, he means you.'

Mitch chuckled. 'They match,' he confirmed.

'Bloody hell,' she said. 'So, we have forensic evidence to tie those two murders together?'

He nodded.

Up until now the tenuous link between Cordell and the dead nurse's mother had been at the very best circumstantial.

'Tell me more,' Kim said, resting back in his seat.

'Textile fibres fall into three categories: Natural, manufactured and synthetic. Your natural ones come from animals, plants, and minerals like wool, silk, hemp and the most common which is cotton. Undyed white cotton is so common it's of little evidentiary value.

'Manufactured fibres come from rayon, acetate, triacetate, raw cotton and wood pulp. Synthetic fibres come from polymers which are substances made up of a series of monomers, single molecules strung together to make longer molecules that can be thousands of monomers long. Nylon and polyester are synthetics.'

Kim knew that, contrary to most popular TV programmes, fibres were lost quickly from a crime scene. The stats said that after four hours you've lost approximately eighty per cent rising to ninety-five per cent after twenty-four hours. Anything finally lifted with tape or a vacuum was like gold dust.

'So, I used my scanning electron microscope—'

'Bloody hell, Mitch, even I'm growing old over here,' Bryant moaned.

Kim crossed her arms. 'Aww, let him talk, Bryant. He doesn't get out much.'

Mitch smiled and continued.

'So, using dispersive X-ray spectrometer with gas chromatography and mass spectrometry I discovered—'

'That you could make up your own words and we wouldn't have a clue?' Bryant asked, as the door opened.

'Mitch, it's almost eight and I'm heading... oh, sorry to interrupt,' Keats said, straightening up his overcoat.

'Okay, see you in the—'

Damn it, Kim thought, realising the day had got away from her. She was going to be in some serious trouble tomorrow.

Unless.

'Keats, can you hang on for one minute?' she asked. 'Need to talk to you urgently about something once we've finished with Mitch.'

'Inspector, I've been here since—'

'It'll take just a minute,' she assured him. 'I wouldn't ask if it wasn't urgent.'

He huffed. 'Five minutes,' he said. 'I'll wait for five minutes and then I'm leaving.'

'Thanks, Keats,' she said to his back as he left the lab.

Kim ignored Bryant's questioning glance as Mitch continued with his explanation of what he'd found.

'The chemical composition of the fibre and any pigments or treatments added during or after manufacture. These chemical determinations can point to the manufacturer of the fibre or match one fibre to another.'

He stopped speaking.

'Please tell me this is where we get rewarded for our patience,' Kim said.

'Oh yes. I can tell you that the microfibres are manufactured by Hollings in Merseyside and they are cloths, Inspector: blue, square cleaning cloths.'

CHAPTER 74

Stacey stared down at the meatball she'd been pushing around the plate for a good two minutes, afraid to look up. One meatball in particular resembled a head with strands of spaghetti flowing from it like a wig.

She could feel Devon's eyes on her and she knew what was coming. Had been expecting it for a few weeks.

The meatball shimmered through her blurred vision as she heard Devon's fork come to rest on her plate. She suspected the woman had eaten little more than she had.

Stacey tried to brace herself against the inevitable.

'I'm losing you,' Devon said, quietly.

Stacey said nothing and continued to stare.

'I'm trying to hang on, babe,' she whispered.

Stacey knew she couldn't raise her head. In those eyes she would see all the love and concern that Devon felt for her. And it would break her in half.

Stacey had been unable to believe her luck that Devon had been interested in her after she'd blown her off months earlier.

But when they'd met again during an investigation into illegal workers, Devon had made her interest clear. And after much prompting from Dawson that she was good enough for this gorgeous, sexy, confident woman, she had found the courage to try again.

And she'd been happy. Happier than she'd ever been or even imagined she could be. Despite demanding jobs, they had made it work. Sometimes Stacey had cancelled due to a pressing case, and sometimes Devon had been called in for a surprise raid or to cover the shift of a fellow immigration officer. But they'd both understood. And Stacey had fallen in love. It had been perfect. Until six weeks ago.

'I love you, babe,' Devon said, gently. 'And I'll fight for what we had, but I can't do it if I'm the only person in the ring.'

Stacey knew she was right. She made hardly any effort to see Devon any more. And when she did she was usually silent throughout. The days themselves took all that she had to give. Turning up for work, concentrating, adjusting, fighting off the grief took every ounce of energy she had. Normality had never taken so much effort.

'Stacey, I know how much you miss him. He was a great guy but he wouldn't have wanted this.'

Stacey fought the tears that were now stinging her eyes.

For a second she was tempted to swallow down the emotion and assure Devon she was okay, that the woman was imagining things and life was fine and dandy, but the words were nowhere to be found. If it was over between them, she had nothing left to lose.

'I don't know how to let him go,' she said, as a sob rose up and choked her.

She felt Devon's arms fold around her and allowed herself to be lifted from the seat and guided to the sofa.

'Sweetheart, you've suffered a loss, it's understandable, especially as you were right there when it happened,' Devon said, pulling her close. 'The two of you were good friends. You always reminded me of siblings the way you ribbed each other but you always had each other's back as well.'

Yes, Stacey remembered when he had sat outside her flat each night after she'd almost lost her life to hateful racists. At first, she hadn't known he'd been risking his relationship with his partner to make sure she was safe. And when she had found out she had loved him for it. And told him to stop.

'But I couldn't protect him, Dee,' she said, as the tears came thick and fast. 'I couldn't stop him from…'

'Stace, what he did was heroic,' Devon said, her own voice thickening with emotion. 'He saved that young boy's life with little thought for his own. There was no way you could have stopped him, and he wouldn't have thanked you if you had because he would have relived that child's death for the rest of his life.'

'But he would still be here,' she protested.

'And that's about your feelings, not his,' Devon said, stroking her hair. She let silence fall between them for a moment before continuing. 'It happened to me, you know,' she said in a whisper. 'Came up through training with a Polish girl named Nicola. A true character she was. We clicked. Best friends from the minute we met. Our first assignment in the field, a Korean greengrocer stabbed her because she was guarding the back of the shop. One wound but it was enough. She died at the scene.'

Stacey reached for her hand. 'I'm so sorry, Dee.'

'It's okay,' Devon said, squeezing her hand in response. 'To start with, I had the immediacy of loss, of grief, but as time went on there was something else. I had thought that we would always roll our eyes across the desk at each other, that she would always open a bag of Haribos and put them on the crack where our desks joined. I had imagined us at each other's weddings and suddenly I knew I had to navigate my own future without her.'

'I get it,' Stacey said.

'I got there eventually but I closed down for a while. Lots of people tried to help, be my friend, but I didn't let them in. To be honest I wasn't all that nice,' she said, holding Stacey tight. 'For a while I wasn't the person I thought I was.'

Stacey allowed the sobbing to subside and just enjoyed the safety of Devon's embrace.

'I love you, Dee,' she said, simply.

'I know you do, babe, and that's why I'll stand and fight.'

Stacey felt another rush of tears as her blessings all came rushing forward. She had a good family, friends, a woman who was in it for the long haul and a job she loved with a passion.

Devon's words had passed through her mind and left a trail of comfort as though coated in soothing balm. Except for one thing. One point had pierced her brain like an arrow and wouldn't pass through.

Devon had allowed her grief to alter the person that she thought she was.

Stacey pulled away and met her girlfriend's gaze.

'Dee, can you help me? There's something I need to do.'

CHAPTER 75

Bryant was still smirking as they left the hospital.

'Really, guv?'

'What?'

'I can't believe you got Keats to X-ray your leg. In the morgue.'

Kim shrugged. 'Woody said an X-ray by the end of the day but he didn't specify how.'

'He wasn't best pleased when you explained why you'd asked him to wait,' Bryant observed.

'He'll get over it. Ultimately he had the equipment and I had the leg. That's all Woody cares about.'

Bryant shook his head. 'Only you would think that was a completely normal request.'

'You'd think he'd be pleased to have a customer without rigor mortis,' she said.

'Fair point,' Bryant agreed. 'Where to now?' he asked.

Kim checked her watch. It was almost nine.

Much as she wanted to carry on working the case after what they'd learned about the fibres, they'd been at it for thirteen hours.

'We'll call it a night, Bryant. I've already sent the k—' she stopped what she'd been about to say. The two of them had often called Stacey and Dawson 'the kids'.

'Stacey and Penn have finished for the night,' she corrected.

'I don't mind,' he said. 'Won't be the first time my dinner has ended up in the dog.'

Kim smiled and shook her head.
Her day wasn't yet over.
Not if she wanted to keep her job.

CHAPTER 76

'Go on, go home,' Stacey said, with her palm on the door handle of the car. 'I'll be fine. I'll get a taxi back.'

'I'll be here,' Devon replied.

Stacey turned to look at her. 'I may be a while.'

'I'll wait for as long as it takes,' Devon said, meaningfully.

Stacey squeezed her partner's hand one more time before she got out of the car and took a breath.

She heard the car window slide down.

'Proud of you, babe,' Devon called.

Stacey felt a frisson of warmth glow in her belly and she didn't push it away. She embraced it.

She regulated her breathing as she headed up the path.

She knocked lightly, mildly uncomfortable at turning up unannounced at almost 9 p.m. But there were things she needed to say.

The door was opened by Penn.

His face creased into confusion. 'Stacey, what are you?... I mean...'

'I owe you an apology,' she said, simply.

He regarded her for a few seconds before he shook his head. 'No, you don't but please come in anyway.'

Stacey stepped into a spacious hallway as an elderly lady appeared from a side room aided by a walking stick. She smiled brightly.

Stacey felt sorry for disturbing them at this hour but she had wanted to talk to him before the courage deserted her.

'Mum, this is Stacey,' Penn said.

'Oh, the nice girl you told me about from work?' she asked, moving her weight from one leg to the other.

Stacey nodded even though the statement was not strictly accurate.

She was from work but she hadn't been very nice at all.

'I'm sorry to call so late but pleased to meet you, Mrs Penn,' Stacey said.

'Likewise, Austin never brings his friends round,' she said as though he was fifteen years old. A wave of sadness passed through her kindly eyes. 'He works so hard and then when he comes back home—'

'Go and sit back down, Mum. I'll make a cuppa once the cakes are in.'

She nodded, smiled and disappeared.

'I know what it is, it's the bandana,' Stacey said, following him through the hallway. 'That's why you look different.' His strawberry blonde curls were hanging free over his forehead. He had changed from shirt and tie to a plain blue tee shirt, jogging bottoms and bare feet.

'I spend a lot of my day looking down,' he explained. 'And hair slides just don't suit me,' he joked.

She followed him into a deceptively spacious kitchen filled with glossy white units and a granite breakfast bar that looked as though a cocaine factory had exploded all over it. A baking tray holding twelve dollops of something appeared to have survived the carnage.

Penn folded his arms and smiled.

'It's okay, Jasper, you can come out now,' he said.

Stacey looked around the empty room wondering who he was talking to.

'Okay, looks like I'm gonna have to come and get—'

'Thurprise,' shouted a boy appearing from behind the breakfast bar.

Stacey immediately saw from the boy's facial features that he had Down's syndrome. She jumped out of her skin, and Penn pretended to. The boy looked delighted. His face creased and his eyes sparkled. Stacey felt his joy from the other side of the room.

He smoothed cake-mixture-covered fingers onto his plastic apron that declared, '*I'm every woman*' in yellow italic writing.

'Jasper, I'd like you to meet Stacey, my friend from work. Stacey, this is my seventeen-year-old brother, Jasper.'

'Pleased to meet you,' he said, offering a gunk-covered hand.

'No, Jasper, you need to wipe...' Penn protested.

Stacey silenced him by reaching over and shaking the gooey hand.

'Nice to meet you, Jasper. What you been making here?'

'Fairy cakes,' he said, proudly.

Penn went around to the other side of the breakfast bar to join him, and Stacey immediately saw the similarities between the two. The blue eyes that held a gentleness she'd not noticed in Penn before. The same fair hair, but where Penn's was unruly, and curly Jasper's hair was neat and straight.

'Okay, bud, I reckon the oven is hot enough now so grab the oven glove.'

Jasper grabbed the glove, put it on his right hand and then formed a mouth like a sock puppet. Jasper laughed and so did she. Penn rolled his eyes tolerantly, as though he'd seen his brother do the same thing a dozen times before.

'Just put them in, bud,' he said.

Jasper copied Penn and rolled his eyes dramatically, which prompted a laugh-out-loud belly chuckle from her.

Jasper laughed at her laughing.

'Okay, I'm opening the oven door now,' Penn said, bending down.

Jasper's face turned serious as he focussed on getting the tray in the oven. Once the door closed he gave a whoop and took off his apron. He lay it over the mess.

'Ahem,' Penn said.

'Ahem,' Jasper repeated.

Stacey covered the smile on her lips with her hand, suspecting that Penn needed to make his point and her amusement would do nothing to help him. Penn held his brother's gaze until Jasper picked the apron back up and hung it on a hook on the back of the door.

'Okay, Jas, go and sit with Mum a bit while I clear up in here,' Penn said, ruffling his hair.

'Ooookay,' he said, bouncing around to her side of the room. He paused as he came alongside her. Very quickly he leaned over and gave her a peck on the cheek before bouncing out of the room.

Penn coloured. 'I'm sorry about…'

'Don't be,' Stacey said.

'He's very affectionate even when it's not appropriate but not everyone…'

'He's awesome,' Stacey said and meant it. She had the sudden feeling that something warm and light had now left the room.

'Yeah, he really is,' Penn said proudly, passing her a piece of kitchen roll for her hand. 'And now you've laughed at his oven glove puppet you've got a friend for life.'

'I'll take it,' she said, smiling.

He pointed to a small bistro table in the corner of the room. 'Have a seat while I clean up.'

She did so. 'Well, that explains the Tupperware box.'

'It's his favourite thing to do,' Penn explained. 'I tell him the people at work love them. He doesn't really get the whole transfer thing. He thinks I've just moved office.'

'You transferred because of your mum?' she asked. 'I couldn't help but notice the stick and the discomfort.'

'Hip operation,' he explained. 'Her second. There's only us two and Jasper, so she needed some help.'

'Will you move out once she's?…'

'No,' he said. 'I'll be staying here now.' He took a deep breath. 'She has lung cancer. It's terminal,' he said, wiping his hands and sitting down.

'Oh my God, Penn, I'm so sorry.'

He waved away her words. 'She's known for a while and we're hoping she still has a while left so…'

'You moved back to take care of Jasper?' she suddenly realised.

He nodded. 'He's my brother.'

Her immediate thought sprang to her lips before she could stop it. 'But, couldn't you consider placing?—'

'No. Never,' he said. 'He's my brother.'

'There's no one to help? No sisters, aunts, wife, girlfriend?'

He smiled. 'No, no and no which is shocking, isn't it?' he said, looking around. 'Seeing as I'm quite the catch.'

Stacey laughed but could just as easily have cried.

'Jesus, Penn, I really…'

'Don't feel sorry for me, Stacey. He doesn't complain, so why should I?'

She took a deep breath. 'Penn, I've been a real cow this week and I am so sorry for not giving you more of a chance.'

She felt that regret down deep in the bottom of her heart. The person she'd been this week was not the person she'd thought she was. And it wasn't the person that Dawson had known.

'You've not been as bad as you think you have. All I've wanted to say is if you don't like me, that's fine. Dislike me for me but not because I'm not someone else. You know how I felt about Kevin Dawson and if I could bring him back I'd do it in a heartbeat.'

Silence rested between them for a moment.

'I'm not proud of myself,' she admitted.

'He was lucky to have a friend like you.'

'Thank you,' she said. 'But this conversation isn't about Kev. I came here to put something right.'

He raised an eyebrow. 'Did you think I expected this to be easy?' he asked. 'I knew what I was walking into. I knew how close you all were but I wanted to work with a good team. And to be honest, Stacey, if I get transferred once this case is over, I'll be glad to have had the chance to—'

'You've gotta stop doing that,' she said, hearing something alien for the hundredth time. 'No one calls me Stacey. It's Stace. Everyone shortens it.'

He laughed. 'Okay, and I prefer the shortened version of my name, so if we could stick with 'Not' instead of the full…'

'Oh jeez, I'm sorry about that,' she said, feeling the heat fill her cheeks for naming him Notkev.

'Don't be,' he said, laughing. 'I'm just mauling you a bit now, for sport.'

The mischief in his eyes matched that of his brother and the resemblance between them was clear.

'I think I'll just stick with Penn,' she said, rising from the chair. She held out her hand. 'Start afresh tomorrow.'

He took it and shook it firmly.

'Yes, but how about we start afresh right now. I've been thinking about Jessie Ryan while I was cooking and I'm bugged.'

'By what?' she asked. They'd already decided to spend time the next day investigating the reason for the three-year gap.

'The severity of her symptoms. Before the healthy spell she was having blood tests, an occasional stay over for observation, the odd X-ray, but after the hiatus she's having scans, catheters, MRIs, angiograms. It's like the whole thing escalated exponentially and…'

Something clicked in her brain as her mind's eye recalled much of the information on the girl's medical records, and Penn was right. The tests on Jessie had reached a whole new level after her period of good health.

But more than that. Penn's meanderings had brought her a sudden realisation.

Someone had been telling her lies.

CHAPTER 77

Oh, Nat, just when I thought you could sicken me no more you took it to a whole new level.

You asked me once to spare the life of your mother but you begged shamelessly for your own life. What was left for you to live for anyway? No family, no husband, no children, no married lover. What was so precious about your life that you gave me your mother's first? What exactly did you want to live for?

You offered no joy to anyone in life, but at least you offered something to me in death.

Every time I felt the blade plunge into your flesh I could hear the tearing sound in my mind, imagining your skin opening up just for me. Small wounds at first. Short, shallow nicks of the flesh which caused you pain. The tears rolled over your cheeks as you tried to clutch your abdomen. The urine slipped from your bladder as the fear took hold.

The thrusts got harder as I saw that the only thing you cared about was yourself.

No consideration for the fact you'd been fucking a married man for years. His family. His children. You've had no children, so would never understand what you did taking a father away from his kids. You could not see past your own wants and needs, and what the fuck did you see in that arrogant bastard anyway?

So the knife thrusts became deeper as I remembered your involvement in shaping the rest of my life. The blade found and twisted your organs as I recalled that false empathetic smile behind which lay a more truthful look of indifference. You didn't care. You were presenting a choice and you were being objective.

Well, let me be objective now.

You're dead, bitch. And you suffered.

But you were my favourite, Nat, and I thank you for that. Your selfish nature offered me the freedom of a completely guilt-free kill. My grief, my hatred, my rage went into every single thrust of the knife into your ageing, pointless flesh.

And still there is more to come.

I have one left to make pay for my loss. And this is the sweetest of them all. It's poetic because I know the choice the last one will make. I know it as well as I know myself. The last one will choose to save the life of the person they love most in the world.

This one will choose to save their child.

And then they will both learn.

That there really is no choice at all.

CHAPTER 78

Stacey knocked on the door that she'd discovered earlier in the week.

After driving her here, Stacey had insisted that Devon go home. Stacey was barely half a mile from her own home, and Devon had a 6 a.m. start.

The drive from Penn's home had done little to stifle her irritation, which was still evident when the door opened.

'Mr Dunn, I think we need another chat about your daughter,' she said, making no effort to conceal her anger.

'Do you have any idea what time?...'

Yes, Stacey knew it was almost ten at night and she didn't care. 'I'm happy to do this on the doorstep, down the station or inside, Mr Dunn, your choice.'

'Come in,' he said, standing aside.

She stepped into the lounge and waited for him to close the front door and join her.

'Is your daughter here, Mr Dunn?'

He shook his head and forced a questioning frown on to his face. 'Why would she be here? I told you I haven't seen her since she was four years old.'

'Yes, I remember that's what you said, but you weren't telling the truth, were you?' she asked, trying to keep the anger out of her voice. It was his daughter she was searching for and he had lied to her.

'You took a look around the house yourself?' he said, evasively.

'And I'm going to do it again,' she said. 'Only this time I'm calling a forensics team to help me and if they find any trace of Jessie here in this house, you are going to be in some serious trouble,' she said, taking out her phone.

Indecision showed on his face. He was wondering if she was telling the truth.

She decided to clear that one up for him.

'You told me about all the tests that Jessie had when the three of you were a family. You mentioned MRIs which Jessie never had until she was in her teens, way after the time you left. You couldn't have known that unless someone told you and I'm guessing it was Jessie herself.'

He looked to the ground and said nothing.

Stacey was not prepared to back down. It had been a long day.

'Mr Dunn, if I call forensics in they will find traces of her if she's been here. Just one hair or DNA sample will catch you out, and then I'm going to wonder exactly what it is you're hiding from—'

He held up his hand. 'Okay, she was here,' he said, slumping down on to the sofa.

She put away her phone and sat in the single armchair.

'But why did you lie?' she asked.

'I didn't want to get her into any trouble. Her mother doesn't know we're in contact and wouldn't be very pleased if she did, but whatever has happened Jessie is my daughter and I love her.'

'How did you find her?'

He smiled. 'I didn't. She found me. On Facebook of all places.' He shook his head. 'Don't get the fascination with it myself but I play for a local cricket team and they put updates about fixtures and dates and stuff on the Facebook page. She sent me a message, and it was one of the happiest days of my life.'

Stacey thought about his reaction to her threat about finding just one hair.

'The other times she ran away, she was here, wasn't she?'

He hesitated before nodding. 'Just one night. I know I should have sent her home both times, but she was here and she wanted to spend time with me. It was a gift I just couldn't turn down.'

'And a part of you wanted to pay back her mother?' Stacey asked.

'If I'm honest, yes. But I sent her away this time. She was here on Saturday afternoon. The day before she disappeared. She wanted to stay for a day or two, and I said no even though I was desperate to say yes. I told her to go home and talk to her mother. I thought it was the right thing to do. I drove by the house later and saw her bedroom light on, so I knew she'd gone home. I thought that would be the end of it.'

'Did she say why she wanted to stay with you?' Stacey asked.

He shook his head. 'Just wanted to be alone, needed some space.'

'Did she ever mention any issues with Emma?'

He shook his head.

'And you're telling me the whole truth this time?' Stacey asked.

'The last time I saw Jessie was on Saturday afternoon and I swear to you that I haven't seen her since.'

Right now Stacey wasn't sure whether she believed him or not.

CHAPTER 79

The case was still running around Kim's head when she pulled up outside Ted's house at ten past ten.

Truthfully, she would have preferred to make a strong pot of coffee and spend the night in her garage building the bike. But today was Thursday and, regardless of murder, Friday was still the end of the week, and Woody had made his timescale clear.

'Come on, boy,' Kim said, opening the car door.

She'd taken him for a walk once she'd got home but after a long day she didn't want to be separated from him again. She suspected he cared less about that than she did.

'Aah, two for the price of one,' Ted observed. He petted Barney on the head and stood aside.

'Sorry to come so late,' Kim apologised, following Barney, who was eagerly sniffing Ted's front room.

'Not the first time, is it, Kim?' Ted observed.

She smiled at the memory: She'd been thirteen years old and suffering. Foster family four, Keith and Erica had recently been killed in a car accident, following the happiest three years of her life. She'd been returned to the care system like a stray cat, where people had prodded and poked her to open up and talk about her grief, her loss. Everywhere she went: school, Fairview, all talking at her, trying to crack her open like a coconut.

One night she had ducked out of Fairview and caught the bus to Ted's house. It was the only place she'd felt she could get some peace.

'You asked if you could come in and just sit a while,' Ted said, sharing her memory.

She recalled it well. Ted had asked if he could help. She'd shaken her head and gone outside to the wooden companion seating set. Ted hadn't joined her. Instead, he had called Fairview to tell them she was fine and that he would ensure she got back safely.

'You know, I still wonder what it was that you were thinking about that night,' he said, filling the cups.

She'd never told him and she never would.

Only she knew that she'd sat in the safety of Ted's garden allowing the memories of Erica and Keith into her brain. Keith showing her how a spark plug worked as they sat on the garage floor amongst a collection of motorcycle parts. Erica making a delicious evening meal while humming tunelessly in the kitchen. Inevitably thoughts of Mikey had tagged along too; the feeling of his warm body against her before he lost his grip on life. And the pain had been unbearable. Somewhere inside herself she had felt something breaking, dying. She had fought for breath as the agony had engulfed her body and she had known that she couldn't live through it, that she couldn't return to Fairview or school and function or even survive.

Any thought of family had the power to weaken her, destroy her ability to focus towards adulthood and freedom.

She had wondered how she could get through the next five minutes, let alone five years.

And then she'd watched the fish. How they swam and swam and swam over the same area, time and time again, the monotony of being on repeat. She recalled having read they had a five-second memory, so each swim was probably a new experience for them every time.

How great to have no memory, to not keep looking back. Only forward to the other end of the pond.

Suddenly it seemed so simple. Just don't think about the things that held the potential to do her harm, to weaken her. Put the memories away. Picture them being placed into a box, sealed away; safe. Keep busy, keep focussed and ignore it.

She had repeated these words over and over as the fish swam and Ted watched her from the doorway.

Eventually her breathing had regulated, the panic had subsided and the pain had begun to fade.

'You pushed past me to leave and I asked if you were okay. You told me you were "sorted",' he said.

'And I was,' she replied, following him through to the lounge.

'Hmm… not so sure about that,' he said. 'But we'll leave that for now. Have you given any thought to the things that were making you so angry the other day?'

Kim shook her head. 'No, I've been a bit busy, and to be fair, there are brand new things that piss me off every day.'

'Yes, quite, but I think some of those things are important to explore.'

Kim felt a dread beginning to form in her stomach. Perhaps she would have been better seeing a force shrink after all.

'I went in hard on a guy today,' she admitted. She wasn't sure why she felt the need to share that with Ted but the words had just come out.

'Why?' he asked.

'I roughed him up verbally, questioned him aggressively. Lost control a bit.'

'Tell me about him,' Ted said. 'The guy you were hard on.'

She shook her head. 'Doesn't really matter. Could have been anyone.'

'But it wasn't. I'm sure you've interviewed many people this week. So, tell me about him. Just three things to describe him. The first three that come to mind.'

She pictured Giovanni Mancini.

'Young, handsome, cocky.'

'Int—'

'Ted,' she snapped.

'He's not Dawson,' Ted said.

'Don't be bloody ridiculous,' she bit. 'I know he's not Dawson. He's a suspect who may be responsible for two or more deaths. That's why I went in hard,' she said, feeling the heat flush her face.

'On some level, he reminds you of Dawson. Those are three words you would have used to describe him. You're angry with him because he died.'

'You know,' Kim said, tipping her head, 'you could get a job on one of those cheap help phones with insights like that.'

He met her gaze. 'Ooh, there's a raw nerve. Always has a direct line to your defences, which blazes a trail to your vicious tongue.'

She opened her mouth to argue, but they both knew he was right.

'Have you cried?' he asked.

She considered lying but then shook her head.

'Interesting,' he said, pursing his lips.

'Ted, you're sounding like a therapist,' she warned as Barney turned twice before lying at her feet.

'So, how are you feeling about elevating your colleague and giving her more?...'

'She's working her own case right now,' Kim declared, defensively.

'Freely?' he asked.

'Of course not,' she snapped. 'She's a constable. It's my job—'

'What kind of case is she working?' he asked.

'Missing girl, probably a runaway.'

'Dangerous?'

She shook her head. 'Unlikely.'

'And the new guy, Penn. You like him any better than you did the other day?'

'He's a good officer,' she said.

'Great answer for someone's question but not mine. I asked if—'

'I heard your question,' she snapped. 'And the answer is no.'

'Why not? Is he aggressive, lazy, arrogant, useless, ignorant, rude?' Ted pushed.

'Jesus, Ted. Are you forgetting how many people have tried to get into my head? I just don't like him. It's that simple.'

'But you did before,' Ted said, unruffled. 'When he was someone else's charge.'

'You make it sound like he was Travis's kid?' Kim acknowledged.

'Interesting that you would say that,' Ted said.

Kim groaned and allowed her head to roll back against the sofa. Her sudden memory of jokingly calling Stacey and Dawson 'the kids' was pushed firmly to the side.

'But that's what it's like, isn't it? Like being given a child you didn't want. Imagine taking Barney to the dog park and somehow he gets out. And then someone gives you another dog, any old dog. It wouldn't be the same. But you came with one dog and left with one dog so what's the difference, right?'

Just the thought of it prompted her to lean down and rub Barney's head.

He paused and regarded her for a few seconds.

'Over the years I've grown used to your obstinate silence. Our sessions normally consisted of you not answering my questions, but I'd like you to answer just one.'

She said nothing. She would never commit without knowing the question.

'How many times have you wished it had been you that had gone up that bell tower instead of Kevin Dawson?'

She gave it serious consideration. Ted rarely asked for anything, but for some reason, he was asking for this.

'A few times,' she answered, honestly.

He nodded.

'You dare say *interesting* one more time...' she warned.

He shook his head. 'I wasn't going to,' he said. 'I was just thinking about your reaction to Stacey becoming more independent. You realise that if a parent loses a child they become more protective of the child they've got left.'

'Oh, Ted, you're—'

'Hear me out, Kim,' he said, holding up a hand to her protests. 'You've admitted that you've wished you'd gone up there instead of him, that you'd died instead of him. That's normally a selfless act reserved for those closest to us. Normally our nearest and dearest relatives.'

She shook her head.

'You really don't see it, do you?' he asked, shaking his head.

She shrugged. 'See what?'

'You were not only building a team, you were building a family.'

She opened her mouth to argue but her opinion wasn't important. Only his was going to Woody.

'I disagree, but even if you're right, did I pass and do I get to keep my job?' she asked, verbalising the only question that mattered.

'Well, Kim, that is between me and your boss.'

CHAPTER 80

'Okay, guys, it's been confirmed that Nat Mansell received twenty-nine stab wounds in total.'

She paused, waiting for some smart-arse comment about her popularity that would normally have come from Dawson.

There was silence.

'As already noted, the majority of wounds were to her abdomen, which has to mean something, but I have no idea what,' she admitted. 'So, we have Cordell murdered, his son dead within twenty-four hours. Nat Mansell dead and her mother, but her mother was killed first. We think Nat Mansell and Cordell were having an affair and both were involved in the complaint against Angelo Mancini. So – ideas, people?'

'Jealous spouse?' Stacey asked.

'Nat Mansell was divorced, and Mrs Cordell couldn't have cared less,' Kim answered. 'As long as he kept it away from her house. And would anyone be jealous enough to murder a family member too?' she asked.

'Unlikely,' Stacey said.

'Ramon Salcido killed most of his family in 1989 when he thought his wife was having an affair,' Penn voiced. 'Took his three daughters to a dump site and slashed their throats. Killed his mother-in-law and two sisters-in-law and then went home and killed his wife.'

Kim knew the case. 'But the jealousy was a delusion. He was on the verge of unemployment and divorce and had started using cocaine,' she said, coolly. 'Most people kill only the object of the jealousy or the person who is a threat and, very occasionally, both, but not normally the loved ones of both people involved in the affair. The only potential suspect in that scenario is Mrs Cordell, and it isn't her.'

'Did anyone else have anything to gain?' Stacey asked.

'Only the Mancinis as far as I know,' Kim said. 'Any luck on the registration number of that van?' she asked.

'Still working through them, boss, and trying to narrow them down geog—'

'Okay, Penn, keep on it,' she said. 'Mancini was questioned yesterday and gave us nothing…'

'Despite the boss's best efforts,' Bryant chirped up.

'But we did establish that their alibis for each other concerning the murder window for Doctor Cordell were a crock of shite. Neighbour confirms they were not at home, and trust me, she knows.'

'Oh yeah,' Bryant ad-libbed again.

'We got a match on fibres from Mrs Mansell's lips and Cordell's wound, so we have that forensic—'

'Yeah, ain't that a novelty?' Bryant said.

Growing increasingly annoyed at his heckling, she turned to him. 'Go on, Bryant. You clearly have something pressing to add.'

'How many cases have we worked where we've had a direct link between victims from forensic evidence?' he asked. 'Looking a bit like *CSI* here.'

Despite her irritation at him she knew he was right. These trace evidence connections were few and far between. And yet she couldn't bring herself to argue with science.

'Bryant, gift horse and mouth is all I'm going to say, as well as Mitch is working round the clock and has come up trumps on this one.'

She turned back to Stacey and Penn.

'Mitch should have emailed the details of the fibres, so get cracking on the manufacturer and who they supply the cleaning cloths to, though I think we know what they're going to say. Hope to have something on the footprint later, but nothing on the hair until we have something to match it against. Everyone clear?'

A nod travelled around the room.

'Okay, Stace, how's your missing girl case?'

'Getting weirder and weirder,' she admitted. 'Jessie Ryan is due to go into hospital today for exploratory heart surgery, which would make me wonder if she has run away because she's scared, but her phone turned up in Emma Weston's bedroom in a very clever and devious hiding place.'

'And her explanation?'

'Her mother was as shocked as I was and called her. Emma claims she didn't know and that Jessie must have put it there.'

Kim frowned. 'Stay on this, Stace. I'm not liking the sound of what I'm hearing. If we get nothing more today I'm gonna speak to Woody about a search team and a press appeal.'

Stacey nodded her understanding. 'I think her parents would appreciate that, boss. They're beside themselves with worry about her health, there's no love lost between the two families, and I'm still a bit concerned about Emma's history of violence.' The constable took a breath. 'Added to that, her absent father hasn't been as absent as we thought and has been hiding her for a night on her previous disappearances. I've searched the house and don't think she's there but can't be totally certain he doesn't know more than he's letting on. Only admitted that much because I caught him out in a lie, but Emma Weston and her mother are raising my hackles more.'

Kim nodded. 'Keep the pressure on the girl. Especially if you think she knows—'

'Sorry to interrupt, boss,' Penn said, looking at his computer. His face creased into a smile.

'What is it?'

'It's the Reeboks, boss. The footprint is a match.'

'Bloody hell, I've never seen an arrest warrant land as quickly as that,' Penn observed as the boss and Bryant headed out of the office at speed.

'She doesn't hang around,' Stacey said, peering around Penn to the printer table behind.

'So, you gonna offer me one of those fairy cakes or what?'

As she'd seen the production line the previous night she felt she was entitled. Penn reached behind and placed the open container on the desk between them.

Stacey appraised them. 'Is that an S?' she asked, pointing to a cake with a swirl of chocolate chips decorating the top.

'Yep, Jasper said that one is for you and that no one else was to have it,' he said, typing something quickly.

'Aww… bless,' she said, plucking it from the box.

'So, what do you think about this three year?—'

'One sec,' he said, looking at the screen. 'Just firing off a few emails trying to track this registration number.'

She took a bite. 'Mmm… nice,' she said, trying to stop too many crumbs landing on her desk.

'Done,' he said, looking her way.

'Last night you mentioned the three-year gap in Jessie's health records. What are you thinking?'

'I just can't work out how a girl who has chronic health problems suddenly gets well for three years and then relapses,' he said, sitting back.

'Some kind of miracle drug?' Stacey asked. 'That wore off and became less effective?'

'One drug for all those health issues?' Penn queried. 'It would have to be some drug or possibly a cocktail.'

Stacey hit a few keys and brought up Jessie's medical records. She shook her head. 'Last thing she was prescribed was a high-grade stool softener for chronic constipation.'

'And nothing after that for three years?'

Stacey shook her head as Penn rubbed at his bandana.

'She didn't go and live with relatives in another county or something for a time, did she?' he asked.

'That would have explained it,' she admitted. 'But her mother said nothing about Jessie having lived elsewhere.' Stacey shook her head. 'I feel so sorry for that poor woman. Losing one child to poor health and having to constantly take care of…' Stacey's words trailed away as Penn regarded her studiously and she realised what she'd said and his own home situation.

'Oh shit, Penn, I don't mean… I didn't…'

'Forget it,' he said, waving away her apology but the frown on his face remained.

'What did I say?'

'What year was the brother born?' he asked.

'In 2013,' she answered.

'And when did he die?'

Stacey looked back over her notes. 'He died in 2016. He was alive when Jessie was ten through to when she was thirteen.'

'So, the only healthy part of her life was when her brother was alive and he was desperately ill?'

Stacey regarded him with an open mouth.

'Oh shit, Penn, what the hell have we found?'

CHAPTER 82

'Guv, will you just wait a few more minutes? If Mancini is our guy we can't risk destroying anything in there.'

She drummed her fingers on the dashboard. A squad car was parked behind them, waiting to take him in, and the arrest and search warrant was safely tucked in her pocket. Only Mitch was missing to secure the scene forensically once they left.

Kim was eager to get Giovanni Mancini down to the station. Both him and his Reeboks. If Bryant thought she'd been tough on him the day before, her colleague might want to shield his eyes this time around.

'He could be destroying evidence right now,' she said with frustration.

'Look, just give—'

'He's here,' Kim said, grabbing the door handle.

Mitch's van rolled in behind the squad car. Her appearance out of the car prompted the two constables to make a move too. They all met at the rear of Bryant's Astra. Mitch and two techies began changing into protective suits.

Kim spoke directly to the constables. 'One knock and if he doesn't answer, force the door.'

They nodded their understanding and headed towards the target property.

They knocked once, and Kim found herself hoping they could barge in and take him by surprise.

The door began to slowly open, revealing Giovanni Mancini.

Kim rushed past, impatient to have him down at the station.

'Giovanni Mancini, I'm arresting you for the murder of Gordon Cordell. You do not have to say anything, but it may harm your defence if you do not mention when questioned something which you later rely on in court. Anything you do say may be given in evidence.'

She ignored his bewildered expression, most likely born of being caught.

'We have a warrant to search these premises,' she said, laying the paperwork on the kitchen countertop.

One of the constables asked him to put out his hands. The request seemed to nudge him from the dreamlike state he'd entered.

'You've got to be fuck—'

'I can assure you we're not joking,' Kim said, as the techies, led by Mitch, entered the home.

'And make sure you get those Reeboks,' she called over her shoulder as Mitch passed behind her.

'You can't arrest me,' Giovanni spluttered. 'You have no proof. You can't have because I didn't fucking do it,' he blasted.

She gave him a half smile and instructed the constables to take him to the car.

'Okay,' Bryant said. 'You ready?'

'Just wanna take a quick look around first,' she said, moving down the hallway.

She pushed open a bedroom doorway on her left. The room was messy, unkempt, like that of a teenager, with the smell of stale sweat and even staler food wafting towards her. The orderly uniform hanging on the door handle of the wardrobe confirmed this to be Giovanni's room. Yeah, good luck in there, guys, she thought of the techies as she closed the door.

By contrast the next room was tidy and ordered. The double bed was made and everything appeared to be clean.

'Hmm, this is a bit strange, eh?' she said to Bryant. 'These two seemed to be incredibly close and when his son appears to be in some serious trouble, Mancini senior is suddenly nowhere to be found.'

CHAPTER 83

Kim took a breath before entering interview room one. With any luck she was at the business end of a case that could not be over quick enough. A long, detailed confession in her hands to end the week was exactly what she needed right now.

Giovanni sat on one side of the table, cuffed and alone.

She sat, began the recorder and spoke loudly, recording herself, Bryant and Mancini as the persons present.

'Giovanni Mancini, please confirm that you have waived your right to be represented by counsel during this interview,' she said.

'I ain't done nothing wrong,' he said.

'Would you please answer the question, Mr Mancini?' Kim pressed.

'Yes, I waived my right,' he said, rolling his eyes. 'Cos, I ain't done nothing wrong,' he repeated, turning towards the tape recorder to tell it directly.

She regarded him for a few seconds allowing the silence to rest between them.

'Mr Mancini, where were you on Monday night?' she asked.

'Told you already. I was... we were at home.'

'Would you like to reconsider and answer the question again? Maybe give it a little more thought so I can be sure you've identified the correct day.'

He shook his head. 'We were at home. Me and my dad. Together.'

'Thank you for answering for your father too, but I have a witness that says otherwise.'

His face coloured. 'Your witness is wrong or lying.'

'My witness is incredibly reliable when it comes to your actions, Mr Mancini.'

He shrugged. 'You ain't tying me to the murder of that arsehole,' he said, trying to fold his arms before realising that he couldn't.

'What about Tuesday night?' Kim asked, thinking about Saul Cordell being run off the road. 'I'm talking late night.'

He shrugged. 'Can't remember. It was days ago. Probably watching the telly.'

'Did you leave home at all, fetch a takeaway, cigarettes?'

'Don't smoke and, no, I never went out.'

'You're sure?'

'Yeah.'

Kim suspected she was going to be returning to his next-door neighbour to confirm that as she seemed to have a better recollection of his movements than he did. She also suspected she was going to get the same response when asked his whereabouts when Nat Mansell and her mother had been murdered too.

Time to change direction.

'Mr Mancini, is there any reason we might find tiny blue fibres on any of your garments at home, say from cleaning cloths?'

He frowned. 'Like them used at the hospital, microfibre or something?'

'Yes,' she answered.

He shrugged. 'Could do, I suppose. My dad sometimes brings...' He stopped speaking, as though his brain registered that was in fact theft. The exact thing his father had been accused of by Doctor Cordell. 'Why, what are you saying?' he asked.

'We believe those fibres may be a match to ones found close to the wound of Doctor Cordell and, additionally, Phyllis Mansell, the mother of Nat Mansell who was the witness in the complaint against your father.'

'Now, just wait a minute,' he protested hotly. 'Who the hell is Phyllis or whatever her name?…'

'I've just explained that she's the murdered mother of Nat Mansell, the surgical nurse at Russells Hall Hospital, who was found yesterday with almost thirty stab wounds to her body but never mind that for now. We're here to talk about Doctor Cordell.'

The colour was slowly dripping from his face.

'Okay, if you can't answer that, would you like to tell me about those Reeboks you like so much? Do those shoes belong to you?'

''Course they do. I ain't no thief,' he said.

Kim was beginning to realise that Giovanni Mancini reckoned he wasn't a lot of things, but given he denied both charges with equal vigour she wasn't sure he wouldn't deny being a leprechaun with the same level of passion.

'And you have a receipt for them?'

He shrugged. 'Maybe… somewhere… probably,' he said.

'And where did you get them?' she asked.

'Dunno, can't remember.'

She looked at him disbelievingly. 'They don't look that old.'

'Couple of months,' he said.

'But you don't recall where you bought them?'

His tongue popped out briefly and licked his lower lip before he shook his head.

He was lying.

'Mr Mancini, it would serve you well to remember,' she advised.

'They're just shoes.'

'That you're not telling me the whole truth about. Now, why is that?'

'Don't remember.'

'I wonder if it would help jog your memory if I gave you a bit of information about them,' she said, opening her folder.

'Made by Reebok for two years only. A total of three hundred and thirty thousand pairs sold and sixty-two of those in the UK.

They are size nine, which was the third most popular size and racked up a total of seventeen thousand sales in the UK.' She looked up. 'They're very helpful at Reebok HQ,' she said. 'They keep all kinds of interesting information, but you wanna know what they couldn't tell me, Mr Mancini?'

He shook his head and then answered 'no' for the tape.

'They couldn't tell me why the boot mark is an exact match for the footprint found on the jacket of Doctor Gordon Cordell, even though you were safe and sound at home. Now, can you help me out with that, Mr Mancini?' she asked, sitting back in her chair.

He met her gaze and held it for a full minute before answering.

'Inspector, I think I'd like that lawyer now.'

CHAPTER 84

'They're all the same symptoms, Penn,' Stacey said, looking at the health records of Jessie Ryan next to her brother Justin who had died aged three years and one month.

'Apnoea, feeding problems, diarrhoea, asthma, fevers, everything,' she said as a cold sensation began to work up her spine.

'So, either they were unlucky enough, genetically, to have two children with the exact same medical—'

'Different fathers,' Stacey observed, wondering if that made a difference.

Penn frowned at her. 'Or we're looking at a whole different scenario,' he added.

'You're not starting to think Mrs Ryan deliberately made her children ill?' Stacey asked although she couldn't manage the appropriate degree of outrage or disbelief for such a claim.

'I am and so are you.'

'Shit. It's definitely possible,' she admitted.

Penn tapped in a few keys.

'Munchausen by proxy. "Where a parent fabricates, exaggerates or induces mental or physical health problems in those in their care to gain attention and sympathy",' Penn read, from the screen.

Stacey recalled the tears and references to her fears and worries when Mrs Ryan had been speaking to her, and Mrs Ryan's reaction when the neighbour had arrived. Stacey had detected a sense of pleasure and read it as relief that someone was helping to look for her child. Mrs Ryan had talked about how wonderful the medical staff had been, how they were on first-name terms.

'Go on,' she said.

'"Most cases present three medical problems in some combination of the 103 different reported symptoms. Most common seem to be apnoea, smothering or starvation".' He paused. 'Weren't there a few references to Jessie being underweight?'

Stacey nodded. 'Which they put down to the constant diarrhoea,' she said.

'Other symptoms include "failure to thrive, vomiting, bleeding, infections or rash".' He paused and read again. '"Commonly inflicted with a cheese grater".'

'What?' Stacey exclaimed.

'Easy to fake, apparently.'

He clicked on a link and continued to read. 'Jeez, I remember this one,' he said. 'A woman named Lisa Hayden-Johnson. Her son was born prematurely in 2001 and needed medical attention immediately. The woman loved the attention and sympathy from having a sick child so much that when her son started to get better she fabricated an elaborate con that he was gravely ill.'

'Why is she known?' Stacey asked, wondering where he was reading from.

'This woman appeared on television, telling everyone that her son had a life-threatening food allergy that left him unable to eat and caused him to have a tube inserted into his stomach. She also said the child was confined to a wheelchair due to cerebral palsy and cystic fibrosis. She convinced the doctors he was sick, as well as the boy himself who ended up having unnecessary operations.'

He read more and then continued. 'Hayden-Johnson got national attention and donations poured in. Money, a car and even a cruise. Her son received a Children of Courage Award and met with politicians and royalty.'

'You're kidding?' Stacey asked.

He shook his head. 'I wish I was. The con lasted for seven years, until 2007, when a paediatrician became suspicious. He ordered more specific tests and on the day of the tests Hayden-Johnson reported that she'd been sexually assaulted. When interviewed by police the whole story came out.'

'And?' Stacey asked. He'd given her the detail and now she wanted the conclusion.

'Pled guilty to child cruelty and was sentenced to just over three years in prison.'

'It really is child abuse but even worse,' Stacey said. 'Most physical abuse entails lashing out at a child, while this takes planning and premeditation.'

'Says here that health professionals are manipulated into a partnership of child maltreatment. They pursue unusual or rare diagnoses thereby allocating even more time and tests to the child.'

He read something else silently.

'Didn't Mrs Ryan ask for a second opinion a couple of times?' he asked.

'Three, I think,' she answered.

'Common ploy if a parent isn't satisfied with level of care as they perceive it. It's called doctor shopping.'

'Jesus,' she breathed. She'd heard the term but had never researched it or come into contact with it before either in her life or career.

'Says here the only cure is to separate the child completely from the abuser, because seeking personal gratification through illness can become a lifelong trait.'

'So, if we're right the only reason Jessie's health improved was because Mrs Ryan was abusing her son.'

'Sickening as it is she probably got more sympathy and attention for the baby.'

Yes, it was sickening but she suspected he was right.

'So, you know what this means about Justin?' she asked.

'He may have been murdered by his own mother.'

She nodded. But more importantly, Jessie was still alive and due to go into hospital for exploratory heart surgery.

'Jesus, Penn, I really hope we find her before they do.'

CHAPTER 85

'I reckon I could drive to this bloody property blindfolded,' Bryant said as they entered Hollytree for the second time that day.

'Or we could sit in the office eating Penn's cakes all morning while we wait for Mancini's brief,' she replied.

'Yeah, what's with that?' Bryant asked.

'Don't know,' she said and just managed to stop herself from adding 'and don't care' suddenly aware of how childish that would sound.

'They're pretty good, though,' Bryant said.

Kim ignored the frisson of irritation that niggled her.

'There's something here, Bryant, I can feel it,' she said as he parked behind Mitch's van, which was this side of the cordon tape strung between two wheelie bins with a constable standing at the midway point. Groups of neighbours stood smoking, drinking and pointing at the Mancini home.

She did a quick assessment of the scene before her and frowned.

'I tell you what's not here. And that's Mancini senior,' Bryant said.

'Yeah, I've been thinking about that and I reckon we'll get him later. His disciplinary is due at three this afternoon and I'm sure he'll be turning up for that.'

'Despite everything that's happened?'

She nodded. 'If Mancini junior has done this in some twisted revenge for the sullying of his father's good name, then senior will be there. And if it's nothing to do with it, he'll be there.'

Bryant made no move to get out of the car.

'What's up?' she asked with her palm on the door handle.

'Remember how the SIO of the Yorkshire Ripper case became fixated on letters and recorded messages from Wearside Jack while the real killer continued to murder more victims?'

She frowned, unsure of his point.

'Bryant, I'm following the bloody evidence,' she exclaimed. 'What do you want me to do, ignore the fact that our guy had motive, opportunity and means and that forensically we can tie his boots to the first victim? Jesus, give the prosecutor the day off and I'll try this one myself.' She paused and tried to swallow her annoyance. 'What the hell is wrong with you? Why are you doubting direct evidence?'

'Nat Mansell said something about making a choice. What did she mean?'

Kim shrugged. 'To have an affair with a married man, to back up a false accusation of theft, what she had for breakfast. How the hell should I know?'

'You always tell me that everything means something, so don't you want to know?' he asked.

'Not at the expense of ignoring forensic evidence that's got Mancini's name all over it.'

'Yeah, you're probably right,' he said, finally getting out of the car.

'Yeah, I probably am,' she snapped, stung by his doubt. What the hell did he want her to do, walk into Woody's office and declare she had chosen to ignore all the evidence because it was making too much sense and was too tidy? She realised that she had added those last two words herself. Bryant hadn't said that. But it was what he had meant. He'd either put the thought into her head or brought her own thoughts to the fore, and right now she wasn't sure which. Yeah, she really needed Woody questioning her sanity the week he was deciding if she was capable of doing her job.

Fucking Bryant and his earworms, she cursed, as she paused at the front door of the property.

She hesitated as she approached the property. 'Sergeant?' she asked an officer giving instructions to two constables.

'Marm?' he responded, surprised.

'If you've not instructed one of these officers to pair up with the guy on the cordon then do it right now. No one stands on Hollytree alone,' she said, brushing past him.

His expression of understanding assured her it would be done.

Mitch met them at the kitchen door with two pairs of blue slippers.

'Anything yet?' she asked, bending down to put them on.

'Done a cursory glance of all the rooms but focussing on the bedroom for any clothing and the kitchen for missing knives to start,' he explained. 'And other than a sizeable collection of soft porn, nothing to report as yet.'

She swallowed her disappointment.

'Mind if we take a look around?' she asked.

He smiled. 'Yeah but just looky no touchy, Inspector,' he said.

'Got it,' she said, heading to the living room.

She stood in the middle of the space and looked around. The room didn't allow for much furniture. The sofas were back against the wall and one coffee table in the centre was in reach of them both. Other than the music centre and the television there was little else present, or of interest. The ugly weed had drooped and shrivelled on the sideboard.

She moved to the doorway of the poky bathroom. A narrow shower cubicle jutted out on her left. A toilet and sink lined the far wall with a waste basket in between.

She opened the shower door and peered inside.

'Guv, you know—'

'Clean,' she observed, closing the cubicle. 'Too bloody clean. Two men live here,' she observed. 'And judging by his room Giovanni isn't the house-proud type.'

'One of them cleans for a living,' Bryant argued.

'Yeah, exactly, how many cop shows you watch in your spare time?' she asked, moving further into the room that only had space for one.

She looked around and almost gagged. 'Yeah, tell your theory to the toilet pan,' she said, looking away.

She opened the small cabinet above the sink by reaching to the top of the mirrored doors and pulling them open avoiding the bottom rim, which would have been more commonly used. She found the usual toiletries: toothbrushes, two different toothpastes, shaving paraphernalia and soap. She closed it again and glanced down at the waste bin, half-full of a few wrappers and lumps of toilet roll.

She glanced back at Bryant who was not so secretly checking his watch.

'Okay, Bryant, I heard you loud and—'

She stopped speaking when her phone began to ring.

'Penn,' she answered.

'Mancini's brief just arrived, boss.'

'On our way,' she said and ended the call.

She stood in the hallway and opened her mouth to concede defeat when something lower down in the wire waste basket caught her eye.

She frowned and took a step back. She squatted down to get a better look at the inch of blue latex amongst the white crumpled tissue.

'Call Mitch,' Kim said, not taking her eyes from it in case it disappeared.

Bryant called, and Mitch appeared almost instantly.

'Yo,' he said, coming into view.

'You say you've been in here?' she asked, straightening.

'Only a cursory glance from the doorway for signs of any-thing— Ooh, I see,' he said, following her pointed finger.

'Lou,' he called. 'Bags.'

It was a small property and Lou appeared promptly with a clutch of evidence bags.

Lou regarded her expectantly, and she stepped back into the hallway.

Mitch nodded at him. He opened an evidence bag as Mitch began to pick out the wadded tissue and drop each piece of rubbish into the evidence bag, exposing more of the blue latex.

Eventually Mitch reached it and held it up for them both to see.

It was clearly a latex surgical glove and it was stained red with blood,

She turned to her colleague. 'So, what do you reckon, Bryant. You think we should ignore that?'

CHAPTER 86

Stacey stood in the same spot that she'd stood the other day and looked up and down the street.

Despite what they'd learned about Jessie's health and the coincidences surrounding her brother, Stacey still hadn't been able to rid herself of the image of the girls arguing and Emma slapping Jessie. The girl had form for violence and she'd also had her best friend's mobile phone, in bits, hidden in a speaker. And that had nothing to do with Munchausen by proxy.

And Emma's mother – so desperate to keep her daughter quiet. Stacey remembered the previous day when she'd found the phone in the speaker. The woman's face had registered surprise, anger and then surprise again.

Stacey knew something had happened here on Sunday night, and she knew that somehow both Emma and her mother were involved; but she needed to see if either of them had exhibited any strange behaviour following Jessie's disappearance.

She looked around the street and spotted the white transit van and she knew exactly where she needed to go.

CHAPTER 87

'And that's where we are, sir,' Kim said, having relayed recent developments to her boss.

'So, we have fibres that match Cordell to his lover's mother, we have a boot print that matches Mancini's shoes, a bloodstained surgical glove at the Mancini residence and you're waiting for a match on the hair found at the first scene and the blood found on the glove?'

She nodded.

'You can categorically tie him forensically to the murder of the doctor but you're on shaky ground with the rest. I'm guessing those fibres are pretty common.'

She nodded. 'Supplied to the hospital and about a thousand other outlets. Unless we find the actual cleaning cloth they came from we're not going to be able to use them.'

'You still feel it's the same killer for all four victims, even Saul Cordell?'

She thought for a moment before nodding. 'His accident is too coincidental for my liking,' she said.

'So, are you going to charge Mancini with the murder of Gordon Cordell?'

She shrugged. 'I've got Penn on standby to start the CPS workup?'

'What are you waiting for?' he asked.

'A confession,' she answered, honestly. 'I want another crack at him. I want him to tell me face to face that he killed all four of them.'

'Okay,' he said, nodding. 'Shake the tree and see what falls out, but don't shake it too hard.'

She understood. He had a lawyer and she was on her best behaviour. If this went to court it would not fail on a technicality.

'Hey, Stone, it's Friday,' he said, meaningfully, as she approached the door.

Yes, she knew. 'And it will be on your desk by the end of the day. As requested.'

That she had no idea what Ted's report would say, she chose not to mention.

'That's not coming from the morgue, I assume?' he said, with amusement in his voice, referring to her leg X-rays.

Her hand hovered over the door handle.

She turned, surprising her boss. Normally, she couldn't get out of his office fast enough once he'd finished with her.

'Sir, Bryant thinks this case is just a bit too tidy.'

He didn't seem surprised. 'And your gut says?'

'I've learned over the years to trust Bryant.'

'And I've learned over the years to trust your gut,' he answered.

Which was a great vote of confidence. If only she could work out what it was trying to say.

CHAPTER 88

'Oh Jesus, not you again,' said van man as he opened the door. 'Are you like one of those recurring nightmares, cos you do realise it's the middle of—'

'Sir, I apologise for disturbing your sleep again but I really need your help. It's important.'

She really wouldn't have bothered him again if it wasn't urgent. She remembered all too clearly her night shifts as a constable. Starting work when everyone else was celebrating another work day completed. Dealing with the night-time problems like drunks, vagrants, assaults. Fighting off the 3 a.m. slump and then taking the work-fuelled adrenaline home with no method of release before crawling between the sheets. Some of her colleagues had enjoyed a beer or two before laying down their heads, but alcohol at 7 a.m. was not a habit she wanted or needed.

Day sleeping had not suited her one little bit, and although her mum and dad had tried to keep the noise down they couldn't prevent real life from happening. The blackout blind in her room had helped to fool her brain into sleep mode, but the laughter of the kids walking to school, the traffic and the postman had not been quite so obliging.

'I really am sorry,' she repeated, meaning it.

He rubbed a big, meaty hand all over his head as though rubbing away the sleep fog and stepped aside.

'Come in,' he said.

Stacey followed.

'May I have another look at?…'

'Here,' he said, plucking the phone from beside his keys on the telephone table.

'Password is "bigboy", one word,' he said, heading towards the kitchen.

'Sir, you really shouldn't just give out…'

'You're the police,' he reminded her.

He had a point.

She keyed in his password and fired up the CCTV app.

The screen was frozen on the last image recorded. She pressed the view option and keyed in Monday's date at 8 a.m.; Stacey knew there was nothing further for Sunday night because bigboy had gone to work his night shift and the dashcam had been switched off and removed.

'What time do you get home?' Stacey asked as he returned with a pint glass of some kind of weak cordial.

'Seven thirty,' he replied.

Stacey keyed in '7.35' and hit play.

The van had been parked in a different place in the street giving her a different angle from the footage she'd viewed the other day.

All she could see was the end of the path and a corner of the Weston's garden.

From the corner of her eye she saw bigboy's head loll back against the top of the sofa.

'I really am sorry about…'

''S all right,' he said, drowsily. 'Just hope it helps.'

She offered him an appreciative smile and turned her attention back to the screen as a pair of legs appeared on the path. Judging by the thick tights and navy skirt, it was Emma, leaving for school. Earlier than Stacey would have expected but maybe she had errands to run.

She continued watching unsure what she was hoping to find, but thinking that surely Emma or her mother would exhibit some kind of changed behaviour if they'd been involved in the disappearance of Jessie Ryan the night before?

Footage of the two of them carrying black bags filled with God knows what had already occurred to her.

A soft snore sounded from the man on the sofa as Stacey saw the same pair of legs return to the house. Emma had been gone for twenty minutes.

At 8.35 Emma's legs appeared again and turned the other way out of the gate.

At 9.10 Mrs Weston, dressed in light blue jeans, headed down the path and out of sight. Damn this partial view. If Snoring Beauty had parked just a few feet back she'd have had a much better line of sight.

Twenty minutes later Mrs Weston returned to the property for a total of fifteen minutes before leaving again.

Stacey sat back and tried to analyse the behaviour.

It was the morning after Jessie's disappearance, following a physical fight with the daughter. They had both left the house, returned and then left again within an hour.

It was like they were checking on something.

'Hang on one minute,' she said.

'What, what?...'

'Not you,' she reassured the half-asleep man.

She keyed in each morning at '7.30' and the van had been parked in a slightly different place every time bigboy had returned from work.

She then checked each evening at around '7 p.m.' before the van was moved again to take its owner to work.

'Oh, my lord,' she breathed, as she saw what had been staring her in the face all the time.

'I've gotta go,' she said, standing and handing the man his phone.

'Did it help at all?' he asked, hopefully.

'Oh, bigboy, you really have no idea,' she said, gratefully.

He closed the door behind her, and with trepidation she crossed the road and headed to the bottom of the street. She hesitated for a second as her hand curled around the door handle of the caravan.

Her hair stood on end as a hand covered hers and a voice spoke into her ear.

'I wouldn't do that if I were you.'

CHAPTER 89

'You are joking me?' Kim asked, incredulously.

Giovanni Mancini shook his head.

'You got the shoes from Lost and Found? At the hospital?' she said, staring at a smug-looking Giovanni Mancini, who hadn't spoken a word since his brief had arrived. But just as he was better prepared, so was she after taking a call from Mitch while Mancini and his solicitor had concocted their defence strategy. This new information would keep for now and would be better served to take him by surprise later.

Kim had groaned inwardly when she'd heard his brief was Norbert Flowers. Habitually he advised his clients to respond with the two-word phrase Kim would like struck from the dictionary.

'No comment,' Giovanni said, proving that the slimy solicitor hadn't changed his tactics one bit.

'My client states he got them Tuesday morning,' Norbert said, blinking rapidly.

'But why didn't he say this when I asked him earlier?' Kim probed.

'Because he thought it would get him into trouble.'

'Yeah cos taking lost property sure trumps murder,' she observed.

'My client was concerned about losing his job. Lost property doesn't always make it through the official channels. He heard about them and managed to obtain them before they entered the logging system of thirty days at which point they can be redistributed.'

'So, basically he's saying he…'

'Apparently it happens all the time and my client is not the only one to take advantage of—'

'I'm sorry but I don't believe you,' she said, addressing the suspect and not his mouthpiece.

'But on to the next point, Mr Mancini, would you like to explain why there's a surgical glove in your bathroom waste bin at home?'

He didn't look particularly surprised as he shrugged.

'Care to answer the question, sir?'

'My father sometimes uses them to clean.'

Flowers shook his head at his client who had obviously broken the 'no comment' rule but if he felt like talking Kim intended to make the most of it.

'And why would it be covered in blood?' she asked.

That did seem to surprise him but he covered quickly.

'Nosebleed, shaving…'

'Which is fine if it's your father's blood, which is being analysed right now; speaking of which. Where is your father, Mr Mancini?'

He shrugged.

She nodded towards the tape.

'I don't know.'

She'd had a plan coming into the room. She had known that she wanted to show him the process of building the evidence against him.

She didn't believe for a second his story about getting the shoes from lost property. The blood on the glove was still being analysed, but there was one piece of evidence that he could not refute and this was her final play.

What she wanted from him now, what she needed from him now to silence Bryant's earworm was a full and frank confession.

She wanted to hear him admit to the brutal murder of Gordon Cordell, to smothering Phyllis Mansell and to viciously stabbing her daughter twenty-nine times. And the murder of Saul Cordell would be a happy bonus.

She needed it, so she could stand outside this room, front up to her colleague and tell him he'd been wrong.

And now to pose the question that had been on her lips since the earlier call from Mitch.

'I'm curious, Mr Mancini, about something. You see, we found a hair at the very first crime scene and I'd like you to explain why that hair matches the one taken from you when you first got here.'

The colour drained from his face. He swallowed. He licked his lips; he looked to his lawyer, who nodded, and then looked down.

Here it comes, she thought. Readying herself for a moment of victory.

'So, how would you like to explain?' Kim asked again.

He took a breath and replied.

'No comment.'

CHAPTER 90

Stacey shook her hand free and turned on Emma's mother.

'What the hell have you done with her?'

'What do you?…'

'You knew Emma had Jessie's phone but you pretended you didn't and…'

'I didn't know about the phone,' she protested.

'But you knew Emma had hit her best friend and you covered it up. You wouldn't even let me speak to her to ask her about Jessie. Now, I understand about protecting your child but what did she do to Jessie?' Stacey asked. 'And what have you helped her cover up?'

Panic and fear shaped her face.

'There's nothing, I swear…'

'What happened between Jessie and Emma on Sunday night that you don't want me to know about? Was there some kind of incident and Emma went too far? Hurt Jessie badly?'

'No, Emma would never hurt Jessie,' she said, moving in front of the caravan door.

'Mrs Weston, if you don't move from in front of that door I will physically remove you and worry about the search warrant later,' Stacey said, meaningfully. She had the feeling that inside this caravan was the body of a fifteen-year-old girl.

Mrs Weston paled and sighed heavily.

'I can't do this any longer. I can't protect her. I've tried and I can't do any more,' she said, moving away from the door.

Stacey's hand moved back towards the door handle, and Mrs Weston didn't try and stop her. When she spoke her voice was a defeated whisper.

'Once you open that door we can never go back. I won't be able to protect her any more. It's all over.'

The tears began to fall from her eyes.

'I'm sorry, Jessie,' she said, loudly.

'Wh-what?' Stacey said, her palm still on the handle. 'Jessie's alive?'

The tears stopped falling, and horror bent her features.

'Of, course she's alive. You didn't think… oh my god… how could you even?…'

'Mrs Weston, you're really gonna have to talk fast.'

The woman glanced at Stacey's hand on the door of the caravan. Stacey dropped it for now.

Mrs Weston moved a couple of steps away and lowered her voice.

'I know you're not going to believe me but Jessie's mother has been making her ill for years.'

Mrs Weston appeared to pause for the exclamation of disbelief.

'Go on,' Stacey said.

'It's got a special, fancy name but the top and bottom of it is that her mother does it to get attention.'

'I'm listening,' Stacey said.

'You already know something, don't you?' she asked. 'That's why you're hearing me out. You wouldn't believe me if you hadn't already got a suspicion.'

'Please continue,' Stacey said, admitting nothing.

'It's a tough thing to believe,' the woman said. 'I've known Jessie since she was five years old and even I struggled to believe her mother could do something like that. But then I started to think about how sickly she was as a child. There was always something wrong with her and then she seemed to get better for a while.'

'When her brother was alive?'

'You do know, don't you,' she asked with relief. 'You've looked at this.'

'Please, carry on,' Stacey said.

'When Justin, that poor little boy, died, it all started up again. But it was different. Her mother was coming up with more and more serious claims. Eventually I asked Jessie about it, and she broke down. It took a lot for her to admit that she thought her mother was making her ill. She actually preferred to think that she was ill. And then last week she received this appointment for the angiogram and it frightened her half to death. She's tried to tell people, but no one will listen to her. She has no control over the procedure because she's a minor. For another three days,' she said, gravely.

'So, that was the plan?' Stacey asked, 'To hide her until the threat of the procedure was over.'

'Until Monday,' she said. 'When Jessie turns sixteen and has some say over what happens to her.'

'Mrs Weston, why did Emma slap her?'

'She's not proud of what she did, officer. She loves that girl like a sister. You really think we'd be doing this if we didn't care a great deal about her? Jessie had decided she wanted to tell her boyfriend about the plan, and Emma got angry. She knew how much trouble I'd be in if anyone found out. She ran after Jessie and apologised. They made up. Jessie went to the caravan as planned, and Emma came home.'

The endless trips up and down the path to take the girl supplies and to check on her.

Again, Stacey touched the door handle.

'Please, if you do that you'll have to take her. I understand that but please know that she will be back with her mother within an hour and then none of us can protect her.'

'But I have to know.'

Mrs Weston stood closer to the door and spoke loudly.

'I would imagine that if Jessie were alive she might find some way to let us know.'

A single knock sounded on the side of the caravan.

'And if she were healthy, and fed and feeling safe…'

Another single knock.

'But I can't just walk away and pretend—'

'You know she's safe,' Mrs Weston pleaded. 'I swear to you that first thing on Monday morning I'll bring her to the station and you can ask her anything. She's in no danger. I won't let any harm come to her but if you take her back…'

'I need to know it's her,' Stacey said. For all she knew it could be Emma knocking back, sitting beside the dead body of her friend.

'Ask something,' Mrs Weston said.

Stacey thought about the girl's medical history. She could picture the list of procedures as though it was imprinted on her brain.

'How old were you when you had your first overnight stay in hospital?' she asked.

Six knocks.

Correct.

'How many times have you been put on an intravenous feeding drip?'

Three knocks.

Correct.

'Damn,' Stacey said aloud, wondering where in the handbook she'd find instructions for this.

The police officer in her cried out to open the door and do what was procedurally correct. To see the girl in the flesh, alive and healthy. Take her to the station and stamp the case closed.

And the human being in her knew that beyond that door was a young girl terrified to go home to a mother who had abused her for years.

She had started this week with Jessie as a runaway. No one had pushed to find the girl except her.

'She's safe. I won't let anyone hurt her,' Mrs Weston breathed. 'I promise.'

Stacey prayed for some kind of sign. Some kind of guidance as to what she should do in this situation.

Suddenly her phone rang, startling them both.

She answered

'Stace, it's Penn. Boss wants you back here. Now.'

CHAPTER 91

'Okay, guys, Mancini ain't talking, so what now?' Kim asked, grumpily.

With the weight of evidence against him the guy should have been either desperate to confess or quaking in his shoes. He was neither. 'Look, folks, we either bugger off on a day trip to the seaside while we wait for the blood results on the glove or we take another look at this thing,' she said.

'But the fibres…' Stacey said.

'Ignore them,' she said.

'And the boot print?' Penn asked.

'Ignore it,' she said, barely able to believe her own ears.

She saw Stacey and Penn shoot a look at each other and part of her agreed with them. But the other part agreed with Bryant.

'And bear in mind that Nat Mansell said something about a choice,' Bryant piped up.

'So, I want you two here thinking outside the box, while Bryant and I go chase up these forensic results from Mitch.'

'Okay, boss,' Stacey said as Kim grabbed her jacket.

Bryant followed her out of the room.

*

'Happy now?' she asked, as they headed down the stairs.

He shrugged. 'You're probably right about Mancini but, be honest, guv, have you ever worked a case that's thrown up so much forensic evidence?'

'I get it,' she said. But by the same token she'd never worked a case where she'd chosen to ignore all the forensic evidence either.

'But why are you so hung up on Nat Mansell's comment about making a choice? It was just something she said.'

'No, guv,' Bryant said, opening the driver's door. 'It was the only thing she said.'

CHAPTER 92

'So, what did the boss say about Jessie Ryan?' Penn asked.

Stacey had updated the boss as soon as she'd got back, ending with her explanation of why she hadn't entered the caravan. The boss had listened, her face showing a mixture of surprise and something that looked like pride.

'So, no one was looking for her except you, cos you refused to let it go?' the boss had asked.

Stacey had nodded.

'And you feel that the girl is in danger if she's returned home in the next couple of days?'

Stacey hadn't hesitated in answering that question.

'And you're convinced Jessie is fit and well and in the care of a responsible adult?'

Stacey had thought about Mrs Weston's fierce protection of a child she had known almost all her life.

'Absolutely.'

'Okay, Monday morning it is,' the boss had said.

'You know, Penn, I think she trusts me,' Stacey said, feeling the weight of that expectation land heavily on her shoulders, and she prayed to God that she'd called it right.

Penn sat back in his chair and eyed her thoughtfully. 'So, this happen a lot around here? You find a missing girl and leave her missing, and then do a complete turnaround on a case that's almost complete when the evidence is telling you exactly what you want to hear?'

Stacey hid her smile at his summary. 'Isn't that how it happens everywhere?' she asked.

Penn raised an eyebrow. 'Not everywhere. But okay, out the box we come,' he said, getting up and heading for the blank whiteboard on the wall by the door.

He took the pen and wrote the name of each victim in a corner. He drew a straight line from Gordon Cordell to Saul Cordell and another straight line from Nat Mansell down to the name of Phyllis Mansell.

Stacey watched as he labelled the lines 'family' and then put two lines stretching from Cordell to Mansell, one marked 'complaint' and one marked 'affair'.

In the middle of the board he wrote the names of Giovanni and Angelo Mancini.

He drew a line from Angelo to 'complaint', which linked him then to Cordell and Mansell.

He listed the evidence. The boot took a line down to Giovanni. The hair took a line down to Giovanni. The fibres took a line down to both of them. He wrote 'blood' and a question mark.

He stepped away and turned to her. 'Anything else?'

She shook her head as a feeling of unease stole over her.

'You know I'm starting to see what Bryant means. Looking at it like that puts a whole new slant on it. The family members. What the hell did they do?'

She carried on looking.

'We've taken everything at face value; the complaint, the affair, the evidence. We've focussed on everything we know: that they were involved in a complaint together. That they were having an affair together.

'And yet we've forgotten a very important third link,' Penn said, tapping the pen against his lip.

Stacey nodded, knowing exactly what he was getting at.

They had forgotten that the couple worked together.

CHAPTER 93

'Carry on up to Mitch,' Kim said, spying someone sitting in the hospital cafeteria.

Bryant followed her gaze and nodded his understanding.

Kim approached the table of a man staring down into a black coffee.

'Hey,' she said, sitting opposite Luke Cordell.

He lifted his head and smiled weakly.

'Sorry about your brother,' she said and meant it. Admittedly, he had been less than courteous this week but his anger had been born of grief. She could only imagine what it had been like to see his brother's broken body in the hospital bed only to watch him slip away.

'How's your mum?'

He shrugged. 'Trying to stay strong for me and I'm trying to do the same for her. We only have each other left. Our family has halved in just a few days.'

'Where is your mum?'

'In the chapel. We had to come sign some papers, and we don't seem to be able to leave. It's so final, like we're leaving him behind.'

Kim understood. While they were still at the hospital they were close to where Gordon Cordell had worked and where Saul Cordell had died. They were still linked to the events. Once they walked out of the hospital for good they had to begin dealing with the 'never agains' as she liked to call them. Never again would Saul walk into the family home. Never again would they be able to just call him on the phone. Remaining at the hospital delayed that final acceptance.

And once they left they would have to adjust to the new landscape of their family.

'Did you always know about the affair?' Kim asked, gently.

'We all did,' he said. 'Although it was more than an affair,' he said. 'They'd been at it for years.'

'But he wanted to come home, didn't he?' Kim asked.

'Only so he could have his cake and eat it,' he answered. 'He wanted to come back for the comforts of a home he bought, and my mother knew that. He had no intention of giving up the affair. My mother also knew that.'

Kim had the sudden sense that this family had endured a lot of pain because of Gordon Cordell's selfishness.

'Can I ask you something?' he said.

'Of course.'

'I overheard one of the nurses who'd spoken to the police say something about not being sure what happened to my brother was an accident. Is that true? I haven't said anything to Mum but I'd like to know.'

Kim thought for a minute before responding.

'The incident with your brother is being handled by the traffic collision team. To my knowledge it isn't under investigation and CID has no involvement.'

'I sensed a great big "but" hanging at the end of that sentence.'

'Most detectives don't believe all that much in coincidences,' she said.

'Are you saying?…'

'I'm saying that if someone else was responsible for the death of your brother, we won't rest until we find them.'

Sensing he was getting no more, he nodded his understanding.

She touched his arm lightly and stood.

'Give my condolences to your mum,' she said.

'Thank you, I will,' he said, as she turned away.

She paused as he spoke quietly.

'You know, strange as it sounds I do get some small comfort from the fact they're now together.'

'Despite everything your father did?' she asked.

'Saul always managed to forgive him. My brother had a generous disposition and tried to give him the benefit of the doubt. I'm afraid I wasn't quite so charitable.'

Kim had nothing left to offer and walked away, leaving the young man alone with his regret.

CHAPTER 94

'Okay, what you got?' Stacey asked.

'Nothing yet, you?'

They had agreed that Penn would continue to work through the van registration number owners, looking for any obvious links to Gordon Cordell, Nat Mansell or the hospital.

Stacey had agreed to interrogate hospital records.

'In total, I've got 120 procedures they worked on together over the years,' she said. 'A mixture of all kinds of procedures but many being hysterectomy or voluntary sterilisation.'

'Okay,' Penn said, waiting for more.

'Of those procedures there are four deaths logged by the hospital administration.'

'Not a bad rate,' Penn noted.

'Depends,' Stacey said.

'On what?'

'How many of them were minor surgeries or standard procedure.'

'But surgery always poses some risks,' Penn observed.

'Agreed, so does stepping outside your door or crossing a road but look at how many times you might do it before you get hit; it's relative, is all I'm saying.'

'You think all this could be linked to one of the operations they carried out that resulted in a death?'

Stacey thought about the boss's instructions to think outside the box.

She looked up at her colleague and nodded.

'I think it's gotta be worth a look.'

Kim gave the camera a hard stare while she waited for the doors to the lab to open. Bryant was leaning against the work surface watching Mitch at his microscope.

'Well?' she asked.

'Nothing yet. The magic is happening in that machine over there, so you could always go stare at it.'

She ignored him, and glanced at the items laid out on the workbench. She could see something from each victim except for Saul Cordell. 'What you looking for?' she asked.

'What I've been looking for all week,' he said. 'A fingerprint, even a partial would be something.'

'Why?' she asked. The forensic evidence was already over-whelming.

'Because you'll struggle to find a techie not a bit in love with a good fingerprint, for a few reasons,' he said, moving over to the table.

Kim realised they were going to hear those reasons.

'One of the earliest forms of forensic brilliance that's as effective today as it was when it was first discovered back in 1891, despite every advancement in the field.

'Every expert loves the lines that are composed of narrow valleys, the grooves and hills. The friction ridges that give traction to the skin every time you pick up a glass or turn a page in a book. You've got whirls, loops, arches, which remains the basis for fingerprint matching today. Then you've got plain arches, single loops, target whorl, tented arch, double loop and sexy spiral whorls—'

'Sexy?' Kim questioned.

'Very, Inspector,' he said, raising one eyebrow. 'But that's not the only reason we love them,' he admitted.

'Go on,' Kim said.

'We love 'em because they prove that the suspect was there.'

'So, you're looking for a fingerprint because you think the case against Mancini is weak?' Bryant asked, with interest.

Mitch looked from one to the other and then burst out laughing. 'Does he really want an answer to that question?'

'I think we both do,' she said, crossing her arms.

'With what you've got on Giovanni Mancini I'd forget the trial, put him straight into a prison cell and throw away the key.'

CHAPTER 96

'Okay,' Stacey said. 'The first death listed was a seventy-one-year-old female called Annie Brewer. Cervical cancer, which was terminal; surgery was to prolong life. Lady had a massive heart attack on the table and died. The risk of which had been made clear to her prior to surgery by Cordell and a second surgeon. Annie Brewer had a seventy-three-year-old husband who died seven months later, leaving behind one adult daughter, who is married and living on the island of Skye.

'No complaints about her treatment and no fault found on the surgery or nursing team.'

'Dead end then,' Penn observed.

'Yep, and case number two was a routine hysterectomy of a forty-four-year-old woman who died during surgery where both Cordell and Mansell were present. Investigation determined cause of death was linked to the anaesthesia administered incorrectly but no fault found with the surgeon.'

Stacey glanced up at her colleague. 'So, that's two down and two to go.'

CHAPTER 97

'Happy now?' she asked Bryant as they exited Mitch's lab.

'Guv, you do know we're on the same side, yeah?'

'Of course, but I told you we were on the right track with Mancini. My only doubt is the involvement of his father, who incidentally, we haven't seen for days.'

Bryant gave her a look that she couldn't read, and it irked her. Right now, *he* irked her.

'Okay, listen, I'm gonna go see if senior Mancini turned up for his meeting with Vanessa, and you should go check both their lockers. I think it would be good to split up for a while.'

Although he just nodded and said nothing, Kim could tell he also thought it was a good idea.

*

Kim shook her head as he walked away, wishing she felt the courage of her convictions about Giovanni Mancini, but every time she fought the corner of his guilt, a warning finger somewhere inside wagged at her.

She tried to remember any point in her training or cases she'd worked since in which completely disregarding forensic evidence had been thought a good idea. Normally it was the 'golden nugget' of an investigation upon which entire cases were won. Not only did it provide a link from suspect to victim but allowed them to put an expert in the witness box, which always went down well with a jury.

There was no doubt that the evidence they had led back to the Mancini household. To redirect her thoughts could only mean that someone with access to the evidence and the household had put it there and that was one hell of a leap she was not prepared to make, she decided, as she reached the admin block just as a smartly dressed woman in high heels was exiting.

'May I help you?' she asked, pleasantly, as she allowed the door to close behind her.

'Is Vanessa Wilson in her office?'

The woman shook her head. 'I'm Sophie, personal assistant to the Nephrology team, is there anything I can do for you?'

Oh, how Kim hated being spoken to with the Friday afternoon tolerance of someone who had no inclination to help her at all and already had eyes on the weekend.

Kim showed her ID. 'Do you know where she is?'

'She may have gone to get coffee. She was here earlier.'

Ah, maybe this woman could help her after all.

'She was due to conduct a disciplinary at 3 p.m. Do you know if Mr Mancini arrived for it?'

She nodded. 'He did, indeed. I took the minutes of the meeting. As it was a simple postponement there was no member of HR required.'

'It's been postponed?' Kim asked.

'Yes. Vanessa is still awaiting advice from an HR lawyer as this is quite a unique situation. She explained to Mr Mancini that although there was no accuser or a witness she couldn't simply sanction his return to work without full authorisation from a higher level.'

Kim could feel Mr Mancini's frustration. He'd probably been hoping that the whole sorry, sordid ordeal would be put to bed today one way or another. Awaiting the verdict was often worse than the verdict itself.

'And how did he take it?' she asked.

'He was upset, annoyed, tried to argue his case, even though Vanessa was quite clear that it would make no difference and that he would have to remain on suspension. That's paid suspension,' she added, clearly for the benefit of someone without any employment law knowledge. It was the law. It had to be.

She would have preferred to hear about the episode from Vanessa herself, but the woman was busy and deserved a ten-minute break down at the café.

'Did Mr Mancini give any indication of where he was going?' she asked one of the only two people who had seen him in recent days.

'I'm sorry but no. It wasn't that kind of meeting,' she answered as footsteps approached from behind. 'Pleasantries were not exchanged.'

'Everything okay here, Miss Potts?' asked the trusty security guard, Tyrone.

'It's fine but this police officer may need help finding her way back to the—'

'I can find it perfectly well,' Kim said, realising that their discussion was over.

'Okay, then. Well have a good weekend,' Sophie said to both of them before disappearing along the corridor and out of view.

'Thanks, Tyrone, but my trail of breadcrumbs should get me back to the lab perfectly safely,' she said.

'It's okay, Inspector. I'm more than happy to take you back to where you want to go,' he said, tapping her arm.

CHAPTER 98

Go and find the lockers, Bryant thought, mimicking her voice in his head. And bloody glad he was to do it, as well.

While she'd been away he'd been counting the days until the team was back together. He'd known that their tight little unit was changed for ever with the loss of Dawson but he had found the disbursement of the team unnerving and discombobulating.

The guys he'd worked alongside at Brierley Hill had been decent enough, hard-working and conscientious but dull, plodding and keeping their thoughts and ideas tightly contained within the box. There had been no moments of brilliance, no flashes of initiative or creativity. He had worked hard but he'd been uninspired.

He'd seen the call back to Halesowen as a return to his own pack, and yet it hadn't been the reunion he'd hoped for.

Perhaps it had been unrealistic to expect them all to readjust back into position without their fourth wheel.

And maybe his expectations in other areas had been too high as well.

He didn't blame his boss for her reaction to Dawson's death. She had done what she always did, retreat to her place of safety. Like a turtle she had retracted her head and reversed into her shell.

It was he who had checked in with Stacey every few days. It was he who had met her a couple of times up at Sedgley and taken her to lunch. He who had been waiting for her after her first counselling session.

He did, not the boss.

And even now, the boss wouldn't talk to either one of them. She hadn't talked to a counsellor and the thing with Ted was a farce. If he was honest, he was most narked because she couldn't even talk to *him*.

There were many things that had aggravated and irritated him over the last few days.

The way she'd just reappeared after six weeks without a word of acknowledgement about Dawson or the effect of his loss on her team. Her coldness towards Penn irked him too. It wasn't the poor kid's fault he wasn't Dawson.

He was annoyed at how she had gone in hard on Mancini. Whether it was him or not, she wanted it to be far too much for his liking. He had never seen her try to bully a confession from someone before. And that was why he'd questioned Mancini's guilt. Simply because she hadn't. And that wasn't like her at all. Normally, she questioned everything.

He knew that the roots of his irritation were buried in hurt. She had shut him out for six weeks and was continuing to do so now.

And so he'd been pleased to be given a break. Another half an hour and he might have just blown. And that probably wouldn't have done either of them any good.

So, yeah, he'd go check the Mancinis's work lockers and, thankfully, he'd just spotted someone who could help him find where they were.

CHAPTER 99

'It's a match,' Mitch said, as the security guard escorted her into the lab and then left them alone.

'Go on,' she said.

'The blood on the glove belongs to Gordon Cordell,' he said.

Although it was what she'd expected him to say, Kim didn't feel the tingle of excitement she normally felt at a major breakthrough. It was what she'd thought the results would indicate, yet there was a feeling of disappointment rolling around her stomach.

Mitch was watching her closely. 'Jeez, why do I feel like I just murdered your puppy?' he asked, deflated. 'I've pulled out every stop to get that result and—'

'It's not you, Mitch,' she said, taking out her phone. 'I'm glad I was right. I'm pretty sure Bryant has found that missing photo from Cordell's place in Mancini's locker. I'll call him and—'

'You'll never get him,' Mitch said, shaking his head. 'If the locker rooms are where I think they are, you're not going to get a signal.'

'But you know where they are?' she asked, as Bryant's phone went straight to voicemail.

'I think so,' he said, standing.

He did a quick check around the room, ensuring all the equipment had been turned off.

Kim was suddenly aware of the hours and effort Mitch had put in for them this last week. Not even spending time at his own lab but transplanting to Dudley to get the results to them as quickly as possible.

'Listen, Mitch, I just want to say…'

'Yeah, you're welcome, now switch that light off on your left.'

She smiled as she did so. People in their profession rarely responded well to gratitude and compliments. Long hours were just part of the job they'd signed up for.

They stepped into an eerily quiet corridor. They passed the morgue on her left which was in darkness.

Mitch took a right and through doors marked *for personnel only*.

Sometimes when she was in this part of the hospital it was hard to imagine the life and activity going on above her head.

She followed Mitch down a set of service stairs: grey shiny concrete and breeze-block walls.

'You know, Mitch, I can kinda see why Bryant has formed the opinion he has about Mancini.'

'Really?' he asked, turning and heading down a second flight of stairs.

'It's almost like it's too much, it's overwhelming. We have hair, fibres, blood, the boot print, everything we need to tie Mancini to three of the murders, but I've never had this before,' she said, as they landed at the bottom of the steps.

There were no flights left and she had no idea which floor or subfloor they were now on.

'Where the hell are you taking?…'

'I swear, it's around here somewhere,' Mitch said, heading along a corridor littered with old and broken equipment.

Every other strip light was not working and the ones that were, were filled with dead insects. The metal suspension chains had cobwebs stretching up to the roof.

Despite her unease Kim continued talking.

'But what I don't get is the glove in the toilet bin,' she admitted. 'Cordell was killed on Monday and they still have damning evidence in their flat on Friday. Why wouldn't they have thrown it away?'

'Forgotten about it?' Mitch said, looking in each doorway as he went.

'Really?'

He shrugged. 'I'm a science man,' he said. 'I deal in facts and figures and tangibles. This case is a dream to me. I believe in the evidence,' he said, turning towards her. 'Don't you?'

She held his gaze. 'Actually, Mitch, I don't know if I do.'

He pointed to a doorway, and she glanced inside. There were a few scattered lockers with doors hanging off. A sink with missing taps and one broken chair.

'Err… Mitch, I don't think they use this place any more,' she observed, as a heaviness headed towards her stomach.

He smiled ruefully. 'Yeah, looks like I didn't know where it was after all.'

CHAPTER 100

'Okay, this one is a beauty,' Penn said, reading from the screen. 'Trudy Lennox was admitted to hospital on the 7th October 2015 to have an ovary removed. Apparently, it was riddled with cysts and was both painful and non-productive.'

'Okay, sounds straightforward,' Stacey said, distractedly.

'Doctor Cordell took out the wrong ovary.'

That got her attention and she looked up. 'You're joking?'

Penn shook his head. 'Nope. She was twenty-six years old at the time.'

'And left without the chance of ever having children,' Stacey observed, returning her attention to her own screen. Jesus, that would be motivation for doing someone harm. 'What happened?' she asked, as something jumped out at her from the monitor.

'It never got to court and was settled for an undisclosed sum; but no one actually died. So, I'm not sure there's enough motive for—'

'Shut up, Penn,' Stacey said, as her eyes read quickly across the screen.

'You got something?' he asked.

'Not much, yet,' she said, trying to take it all in. 'This one is still tied up in legal.'

'Hit me,' he said.

'Bear with me, I'm piecing stuff together here as I talk. From what I can gather, eight months ago a woman was rushed into A & E in a bad way after a car accident. She was heavily pregnant, and despite Cordell performing emergency surgery, the woman died.'

'How heavily pregnant?' Penn asked.

'Eight months, I think,' Stacey said.

'Did the child survive?' he asked.

'Don't know yet,' Stacey said. 'But guess who was in the surgery with him?'

'Nat Mansell?'

Stacey nodded as she flicked between documents and newspaper reports, though information was limited.

She felt heat surging into her body.

'Penn, what did Nat Mansell say to the boss before she ran away?'

'Something about making a choice and living with it.'

'Oh shit. He had to make a choice,' Stacey breathed. 'The next of kin, presumably the husband, had to choose whether to save the life of the wife or the child,' she said dumbfounded.

Penn stood and looked at the board.

'So, you're thinking he made them choose?'

Stacey nodded as she continued to tap.

'But if Cordell made the choice to die himself then why is his eldest son still dead? And Nat Mansell's mother died before she did.'

'Hang on, hang on,' Stacey said, standing beside him. 'Let's say Cordell chose to save his son's life over his own. Explains why he was so easy to move around. There was no force involved. He'd accepted his own death in place of his older boy, who ended up dying anyway.'

Penn followed her train of thought. 'And, what if Nat Mansell was given the choice of herself or her mother and she chose to save herself?' he asked.

Stacey was horrified. 'You think she could do that to her own mother?'

Penn shrugged. 'Her mum was getting on, in an old people's home. Maybe she thought she deserved the chance to live more. Didn't she say about having to live with the choice she'd made?'

'Yeah but she didn't have to live with it for very long, did she?' Stacey asked, returning to her desk and throwing some search words into Google.

'We're missing something,' Penn said, pacing in front of the board. 'If he's giving them a choice of who dies, and they die anyway, then it's really not a choice at all.'

'Bingo,' Stacey cried out.

'Huh?' Penn said turning.

'It does make sense,' Stacey said, turning her screen towards him. 'If after making such a horrific choice between his wife and child, the one he saved died anyway.'

CHAPTER 101

The call from Stacey rang through to her mobile as she and Mitch reached civilisation.

She stood away from the lift to take the call as Mitch motioned that he was going back upstairs. His proximity down in the bowels of the building had unnerved her and made her realise that she didn't always know people as well as she thought she did.

'Go on, Stace,' Kim said.

'Boss, we don't think Mancini is our guy.'

'What're you talking about? It's been confirmed that the blood found on the glove is Cordell's,' she stated, with no real conviction. There was a buzzing in her stomach that she couldn't ignore.

'You said think outside the box, and we found something.'

'Tell me,' Kim said.

By the time her colleague had finished speaking, Kim had forgotten the blood completely.

'What's his name?' she asked.

'Don't have it yet, boss. His details are tied up in legal, but I hope to have—'

'So, you're saying that Cordell and Mansell were the people that gave the guy the choice. They took him into a room and made him choose between his dying wife and his dying child?'

'It's looking that way,' Stacey said, and Kim could hear her tapping.

'Just those two?' Kim asked, doubtfully.

Stacey's voice sounded over the noise from her fingers. 'I'm sure there would have been a hospital representative…'

Kim turned cold.

'Stace, tell me right now. Who else was in that room?'

But Kim already knew.

'Err… it was the Operation Medical Director. A woman called Vanessa Wilson.'

CHAPTER 102

Kim banged hard on the admin block door. It would either bring Vanessa scurrying out of her office or a security guard to tell her off.

She knew which one she preferred but it wasn't the one she got.

'Excuse me, but...'

This guy looked like he'd slept in his uniform, with creases across the middle and a tea-stained tie.

She shut him up by presenting her ID.

'Where's Tyrone?' she asked. She'd felt the two of them were becoming quite close.

'Finished his shift for the day.'

'Where's Vanessa?' she asked, urgently.

He shrugged. 'She's not in there. It's all locked up for the weekend.'

Kim had a sudden, terrifying thought.

'Did Vanessa have her child with her today?'

He frowned, 'I'm sorry but what does that have?...'

'A lot. Now get on your radio and find out,' she demanded.

He radioed through, and after a brief pause the voice confirmed that Vanessa had arrived at nine with her child.

Kim tried to stop the panic and think logically. Right now, she had no idea if Stacey's theory was even correct. Despite all the forensic evidence against Giovanni Mancini, there was something in her gut that had connected with this new information.

Some sicko was making people pay for a choice he'd had to make. If Stacey was to be believed, Cordell had been offered the choice of himself or his eldest son. He had committed the one selfless act of his life and chosen to die instead of his son, thinking he was giving his own life to save Saul's. But Saul had died anyway. Nat Mansell had been given the same choice and had chosen to save herself. Her mother had been killed and then so had she. So, two of the people involved were already dead, and Vanessa had been in the hospital with the person she loved most in the world and was nowhere to be found.

But maybe the killer hadn't known that. Perhaps Vanessa had left right after the disciplinary to take her sick child home or to a doctor's appointment.

'Sorry, but can you find out for me what time Vanessa left?' Kim said, trying to calm down.

It shouldn't take too long to work back through the camera footage. She said a silent prayer that Vanessa and her child had left the building.

He went to key the radio and then changed his mind.

'I don't need to check with control for that,' he said.

'Why not?'

'Cos I started my shift fifteen minutes ago and I parked right next to her car.'

CHAPTER 103

Kim scrolled to Stacey's number and pressed.

'Stace, tell me you've got something,' Kim said, urgently. 'Because I've got an unaccounted for Medical Director who has her six-year-old daughter with her.'

Kim tried not to show her frustration but she was beginning to feel like a cage was being erected around her. What she wanted to do was hit the fire alarm button and alert everyone to the fact that Vanessa and her child were missing and possibly in danger, but this was a hospital, filled with sick people on ventilators and heart monitors. Patients in operating theatres and treatment rooms. She couldn't throw an entire hospital into an emergency situation because someone was missing.

'I need a name... something... anything to help me identify who the hell I'm looking for.'

'I'm trying, boss,' Stacey answered, breathlessly. 'Give me just another few seconds. I'm close to accessing the legal...'

'Hey, David, hang on, I might need you,' Kim said, as the security guard began to walk away.

He turned and rolled his eyes. 'Fine, but my name isn't...'

'Got it,' Stacey said, excitedly. 'You're looking for a thirty-five-year-old man named Richard Chance.'

'But how the hell am I supposed?...' her words trailed away as she looked at the name badge of the security guard.

The events of the week flashed before her eyes and she remembered something Bryant had told her.

'Stace,' she said, quietly. 'Does Richard Chance have a middle name?'

She didn't need to wait for Stacey's answer.

She already knew the name of the man she was looking for.

CHAPTER 104

Bryant thanked his guide and passed through a refreshment area with vending machines, a sink and a few wooden tables and benches. *The Sun* and *Daily Star* were strewn between empty plastic cups and crisp packets.

He opened the locker door of Angelo Mancini by snapping the tiny padlock. His was labelled second one down in a tower of four lockers all lining the walls of a plain, brightly lit functional space. The crude labels were simple sticky squares. Some had been overwritten with the previous name scribbled out. Some had been written directly onto the metal and some had been stickered over and over again, causing Bryant to wonder at the rate of staff turnover.

Inside Angelo's locker he saw an old tee shirt, a can of deodorant, a spare pair of rolled-up socks and a car magazine.

He moved along the row until he found Giovanni's locker. There was no padlock and the door was ajar by about an inch. He opened it cautiously and took a breath. On the inside door was a topless woman astride a motorbike but it was what lay inside that had caused his breath to pause.

Beside a blue microfibre cleaning cloth was the photo of Cordell's two sons, taken from the photo frame used to smash the doctor around the head.

He took it out and looked at it for a second. The final piece of the puzzle. Indisputable proof that the man they had in custody was responsible for at least three murders and possibly a fourth.

He heard the unmistakeable sound of footsteps approaching from the refreshment room.

'You all done, officer?' asked his guide.

'Yep, all sorted, mate. Thanks for showing…'

Bryant's words were cut off as Giovanni Mancini's locker door smashed against his head.

CHAPTER 105

'He's not answering,' Kim growled as Bryant's phone went straight to voicemail for the third time. 'Where the hell is the locker room?' Kim asked the guard.

'It's right at the other end of the building,' he said.

Her fast walk turned into a trot. David had already called the control room and alerted them but her mind wouldn't slow down. All staff members within radio contact were now looking for Vanessa and her daughter.

'If we get to the next staircase, it'll take us all the way down,' he said.

Kim nodded her agreement, but something was tugging at her mind.

Cordell had chosen to die, so he had died first and his son later. If Nat Mansell's choice had been to sacrifice her mother, the older lady had died first and Nat Mansell after.

Kim didn't need to think about Vanessa's choice. She would give her own life for her child. There was no doubt in her mind about that.

So, he would kill Vanessa first and then go take care of her daughter.

Her legs slowed.

'Come on, it's along the next hall,' he said.

Yes, she knew it was and even though every muscle in her body ached to follow him to the stairwell and go after her colleague, she knew she couldn't do it.

If she made the wrong decision now Bryant would never forgive her and she would never forgive herself.

'We need to find the child,' Kim said, slowing down and turning left.

'But how are we?… I mean, where?…'

Kim had a sudden thought.

'I think I know where he's put her,' Kim said.

'How would you know that?'

'Because it's where he took me at the beginning of the week.'

CHAPTER 106

Bryant focussed through the pain in his head to stare into the face of Terry, the red-tee-shirted volunteer.

'What the?…'

'Stay still, or I'll hit you again,' he said in a voice that Bryant didn't recognise.

They had talked amiably as Terry had shown him to the locker room. They'd chatted about the weather, about the hospital, and Bryant had never suspected a thing.

But his voice was different now; cold, hard, emotionless.

He tried to think through the fog that was bearing down on his mind from the bang to the head. What the hell did Terry have to do with anything? He was an invisible, someone who moved around the hospital unnoticed by staff, patients and public. Was he trying to help or protect Giovanni Mancini? Nothing was making sense to him.

A sudden cry sounded from the other side of the room.

Bryant squinted his eyes and saw Vanessa Wilson, tied and gagged against the opposite wall.

'What the hell is?…'

'I'm going to give this bitch a chance to apologise before I cut her throat,' Terry said, reaching down and ripping the gag from her mouth.

Apologise for what? Bryant wondered, trying to understand this alternate reality in which he'd found himself. For a second he wondered if he had woken up, but the throbbing from the back of his head confirmed this was no dream.

'You bastard, where's my daughter?' Vanessa spat.

'She's safe,' he said. 'For now.'

Bryant was desperately trying to play catch-up but realised he was running a completely different race. He knew this man had knocked him out but he had no clue why.

'Come on, bitch, tell him what you did. Tell him how you ruined my fucking life.'

'Richard, there was no way we could save…'

'Fuck off,' he cried, kicking her ribs, hard.

She cried out with pain as her body fell to the side.

Who the hell was Richard? Bryant wondered watching the exchange between the two of them and trying desperately to understand.

'You didn't even try. You gave me the choice: my wife or my child,' he cried. 'You quoted statistics, fucking numbers at me while my wife lay dying on the operating table. All three of you gave me percentages and mortality rates when I couldn't even think. That's all we were to you, just numbers. You wanted me to make the decision; you wanted me to make the choice. You told me my child would have the better chance.'

Terry glared at her as she held her side and coughed. 'Who the hell can make that kind of choice?'

Bryant tried to keep up while appraising the room. It was clearly no longer used as a ward but would once have held four beds judging by the equipment on the wall. A metal bin sat beside a small hand basin next to which was a door.

And why was she calling him Richard? His name tag referred to him as Terry, which was doing nothing to help Bryant's confusion; but he knew one thing for sure. If he was in the room and having trouble trying to work it out, his team didn't stand a chance. He was on his own and no one was coming.

His boss knew he'd gone to check the lockers but he'd been knocked out and had no clue where he was now. The hospital was a warren of corridors and staircases, dead ends, and outdated wards not used any more. They'd never find him.

'Okay, so there's no point wasting any more time,' Terry said, moving towards Vanessa.

'But what about your baby?' Bryant asked, trying to keep up. He'd said something about a choice between his wife and child.

'Two weeks,' he whispered. 'And then my son died anyway.'

'Wait,' Bryant said. 'Give her another chance.'

Terry shook his head.

'No, she's already made her choice.'

'Open the door slowly,' Kim instructed, standing beside the door to the empty office.

David produced what looked like a master key and slid it into the lock.

The room was in darkness. Kim remembered a light cord to the left of the door. She reached for it and pulled. Nothing.

No light and no sound.

Kim's heart rose in her throat. If she was wrong about anything at all then the child might already be dead.

'Mia,' she said, stepping into the small space.

Nothing.

She took another step as a torchlight from David shone past her and began to search the room.

A whimper sounded from the darkest corner.

Thank God.

'It's okay, Mia. My name's Kim and I saw you yesterday in your mummy's office. It's okay, you're safe now,' she said, as David's torchlight found the child.

Mia's small body was folded into the corner, her legs pulled up, a small pony toy clutched to her chest.

The one that Bryant had played with.

Bryant.

Kim ached to turn away and go searching for her partner, but the child before her trembled with fear.

'It's okay, Mia. You're safe now,' she said, lowering slowly to her knees. She heard voices at the door, asking David what was going on, and thankfully one of those voices was female.

'Mummy... I want Mummy,' the child whimpered and squeezed the pony tighter.

'Mia, do you know where the man took your mummy?'

The girl whimpered louder and shook her head.

Kim moved forward and touched her leg gently.

'Mia, there's a nice lady behind me who is going to look after you while I find your mummy, is that okay?'

The whimpering stopped. 'You'll find my mummy?'

'Yes, sweetie, I'll go find mummy but I need to make sure you're okay. Can you come with me so I can go look for her?'

Kim held out her hand, and the child took it.

Kim gently pulled the girl to her feet and brought her closer towards her.

David's torchlight stayed on them both.

Kim held the small hand loosely and guided her towards the door.

Kim glanced at the woman in the security uniform questioningly, wondering why she was breathless and there at all.

'Panic alarm,' she said, pointing to the cord Kim had pulled. 'Linked to the control room.'

Kim nodded to the woman and then turned to the child.

'This lady is going to take you somewhere safe while I go and find your mummy, Okay?' she said, letting go of the small hand, trying to keep the urgency from her voice. Vanessa Wilson was not the only person she was desperate to find. Bryant was in the hands of someone who would stop at nothing to get his revenge on the people he felt were responsible for the death of his family. And even worse, her colleague had no clue what was going on.

The woman took the girl's hand. 'Oh, my daughter has that exact same pony,' she said, guiding the child away.

Kim turned to the security officer.

'Okay, David, where are these locker rooms and how do we get there fast?'

CHAPTER 108

With both his hands and feet bound, Bryant did the only thing he could think of to get Terry's attention.

'So, how'd it happen, then?' he asked, as Terry bent down towards a trembling Vanessa. Bryant could see the fear in her eyes and after what Terry had done to Cordell and Mansell he could understand why.

'I w-want my child,' she rasped, trying to hold her rib steady.

Bryant had no clue what Terry had done with Mia but he could only deal with what was before him right now. One problem at a time.

'The accident?' he asked Terry again.

'The wh-what?' Terry asked, confused. His mind was already focussed on taking this woman's life.

'The car accident with your wife… what was her?…'

'Her name was Sarah,' he offered.

That was exactly what he'd wanted. To put thoughts of his wife into his head. If there was any tenderness, any humanity left behind by the need for vengeance, it would be attached to his wife.

'How'd it happen?' Bryant asked, using his behind to scoot a short way along the wall. He knew where he had to go. It was his only chance but the challenge lay in distracting Terry for long enough.

He'd already worked out how easily Terry had been able to frame the Mancinis. Next to the locker room was a bathroom where people cleaned up. In Mancini's locker had been a comb where he'd been able to get a hair or two. He'd used the Reebok shoes, then handed them in to lost property and mentioned his find to Mancini, who had gone and pilfered them before they entered the system. And older Mancini had mentioned his colleagues dropping by to offer support and a half-dead weed. He was betting that person had been Terry planting the bloodied glove.

As a volunteer, Terry had been able to move around the building virtually unchecked, dropping a file here, a piece of paper here; an invisible helper that no one noticed or remembered.

'It was dark,' Terry said. 'We'd been to a friend's wedding reception. My friend, not hers,' he said.

Bryant scooted across one small inch at a time.

'Sarah was just a couple of weeks away from giving birth. She didn't want to go,' he said tapping the flat side of the blade against his palm.

Bryant could see Vanessa's terror-filled eyes on the gleaming blade.

'She was tired, felt huge and uncomfortable and I promised her we wouldn't stay long. And I promised her I wouldn't drink.

'She was fine for the first couple of hours, but then she started to moan. The more she complained the more I drank. Beer and whisky shots.'

Bryant was almost at the doorway to the single bathroom that would have served the four beds in the ward. Terry paced back and forth, and each time Terry turned away Bryant had gained another few inches.

'We left around eleven; she was angry. I was annoyed she was angry. It was hard for her to drive but she wouldn't let me get behind the wheel.'

Bryant glanced into the doorway, his eyes searching the space. What he sought was just inside on the left-hand side of the room.

'She was crying, her vision was blurred and she never saw the other car coming. The steering wheel…' he said, looking down at his stomach.

CHAPTER 109

'Where is he, David?' Kim asked, between breaths.

They had travelled all the way to the locker rooms to find an empty space and the photo of Gordon Cordell's sons on the floor in front of a locker holding a blue microfibre cleaning cloth. Kim had pushed her leg as hard as she dared before passing out.

'I'm sorry I don't...'

'Look,' she said, pointing to the locker door. 'That's blood. My colleague's blood. Now think, David,' she said, urgently. 'Where could Terry have taken him?'

He shook his head, and Kim wanted to reach over and smack him. She knew that wasn't fair but what she needed right now was either a mind reader or a miracle. She'd take either one.

The whole thing was beginning to make sense to her. Terry had managed to take Vanessa somewhere and restrain her. He'd then taken Mia and locked her in the abandoned office for later so he could have his time with Vanessa. No one would have been suspicious of Terry, a red-tee-shirted volunteer, walking the corridors with a little girl.

He'd seen Bryant, who had probably asked for directions to the locker room. And Terry had taken him. And then maybe smashed his head against the locker.

If that's what had happened, how far could he have got with an unconscious man, and how badly was her colleague hurt?

And did Bryant yet have any clue what was going on?

All she knew was that she needed to find him. Now.

'David, I swear if you don't…'

Her words trailed away as his radio crackled into life.

'What's that?' she asked, unable to hear the incident code or location.

He held up his hand to listen.

'Another panic alarm in the abandoned day surgery wing.'

'Take me there,' Kim said, knowing it was Bryant.

It had to be.

CHAPTER 110

'What the fuck did you just do?' Terry roared, glancing Bryant's way for the first time in minutes.

After making it to the doorway of the bathroom he had managed to grab the panic cord in his teeth and pull, while praying it was still linked up to something. It was his only chance to save either of their lives.

Vanessa cried out as Terry rushed towards him.

'I knew I should have killed you first,' he growled. 'I should have just cut your throat before she got what was coming to her,' he said, hauling Bryant to his feet.

Bryant thanked God the man had moved away from Vanessa. That knife had been just inches from her skin.

Bryant had to play for more time. If his plan had worked, all he needed was a couple of minutes.

But he knew he was dealing with a man who had nothing to lose. Terry didn't expect to live. He didn't want to live. He had nothing left to live for. He was no longer trying to hide his crimes and another dead body meant nothing to him.

'But it's not her fault, is it, Terry?' Bryant asked, locking the man's gaze with his own. Anything to keep him from looking at Vanessa. His only option was to bait Terry as his bound ankles and wrists locked behind him meant he couldn't take the man physically.

He knew he was vulnerable to the knife, his body open and exposed, but he had to keep Terry away from Vanessa.

'It wasn't Cordell's fault. It wasn't his son's fault. Neither Nat Mansell nor her mother were to blame. And Vanessa isn't either. You're right that they couldn't save Sarah or your child, and you were offered the worst choice imaginable,' he said, trying to picture having to make the same choice himself. 'But the choices that mattered, Terry, were all yours. You chose to go to the wedding reception,' Bryant said, wishing he could hear voices or movement in the corridor. 'You chose to have a drink or two despite your promise to Sarah. It was you who chose to let Sarah drive instead of insisting on getting a taxi so—'

'You think this is my fault?' Terry asked, incredulously, as though the thought had never occurred to him.

Bryant could sense the blade hovering between them attached to a hand that wanted to use it.

He realised that no one was coming and he'd played all the hands he had.

Now he too had nothing to lose.

'I think the choices you made—'

Suddenly the door burst open, and Bryant didn't need to look to know who was there.

Terry held his gaze with hate-filled eyes.

Thank God she's here, Bryant thought, as the blade was thrust into his flesh.

CHAPTER 111

'Someone help him,' Kim screamed as she lurched forward, reaching him a second after he fell to the ground.

Her hands found the wound site on his stomach, and pressed down hard. The warm stickiness oozed against her palm and over her fingers.

David had kicked the knife behind and had placed himself between herself and Bryant's attacker.

More footsteps sounded behind her; the noise level increased as people behind her wrestled Terry Chance to the ground. Others moved around her but she didn't look up and she didn't move as the blood gurgled through Bryant's shirt and onto her fingers.

'Get someone quickly,' she cried out over her shoulder.

More footsteps, voices on radios but all she could see were Bryant's fluttering eyelids.

'Don't you fucking dare,' she screamed, feeling the rage rampaging around her body.

'Bryant, you hear me?' she said, as the voices around her began to quieten.

'I mean it, Bryant,' she cried, bearing down as hard as she could.

'I'll never forgive you, you bastard,' she screamed into the silence around her as the emotion clogged her throat.

'What can I do? Can I take over?' Vanessa asked, appearing beside her.

She shook her head, as she heard a trolley being pushed at speed along the hallway. No one was touching him except her.

'Stay with me, Bryant. Just stay with me,' she commanded.

'He saved my life,' Vanessa breathed.

Of course he had. Kim wanted to find the words to tell her that Mia was fine, but she couldn't. She only had words for her friend.

'Bryant, I swear if you leave…' her voice trailed away as a silent tear rolled over her cheek. She couldn't even bear to finish the thought.

'Move aside, please,' said a voice as her hands were physically removed from his stomach.

Within two seconds Bryant had been lifted up and on to the trolley. A doctor checked him over and then nodded.

'Theatre 1, now,' he commanded.

Kim felt powerless as she watched him being wheeled away.

She looked down at her trembling hands, coloured red by Bryant's blood, through the tears that were blurring her eyes. A vision of Dawson's broken body at the foot of the bell tower broke into her mind.

No, this could not be happening. She couldn't lose Bryant. She could not make a box in her mind for him. Not ever.

'Save him,' she cried out, falling back against the wall.

The tears rolled openly over her cheeks as she called out to the team rushing down the hall.

'Please, you just have to save him.'

CHAPTER 112

Kim continued to stare at the noticeboard. She now knew by heart the signs of diabetes, the effects of smoking and the ten top tips for preventing heart disease.

Richard Terry Chance had been transported to the station and was suddenly not so talkative and had not said a word since asking for a solicitor. Penn was gathering all the forensic data ready for her to join him. She intended to be front and centre in the interrogation of the man who had begun the week helping her and had finished it by stabbing her friend and colleague.

Stacey had arrived an hour earlier and talked to her before Kim had sent her to get coffee. Stacey had urged Kim to come with her, to get a break, but she wasn't going anywhere. Not yet.

'He wants to see you,' Jenny said, appearing in front of her. She hadn't heard the ward door open or Bryant's wife approach her.

The woman's kind face was riddled with fear and worry.

'He knows I'm here?' she asked, standing.

Jenny smiled sadly. 'Where else would you be, Kim?'

The woman opened her arms, and Kim stepped into them. They hugged each other tightly but said nothing. No words were needed. They each understood in their own way the significance of the man beyond the doors in their lives. Both needed and loved him in different ways.

Jenny squeezed her tightly before letting her go.

'Laura will be here soon. I'll take her for coffee and then come up.'

Kim nodded and took a deep breath before she entered the room.

Her colleague lay against stark white pillows highlighting his own pale expression. He looked shrunken, vulnerable, weary but alive. Definitely alive.

His eyes fluttered open as she stood beside his bed.

'Bryant, you absolute fucker. I could kill you,' she said, swallowing back the tears.

His eyes softened at her harsh words. 'Yeah, I'm glad I'm alive too,' he said.

'I swear to God, I'd have haunted the bloody life out of you,' she said.

'Not sure that's how it works but you'd probably find a way. Doc says the blade just missed my liver. Another two centimetres and I'd be dead. Great bedside manner. Reminds me of someone.'

Kim knew every detail of his injury. She'd interrogated everyone who had gone in and out of the ward. Significant blood loss, intestinal damage, three staples inside and seven stitches outside.

'But if anything…'

'Kim, I'm fine. Just a scratch.'

'Yeah, always the drama queen, aren't you?' she said.

'Yeah, and you're the fucking Ice Queen,' he growled.

'The what?' she asked, shocked at his language.

He winced. 'Won't let anyone in. Won't tell anyone how you're feeling. Not even me.'

She was stunned. 'You're joking. Is that why you've been moody this week?'

He shrugged and winced again.

'Bryant, we'll talk about this another time once you're—'

'No, we'll talk about it now, and you can hardly refuse me. You don't take counselling, you don't even take Ted's counsel cos I can imagine how those sessions have been going. So, I wanna know which hook you've found to hang your guilt on.'

'Jesus, Bryant, this isn't fair and now isn't the right time to do this.'

'I know that but I want an answer.'

She thought for a moment. She had to give him something. He deserved that.

'I couldn't stop him,' she said. 'I couldn't stop him from making that choice. I should have been able...'

'I was right there in the bell tower with him and couldn't stop him. But that's not it, Kim. That's not what keeps you up at night. That's not what haunts you about Dawson's death.'

Damn him. He was right. It wasn't.

'He wanted something from me, Bryant. Something I never gave him. I let him down. He wanted me to tell him he was ready for promotion, and I never did. He was desperate for my approval. I could see it in his eyes, and I still couldn't say the words. I couldn't tell him he was ready.'

There. It was out. That's what kept her up at night. Dawson had wanted to hear her say those words, and she never had.

'Because he wasn't, Kim,' Bryant said, surprising her. 'You never said it to him because it wasn't true. The lad had matured a lot, grown a lot, but he wasn't ready to lead a team, and you knew it. So, whether he's here or not doesn't change that fact. You were just being honest.'

And there it was. In all its simplicity, communicated by her friend. He hadn't said it to take the beating stick from her hand. He'd said it because it was a plain and simple truth that in light of Dawson's death she couldn't bring herself to face.

She met his gaze and smiled.

He raised an eyebrow. 'And don't go replacing it with this. You couldn't have stopped this from happening either.'

'Fuck that,' she said feeling the cage of guilt begin to slip away. 'You're definitely old enough and ugly enough to look after yourself.'

A moment of easy silence settled between them.

'Just one question,' Bryant said. 'Something been bothering me all week.'

'Go on,' she replied.

'Zoe and Liz.'

'Who?' she asked, frowning.

'The kids at the children's home when you were ten. That story you told me when we were talking about Stacey and Penn. The sardines in the bed of the young, new kid. You really just leave them to sort it out themselves?'

Kim laughed out loud. 'Seriously? What do you think?'

He smiled. 'I think you kicked her ass into the middle of next week.'

'Close enough,' she said, as Stacey tore into the room.

'Bryant,' she exclaimed, rushing towards the bed.

She just stopped short.

'Is it inappropriate for me to want to squeeze you right now?' she asked.

Bryant laughed. 'More painful than inappropriate, Stace,' he said, holding out his hand. 'Squeeze this instead.'

'Ahem, am I interrupting something?' asked Woody from the doorway.

Bryant automatically tried to sit up straighter.

He raised his hand. 'I'm not staying,' he said, taking a few steps forward. 'Just wanted to see how you were doing.'

'I'm fine, sir,' he said.

'I'm not sure internal staples and seven stitches is fine, but you'll live and for that we're all grateful.'

'Thank you, sir.'

'And Laura has just arrived and will be up with her mum in about ten minutes.'

A smile lit up his face, and Kim knew that for Bryant there was no better medicine than his family.

'Stone, a word outside,' Woody said.

Kim followed him to the corridor.

*

'Bloody good job, Stone,' he said, regarding her seriously.

'Four people died, sir,' she said, unable to share his joy. 'And it was Stacey and Penn who found the strand and unravelled it.'

Maybe if she'd been less focussed on the Mancini family she'd have spotted it sooner and less people would have lost their lives.

'Vanessa Wilson is at the station, right now, giving her statement. Her six-year-old daughter is sitting beside her clutching a small pony. They are emotional, they are shaken up, but do you know something? They're alive – and that's because of you and Bryant and Wood and Penn. This day could have ended very differently, and sometimes, Stone, you've got to allow yourself to take the good.'

'I know, sir,' she said. Bryant was alive and that was enough good for her.

She wasn't sure she would ever rid herself of the vision of that knife being plunged into Bryant's torso.

She shook it away. He had come too close, way too close.

'Talking of Penn, sir, you knew about his personal circumstances, didn't you? You knew why he'd transferred back to West Mids?'

Woody didn't hesitate. 'Of course.'

'And you didn't think to share that information with me?'

Stacey had told her everything as they'd sat together and waited for news on Bryant.

He shook his head. 'Not at all,' he said. 'Because that shouldn't be the reason you keep him on your team. That's a decision for another day.'

She nodded her agreement.

He smiled and inclined his head towards the ward. 'Now go back in there with your team.'

He walked away, and she re-entered the room.

For a moment, she just stood and enjoyed the sight of Stacey holding onto Bryant's hand while she told him all about Jessie Ryan. And she watched Bryant pretending to care.

Yes, her team was small and needed a fourth member. She accepted that now, and although it would never be the one she wanted, it had to be someone.

But this was not a decision she would make alone.

Kim stepped forward. 'Okay, guys, I think it's time we took a vote.'

CHAPTER 113

It was almost nine when Woody got the call he'd been expecting. He'd told Stone the end of the week and he'd known it would be done.

'Come in,' he called as a soft knock sounded on the door.

He stood as the door opened and offered his hand. 'Mr Morgan?'

'Inspector Woodward,' he said, shaking the hand firmly.

Woody pointed to a chair and sat himself.

Strangely, the man was exactly how he had pictured him. Standing at about five foot six he wore a grey rain mac with a scarf tucked beneath. He had a skirt of hair from ear to ear but was completely bald on top. He had a kindly face with gentle eyes, and Woody liked him immediately.

'Thank you for agreeing to see Detective Inspector Stone, Mr Morgan.'

'Ted, please,' he said. 'And it really was no bother. Any reason to spend time with her is a joy.'

Woody waited for the sarcastic tilt of the mouth or amusing rejoinder. It didn't come. The man meant it, and he wasn't sure he'd met many people who would say that about Kim Stone.

'Oh yes, I still enjoy the challenge,' he said, with a smile.

'And was she?' Woody asked. 'Challenging?'

'You know her well enough to render that question rhetorical.'

'So, has she ever opened up to you over the years?' Woody asked, intrigued. Not least because she returned to this man time after time. And she trusted him.

'Opening up and revealing are two completely different things but that's not…'

'Of course,' Woody said. It had been an idle question born of his own curiosity, and he could understand the man's refusal to answer, and respected it. 'Did she explain the reason for the report?' he asked.

'Her suitability to return to work.'

'Partly,' Woody said. 'But I was also hoping she would talk to you about Dawson's death,' he admitted.

'Then that was wishful thinking on your part, sir,' Ted observed, wryly.

'So, she didn't open up…'

'As I've already said, opening up and revealing are two totally different things. Losing Dawson was like losing her brother all over again. She takes it upon herself to protect her team as though they're family, and she doesn't even realise it. Dawson died, just like her brother, which is purely her failure.'

'But she couldn't have prevented…'

'Play that thought on a loop into her head for the next twenty years and she still won't accept it, just like she's never accepted that Mikey's death wasn't her fault.

'You see, she'd allowed the young man into her world. Dawson had become a part of the fabric of her daily life. He was a constant. She knew how he would act, the things he would say. Those constants give her stability. They keep her world safe. She trusts them. Same goes for Stacey, yourself and especially Bryant.'

'Who almost died today,' Woody said.

'God help you if he had, because we'd be having a very different kind of conversation.'

'How so?'

'Call me if anything ever happens to Bryant and I'll let you know, but as long as he's alive, she'll be fine. She handles near misses very well.'

'And your report?' Woody asked.

'Aah, well that's where it gets interesting,' Ted said, reaching into his pocket. 'Because I have two,' he said, holding them both up.

'Why?' asked Woody, perplexed. Either Kim was fit to return to work or she wasn't.

'One explains why she's fit for work and one explains why she isn't. But let me explain. These reasons are not going to change no matter how much counselling you try to force upon her.'

'I don't understand,' Woody admitted.

'Kim's a paradox. It's basically the same reasons in both,' he said. 'The reasons she's not up to the job are the reasons she's so good at it. Her lack of emotional connection and understanding might appear a shortfall to you but they mean she can often remain more objective and less involved than others. Her ability to box things up and close them away also means she can dispose with nonsense while hanging on to the important stuff. Her inability to play nice with others also means she won't be easily fooled or led. Her brusqueness and lack of manners discourages people from trying to deceive her. Her directness can be rude but it gets to the truth. Now do you see what I'm saying?'

Woody nodded. 'I think so.'

'Imagine a baby born premature. The baby survives but will never catch up. It will always be smaller than average. Look young for its age. That's the same with Kim but on an emotional level. She never got the chance to grow those higher emotions in the way that we did. It's like the computer crashed before the whole programme had downloaded.'

'But surely she can learn—'

Ted cut him off by shaking his head. 'You know that children have an optimum time for learning certain things but once that door closes it's gone for ever. I'm afraid that's likely to be the case with Kim. Her ability to express and feel emotion is as good as it's going to be.'

Woody found this difficult to accept. 'I'm sorry, Ted, but…'

'Please don't make that mistake with her,' Ted advised. 'She's spent much of her life surrounded by people trying to make her into what they think she should be, force her to behave a certain way based on their perception of her experiences.'

Ted regarded him for a couple of seconds, weighing something up in his mind.

Woody waited.

'I'd like to share something with you but it must stay right here.'

'Of course,' Woody replied. He would never break this man's confidence.

'I wasn't Kim's first counsellor back when she was six years old. A woman who was nearing the end of her career and was resolute in her beliefs and practices got her first. She firmly believed that Kim needed to cry out her grief. The girl hadn't shed a tear since the cold, dead body of her twin was ripped from her arms. She tried everything to make Kim cry because that's what she thought the child should do. That once the tears began she would find solace in them. Didn't matter if they were tears of grief, hurt, sadness or pain.'

'You're not saying the therapist hurt her?' Woody asked, horrified.

Ted nodded. 'Pinches and pinpricks on her arms and legs.'

'Did Kim report it?'

Ted shook his head. 'That's all I'm going to say, but more importantly, I'm trying to explain that she still didn't cry. The day she lost her brother, something died which cannot be brought back, and you can't fix her. Kim will always equate love with loss and so will try to avoid it. That's a choice that she has made herself, despite the help and advice of every mental health professional she's ever met, but she now refuses to explain or justify it to anyone. To accept Kim is to accept who she is and allow her the level of contentment that she has allowed herself.'

Ted took a breath, allowing him a moment to consider everything.

'The person that she is seeps out in spite of herself. In her passion for her job, her commitment to her team. Her fierce protection of the people she cares about. Her drive and determination to do the right thing. She is a good person and she connects as much as she is able to.'

'I understand,' Woody said and silently thanked God for this man who appeared to know Kim Stone better than she knew herself.

'So, given all that I've said and the fact she's never likely to change, which envelope do you want me to leave?'

There was no hesitation from Woody as he pointed and made his choice.

'Okay, guys, you sure about this?' Kim asked, looking at both of her colleagues.

Stacey nodded emphatically, and Bryant followed her lead. And then winced.

Kim caught it. 'S'pose you're going home after this is done, eh?'

'Doctor's orders,' Bryant said. 'Well, most importantly, the wife's,' he admitted.

Bryant had been discharged from hospital Sunday afternoon but had insisted on coming in to the office to finalise his statement.

Richard Terry Chance had confessed to everything, against the advice of his brief, when she'd questioned him. Throughout the case she'd been seeking a full confession, but she hadn't expected it to come from the man who had been kind and helped her on Monday afternoon.

But that had been the chilling part. He had recited everything he'd done, while, not with a sense of pride, but with an expectation of understanding and empathy. He genuinely felt that he'd done nothing wrong and that a jury would agree with him.

She had spent Saturday afternoon visiting with the Cordell family and talking them both through the whole thing.

Afterwards she'd visited the Mancini home and sincerely apologised to them both. They had accepted gracefully still unable to believe the man they'd both classed as a friend had been capable of such a crime, never mind trying to frame either one for the murders. Richard Terry Chance had shrewdly tried to frame father and son under the shroud of kindness. He had brought the sad-looking, cheap plant as an excuse to get into the property. Once there he'd dropped the blood-soaked glove into the waste bin and covered it over while telling the younger Mancini about the Reeboks he'd handed in to lost property, knowing full well the man would claim them at the earliest opportunity. Richard Terry Chance had fooled them all.

Vanessa and Mia were still shaken but thankful. With her husband back from his business trip, Vanessa had decided to take a leave of absence to spend some time with her family, which Kim suspected was a little bit overdue, but most definitely a loss for the hospital.

And just a few moments ago Stacey had received a call that Mrs Weston was waiting downstairs with her daughter and Jessica Ryan, all ready to make statements about the abuse, as promised.

Stacey had offered to pass it along, and Kim had refused. Only Stacey's tenacity and Penn's assistance had uncovered the poor girl's history and her mother's actions. Stacey would take the statement and work with the authorities to keep the girl safe and well. It was her case and she would finish it.

Which brought Kim nicely to something that was long overdue.

She cleared her throat. 'Guys, listen, before Penn gets here, there's something I'd like to say.'

All eyes were on her as she took a breath.

'We all miss him,' she said honestly. 'Dawson was important to us all in one way or another. He was a part of this team and will always be with us. We were lucky to know him and watch him grow.' She took a deeper breath. 'But now it's time to let him go, okay?'

Stacey wiped a tear, and Bryant looked away.

'Okay?'

'Okay, boss,' Stacey said.

'Got it, guv,' Bryant said.

And there was something else overdue too.

'Hey, Bryant, you popping round tonight? Barney misses you.'

'Aww… sorry, boss, I can't. I'm washing my hair,' he said.

'Great, bring pizza,' she said, as Penn entered the office.

'Hey, am I late?' he asked, colouring.

'No, you're okay,' Kim said, as he walked past carrying his Tupperware box.

'Hey, Penn, great work with the forensics on Chance,' she said.

He looked around as if it was some kind of joke. But it wasn't.

Every detail had been organised and noted and ready to hand. His bullet points had been chronological, succinct and relevant. He had sat beside her handing her information before she'd even known she needed it.

Later, she had watched back the footage of the interview they'd conducted together. In the interview room, away from the office, away from the desk, she had watched Penn the officer and not Penn the replacement.

The kid had his own problems and a whole heap of responsibility to come but he'd just done his job in the face of a wave of hostility and never once fought them back. Because he had understood.

He placed his man-bag on the floor and moved the set of trays that Stacey had artfully rearranged.

His brow furrowed in confusion. 'What's that?'

Kim stepped forward. 'It's a plant, Penn, and her name is Betty.' She smiled and offered her hand.

'And I'd like to formally welcome you to the team.'

A LETTER FROM ANGELA

First of all, I want to say a huge thank you for choosing to read *Fatal Promise*, the ninth instalment of the Kim Stone series.

Most of my readers will know that I like to explore a psychological aspect within the motives for my killers, and in this book I wanted to consider the repercussions of having to make a horrific choice of life and love. What might that do to someone? Who would they blame? How extreme their need for revenge?

No spoilers but I also wanted to explore the reaction of the team in response to the traumatic events of *Dying Truth*. How out of character would they act while facing a painful loss? How would they regroup? How would they react to a newcomer? How would they adapt to each other? And would they finally be able to come back together as a unit?

I hope you enjoyed it.

If you did enjoy it, I would be for ever grateful if you'd write a review. I'd love to hear what you think, and it can also help other readers discover one of my books for the first time. Or maybe you can recommend it to your friends and family…

If you haven't read any of the previous books in the D.I. Kim Stone series, you can find them here:

Silent Scream
Evil Games
Lost Girls
Play Dead

Blood Lines
Dead Souls
Broken Bones
Dying Truth

Thank you for joining me on this emotional journey.

I'd love to hear from you – so please get in touch on my Facebook or Goodreads page, Twitter or through my website.

And if you'd like to keep up-to-date with all my latest releases, just sign up at the website links below.

🖥 www.angelamarsons-books.com

 angelamarsonsauthor

🐦 @WriteAngie

Thank you so much for your support, it is hugely appreciated.

Angela Marsons

ACKNOWLEDGEMENTS

As ever, my first acknowledgment must be to my partner, Julie. No book sees the light of day without her extensive involvement in every part of the process. She adds excitement to my initial ideas, grieves with me when some inevitably die and is always ready to enthusiastically embrace the next. She has learned recently that when I am twirling Bic pencils into my hair to make dreadlocks the process is not going well and has learned to take me outside for some air, space and a chat, which inevitably leads to me using the pencils for the purpose they were intended. She loves these characters as much as I do, and I am thankful for her every single day.

Thank you to my mum and dad who continue to spread the word proudly to anyone who will listen. And to my sister, Lyn, her husband, Clive, and my nephews, Matthew and Christopher for their support too.

Thank you to Amanda and Steve Nicol who support us in so many ways, and to Kyle Nicol for book spotting my books everywhere he goes.

I would like to thank the team at Bookouture for their continued enthusiasm for Kim Stone and her stories. In particular, the incredible Keshini Naidoo who never tires in her encouragement and passion for what we do. Without this woman there would be no Kim Stone stories and working with her has been a pleasure and an honour.

To Oliver Rhodes and Claire Bord who gave Kim Stone an opportunity to exist. To Kim Nash (Mama Bear) who works tirelessly to promote our books and protect us from the world. To Noelle Holten who has limitless enthusiasm and passion for our work.

A massive thank you to Natalie Mansell who won the bid for charity to have her name in this book.

Thank you to the fantastic Kim Slater who has been an incredible support and friend to me for many years now and to the fabulous Caroline Mitchell, Renita D'Silva and Sue Watson without whom this journey would be impossible. Huge thanks to the growing family of Bookouture authors who continue to amuse, encourage and inspire me on a daily basis.

My eternal gratitude goes to all the wonderful bloggers and reviewers who have taken the time to get to know Kim Stone and follow her story. These wonderful people shout loudly and share generously not because it is their job but because it is their passion. I will never tire of thanking this community for their support of both myself and my books. Thank you all so much.

Massive thanks to all my fabulous readers, especially the ones that have taken time out of their busy day to visit me on my website, Facebook page, Goodreads or Twitter.

Read on for the beginning
of *Dead Memories*, the next book in
Angela Marsons's Detective Kim Stone series.

PROLOGUE

17 June

Amy Wilde's eyes closed as the liquid gold entered her vein and travelled around her body. She could visualise the trail of white hot beauty hurtling towards her brain.

The effects were almost immediate. The pleasure suffused every inch of her being, almost painful in its intensity. The euphoria transported her to another planet, another world, somewhere undiscovered. Nothing in her life had ever felt so good. Elation pumped through her body. Wave after wave of ecstasy surged through her skin, muscles, tendons – right through to the centre of her bones. She tried to hang on to it as it weakened in strength.

Don't go. I love you. I need you. Don't go, her mind screamed, pleaded, begged, desperate to hang on to the sensation for as long as she could.

As the last tremors of happiness faded away she turned her head to her left to share that secret smile with Mark, her lover, her friend, her soulmate as she always did after a shared hit of heroin.

But Mark didn't look okay, she realised, through the fatigue that was pulling her into the welcoming dark oblivion that always followed the hit.

She knew they were sitting on the floor in an unfamiliar room. She knew the radiator was warming her through the denim jacket.

She knew there were handcuffs around her wrist but she didn't care. Nothing mattered after a hit like that.

She tried to say Mark's name but the word wouldn't crawl out of her mouth.

Something was wrong with Mark.

His eyes were not closed, already succumbed to the warm drowsiness. They were wide: staring, unblinking, at a spot on the ceiling.

Amy wanted to reach across and touch him, shake him awake. She wanted to share that smile before she gave in to the dark.

But she couldn't move a muscle.

This wasn't normal. The usual heaviness that soaked into her bones made her feel lethargic and weighted down but she could always muster enough energy to turn and snuggle Mark.

The exhaustion was trying to take her, pulling at her eyelids, willing her to sleep, but she had to try and touch Mark.

Through the descending fog she tried with all her might to move a single finger, but there was no response. The message was not making it out of her brain.

She tried to fight the creeping drowsiness, but it was like a blanket being pulled up over her head.

She felt helpless, weak, unable to shoo away the blackness, but she knew that Mark needed her.

It was no use. She couldn't outrun the shadows that chased her.

Her eyes began to droop as she heard the door to the flat slam shut.

CHAPTER 1

Kim felt her jaws clench at the incessant tapping sound niggling her left ear.

A moth had entered her garage space through the open shutter that was capturing little breeze from the storm-heavy June air. The insect was launching itself repeatedly against the 60 watt bulb.

But that wasn't the tapping that was annoying her.

'If you're bored, piss off,' she said, as a few flecks of rust dislodged from the wheel spokes and landed on her jeans.

'I'm not bored, I'm thinking,' Gemma said, tipping her head and looking up at the moth, who was giving himself an aneurism.

'Convince me,' Kim said, drily.

'I'm trying to decide whether to take the flowers with me or arrange them in a vase at home.'

'Hmm...' Kim offered, helpfully, as she continued to scrape.

She knew that Bryant and many other people questioned her relationship with the teenager who had been sent to kill her, manipulated and used by Kim's nemesis, Doctor Alexandra Thorne.

Bryant's view was that the girl should be locked up at Drake Hall prison, where her mother was currently residing and where the girl had come into contact with the sociopathic psychiatrist who had made it her life's work to torment Kim at every opportunity since she had put an end to her sick experiments on her vulnerable patients.

As far as Bryant was concerned there were no circumstances under which you could befriend a person who had wanted you dead. It was simple. Except it wasn't. Because Kim understood two things perfectly: how skilled Alexandra Thorne was in manipulating every weakness or vulnerability a person had – the ones they knew about and even the ones they didn't. And that the girl had suffered a shit childhood through no fault of her own.

She wasn't being facetious in not responding to the girl's comment. It just wasn't something she could see happening.

Gemma's mother had been in and out of prison all the kid's life, palming her child off onto any relative who'd have her, until no one would take the child. Gemma had resorted to selling her body in order to eat. Yet, for some reason, the kid had maintained regular contact with her mother and visited at every opportunity.

The woman was due for release the following week but somehow she always managed to get herself into some further trouble that extended her sentence.

Kim had offered Gemma a loose invitation that whenever she was in need of a meal to come round, instead of heading for the streets, and while she couldn't offer a gourmet meal she could throw in some oven chips or a pizza.

And Gemma had taken her up on the offer, even after she'd secured a job a month ago working part-time at Dudley Library.

'So, how's work?' Kim asked, avoiding the subject of her mother completely.

Gemma blew a raspberry, and Kim laughed.

There were days Gemma was an old eighteen-year-old hardened by choices and what life had thrown at her already and other times she was just eighteen.

And Kim hadn't minded the unexpected company today. Of all days.

'Look, Gem, it might not be brain—'

'Numbing,' she cut in. 'It's brain numbing,' she said, pulling a face.

'I check books out; I check books back in. I put 'em back on the shelves. In the evening before we close I get the coveted job of wiping over the keyboards of the communal computers.'

Kim hid her smile. It was much more entertaining hearing Gemma complain about her job than moaning she couldn't get one.

'Oh, and yesterday I had this lovely old dear approach me,' she said, standing. She hunched her back and pretended to walk with a cane across the space. '"Excuse me, love, but could you show me how to send these photos to my son in New Zealand?" she asked thrusting her ancient digital camera at me. I swear…'

'Hang on,' Kim said, as her phone began to ring.

'Stone,' she answered, brushing rust off her jeans.

'Sorry to disturb you, Marm, but something happening over at Hollytree. A bit garbled. Got an address and one word,' said a voice from dispatch.

'Give me the address,' she said, getting to her feet.

'Chaucer block, flat 4B,' he said.

Her stomach turned. Same block, three floors lower. Today, of all fucking days.

'Okay, I'm on my way. Get Bryant en route too.'

'Will do, Marm.'

'And the word?' she asked. 'What was it?'

'It was "dead", Marm. The word was "dead".'

CHAPTER 2

Kim negotiated the maze of streets, dead ends and shortcuts with ease on the Ninja, drawing curious glances from the groups of people congregating on the pavements wearing as little clothing as possible in an effort to catch the night-time breeze.

The sun had set fifteen minutes earlier leaving a red marble sky and a temperature still in the high teens. It was going to be another long, sticky night.

She wound the bike around the bin stores and headed for Chaucer House, the middle block of flats at the bulging belly of the sprawling Hollytree housing estate.

Chaucer was known for being the roughest of the tower blocks, home to the worst that society had to offer.

It had also been home for the first six years of her life. Normally, she was able to keep that thought pinned to the noticeboard at the back of her mind. But not today. Right now, it was front and centre.

She eased the bike through two police cars, an ambulance and a first responder bike and parked behind Bryant's Astra Estate. He lived a couple of miles closer and it had taken her a few minutes to shepherd Gemma out of her house. The girl had been wide-eyed with curious questions about what she'd been called to.

Not that Kim would have told her but she hadn't known herself.

'Oi, pig on a bike,' shouted a voice from the crowd as she removed her helmet.

She ran a hand through her short black hair, freeing it from her scalp, while shaking her head. Yeah, she hadn't heard that insult for at least, oh, three days or so.

The crowd around the voice laughed, which Kim ignored as she headed for the entrance to the tower block.

She'd passed an outer cordon, an inner cordon and then met a wall of constables at the lifts and staircase.

The lift on the right had dropped below floor level and its doors gaped open, obviously out of order.

'Evening, Marm,' said a WPC stepping forward. 'One working lift,' she said, pointing to the display which told her it was currently on floor five. 'We're clearing the floor above and the floor below, Marm.'

Kim nodded her understanding. The stairs were being kept free for police use, while the lift was being kept as a means of access for the residents.

Evacuating the whole building for an incident on one floor was not an option, so the situation had to be managed.

She headed for the stairs and began the ascent to the fourth floor.

Thank goodness her left leg was now in a stronger state to deal with it, following the fracture she'd sustained after falling from the roof of a two-storey building in a previous case three months ago.

Officers were stationed at each floor to ensure no one tried to get closer to the incident. One of the officers at the fourth floor smiled and held open the door into the lobby.

She approached the open doorway.

Inspector Plant blocked her way.

'What the?...'

'If you can just hang on?' he said, looking behind him.

She gave him a hard stare. She knew this guy well, had worked with him a few times. What the hell was he playing at?

'Plant, if you don't move yourself from that—'

'Your colleague, Bryant,' he said, uncomfortably. 'He doesn't want you in there.'

'What the fuck are you on?' she raged. It was a crime scene, she was the SIO and she wanted access.

'I don't give a shit what...'

Her words trailed away as Bryant came into view behind the inspector, who moved out of the way.

His face was ashen and drawn, his eyes full of horror. He hadn't looked as bad as this when he'd been lying on the floor with her hand in his stomach to stop the blood that was oozing out of him on their last major case. If he wasn't known to the constables as a detective sergeant someone would be wrapping him in a foil blanket.

'Bryant, what the?...'

'Don't go in there, guv,' he said, quietly.

Kim tried to understand what was going on here.

Together they had witnessed the worst that mankind could do to each other. They'd viewed bodies where the stench of blood clung to the air. They'd seen corpses in the worst state of decay, alive with maggots and flies. Together they had unearthed the bodies of innocent teenage girls. He knew her stomach could handle just about anything, so why was he trying to stand in her way now?

He ushered her to the side. 'Kim, I'm asking as a friend. Don't go in there.'

Never before had he used her first name on the job. Not once.

What the hell had he just seen?

She took a deep breath and fixed him with a stare.

'Bryant, get out of my way. Now.'